THE DREAMER'S LOTUS

Margaret and Gordon,

I'm so grateful to know you both.

Warm wishes,

Mike Dickerson

The Dreamer's Lotus
Copyright © 2014 Mike Dickenson
ISBN 978-0-9908983-0-6

Cover Design by Kassia Borycki - www.kborycki.com

Published by Commonlink Productions

To contact the author email: mike@themapmakers.org

For more information please visit: www.michaelcdickenson.com

Acknowledgements

Like so many things in life, this book is the product of a collective effort.

First and foremost, I would like to thank my wife, Amy, for her help and support throughout this journey. Your passion and dedication were the fuel that kept me going - truly, this would not have been possible without you.

Thank you Matt for your time, advice, service, and friendship. I am so grateful that we have reconnected.

Thank you Mom for reading pretty much every draft I gave you and for saying that each one was perfect.

Thank you Kassia for your incredible artwork and unwavering professionalism.

And lastly, to the forest - thank you for your teachings, your inspiration, your beauty, and everything that you provide for this world.

To mom, for showing me the magic of nature.

Part One:

The Boy With Grandfather Eyes

Chapter One

At the top of the hill stood a tall pine tree where the boy with grandfather eyes would sit and overlook the village. The tree was old and had once been struck by lightning, leaving it only half alive. Crows floated above and among the broken branches and occasionally dropped to the lower branches to overlook the boy. He could see everything from where he sat. His vantage point gave him a fresh perspective, allowing him distance and a reprieve from the village and the beliefs of the villagers. Today he was waiting for a sign, or a guide, or perhaps both.

He gazed out at the mountains that surrounded the village like a powerful dream. Beyond the meadows that crept to the edge of the forest, the mountains climbed higher and farther and deeper away, until they sealed back the horizon, crawling behind the curve of the earth. A green crescendo of beautiful trees blanketed the steep hills, their canopy radiant and inspiring, yet so dense that only the faintest trickle of light made it down to the floor of the forest.

Near the bottom of the hill, The White Village seemed small enough to fit in the palm of a child's hand. Still, one could see dim outlines of people below, walking through the cobblestone streets on their way to the church. His dark eyes observed and followed the patterns in the distance, because he, like all of the inhabitants of the village, read the signs of the universe like a book. He could hear the soft muffled tune of the church bells and he looked up above him, hoping for a harbinger of meaning. His eyes scanned the sky, but no dove appeared. He had never seen a white dove before, but he thought that one day, he might.

At the edge of the village, fallow fields waited for the winds of spring to come down the mountains. The boy pulled his white coat over his white shirt to shield himself from the sharp breeze. The last days of winter dragged on, but the cold weather would soon be over for good. In no time, the fields would be plowed and planted and the season of spring would jump into gear - The Festival of the Ax was just around the corner. His eyes perked up and he smiled as he thought about the coming festival. It would be nice to participate in The Cut this year, if he was allowed.

The boy's brown hair blew in the wind. He was short for his age and the tree towered over him like an old retired sentinel. He whistled softly and one of the crows descended from the old tree and landed in the grass before him. He whistled again. The bird ruffled its feathers and paced back and forth. The boy had fashioned a unique whistle for each of the crows. He would whistle their song, and they would come to him, perhaps thinking that the song was their name. He had no idea what his whistling meant to the crows. All he knew was that they responded to it. The crows never let the boy touch them, but they would come within arm's reach, until he reached out his arm.

He watched the crow carefully, admiring the intelligence behind its eyes. "Hi there," he said to the crow. "Perhaps I should teach you to bring me food from the village, *that* way I won't have to leave every time I get hungry. I am sure you have other tricks though, right? What *can* you do, Oritus?"

The crow squawked and hopped forward. It lowered its beak and pushed a pinecone toward the boy. It did this for a few feet and then retreated nearby to the crest of the hill.

The boy smiled and whistled again, thanking the bird. "The pinecone," he thought to himself, remembering that The Book of Signs defined the pinecone to be a riddle, a dormant magic inside a perfect design. "*Another* riddle?" he asked and laughed, looking up at the tree.

The tree remained silent and stoic, its upper branches hanging hundreds of feet off the ground.

"Make pinecones, drop pinecones," the boy said with a grin. "At least you know what *your* purpose is," he said, still gazing at the tree in awe. He shook his head, wondering how anything could grow so tall. "Always riddles under the pine tree," he chuckled to himself. "Imagine that."

The crow on the crest looked down the hill. The hill was steep and devoid of living trees, but massive stumps lay hidden beneath the tall grass, remnants of another time. Few villagers came out this far or up this high.

"Maybe one day we will actually understand each other," he said to the crow affectionately. The black bird squawked again and returned to its perch on the tree. The boy turned and counted the crows. Twelve. He stared at them for a long while thinking about their symbolism, wondering why they came, wondering why they followed him...

Suddenly, the crows on the tree began to caw one after another, filling the air with their abrasive speech. The boy knew – his wait was over. He squinted his eyes and searched for the approaching arrival.

A black dot emerged out of the forest and into the sky, sailing in his direction like a current of wind. On the first day of each new year of the boy's life, a crow would materialize out of the forest and find him. This would be the thirteenth. Even from faraway, he could see that the bird was much larger than the others. The boy's heartbeat quickened and the palms of his hands began to sweat. He kept his eyes trained on the bird until it was gliding gracefully above him, circling the old tree, watching him and the other crows from above. After what seemed like an eternity, the crow landed on the ground before him.

A gentle breeze blew through the boy's hair. The crow was less than ten feet away. Suddenly, the breeze ceased to blow and even the crows in the tree had become eerily quiet. He looked into the jet black eyes of the bird, eyes that so strikingly resembled his own, and waited for the sign to unfold. The boy had so many questions for this new crow. He considered speaking all his thoughts at once, sensing in his heart that this crow could understand his words, yet knowing in his mind that it never would. From the boy's perspective, no one understood him. He was an outcast because of these birds, but after years of being alone, he had become accustomed to it, and in a way, he enjoyed his solitude.

The crow in front of him remained still as a statue. Above him, the boy could hear the birds in the tree moving restlessly, agitated perhaps by the suspense. Finally, the crow took a step toward the boy and began to shake its body back and forth almost like a dog. Delicately, the crow reached its beak into its feathers and pulled out a single black plume. It held the plume in its beak, as if showing it to the boy, and then set it on the ground in front of him. With that, the crow squawked loudly and flew into the tree to join the rest of the birds.

The boy quickly crawled over to the feather and picked it up. The feather was twice the length of his hand and nearly as wide. He traced the long white quill with his fingers until it disappeared among the soft velvet material of flight. In a world where everything was symbolic, this was a powerful sign.

His laughter ruptured the silence and he turned and faced the crows in the tree, waving the feather as he laughed. "Look!" he yelled up at them. "A gift from the forest! This is a wonderful sign, indeed. I will think about it much, in the days to come."

The church bells began to ring. The boy clasped the feather in both hands and darted down the hillside toward town. The crows circled in slow circles in the air above while he ran to the village. When he arrived, the streets of the village were as empty as the houses. It was only the boy who did not attend the church services, and it was only the boy's footsteps that could be heard walking upon the cobblestone steps with a soft *clop clop* that echoed against the white brick buildings.

The plaza was empty as he entered it. One by one, the crows glided to rest about the rooftops around the plaza. The boy walked slowly and calmly over the white stones until he came to the charred center of the ash eye. It was here that the wood from The Festival of the Ax was ritually burned. He stepped around the large black stone and made his way to the north end of the plaza where the Tree of Truth stood. No one knew for certain just how many years the old olive tree had grown here, but it was most certainly the oldest living thing in the village.

The crows glided down to surround the boy. Some of them stood on the white stones of the plaza while others rested in the branches on the Tree of Truth. The boy sat down in a bench with his back to the tree. The Tree of Truth was a powerful symbol in the community, though the boy gave it little regard. As far as he could tell, however, he was the only one with that sentiment.

He patiently waited for the service to end. He had only been inside the church as a young child in the company of his aunt, but by the time he had attracted a flock of four crows, Elder Mallory had asked his aunt to leave the boy at home. The boy resented the Elder's decision, though for Mallory it had been an unfortunate necessity. How else should the Elder have responded to a crow flying through a stained glass window during a Sunday service? Naturally, the incident was no longer present in the boy's memory, though Mallory thought of it often.

The Elder's face carried the scars of a leader who had seen much destruction. He was a tall and heavy man and old in his years, with dark sunken brown eyes and black-stained teeth from years of tea and neglect. Most people considered Elder Mallory to be the spiritual leader of The White Village and a master reader of the signs. He had status and experience. Mallory had saved the village once before and the villagers believed that he would do so again if need be. It was obvious that he cared deeply about the integrity of the community and the individuals within it. He had no living relatives and so he looked after the villagers as if they were his own children.

A firm believer in the power of the collective, it had been Mallory's idea to form a council of Elders to assist the community by providing insight into the language of the signs. Mallory's council consisted of five Elders who oversaw most aspects of life in the village. They decided when it was time to plant, when it was time to harvest, what was taught in school, and what daily rituals were supposed to be followed. Mallory considered the individual insignificant in comparison to the strength of the collective. "For while the individual is mortal and finite," he said during his sermons, "the collective lives forever and thus must be protected."

The church bells began to ring again, bouncing off the brick buildings and sailing through and against the mountain slopes like delicate afterthoughts. The people filed out the church door and dispersed into the streets. The villagers smiled back and forth as they chatted about this and that, making their way back to their homes for supper. As the people walked across the plaza they avoided the boy's eyes and quickened their pace until they were safely away from his perimeter of crows.

Exiting last out of the church was the boy's aunt and only guardian, Sarah. Sarah was a tall and thin woman and she walked with a stiff and mechanical gait. Her younger years of beauty and appeal were gone and left in their wake was a silent sternness which she wore like a tight belt. Sarah knew her nephew would be waiting for her in his usual spot. She walked slowly through his flock of crows. When she came to him she did not meet his eyes.

"Come, Corvus," she said, looking over his shoulder. "It is time to go home."

They walked the cobblestone steps in silence, he following behind his aunt, the crows following behind him.

When they got home, which was like every other home in The White Village - simple, whitewashed, built of stone, Sarah began to make dinner.

"Fetch me some water from the well," she said to her nephew.

Corvus walked down the alley to the communal well and pulled up the bucket. Inside of the bucket was a red snake. The snake was long and hung halfway over the edge. Corvus looked at the snake and did not speak. He lowered the bucket into the water, and when he pulled it back up, the snake was gone.

When he returned he set the bucket of water on a table beside the washbasin and sat and watched his aunt peel potatoes. She placed a potato in front of him. "Make yourself useful if you are just going to sit there," she said.

They peeled the potatoes in silence.

"Set a fire," she told him quietly.

Corvus gathered kindling and set a small fire. When the water reached a boil his aunt put the potatoes in the pot and began cutting carrots. He could see his aunt's hands in his peripheral vision as he watched his own. For the most part, Sarah was his only form of human contact, which was fine by him. They tolerated one another as best they could, despite the fact they had nothing in common besides blood. Though he would never admit it out loud, he was still grateful for her company.

Corvus quietly pulled the crow's feather out of his pocket. He rubbed it with his fingers as he examined its black sheen.

"Where did you get that?" Sarah asked, her voice just above a whisper.

He looked at her. Mimicking the volume of her voice he said softly, "It was given to me. The thirteenth crow came today, Aunt Sarah. It came from out of the forest like the rest of them. It gave me this feather." He offered the feather to her and for the first time ventured a smile. "It is a wonderful sign."

"It is no such thing," she said, raising her voice. "It is a burden on this household is what it is. Put that thing away before someone's prying eyes see it."

He scowled. "But Aunt Sarah, it was a *gift*."

Sarah looked into the boy's eyes. His eyes were deep and black, but from that blackness escaped a vision of light and ageless wisdom. His eyes were so peculiar that they offset everything about his face making him a blaring incongruity. His nose was small, as was his mouth, and his small teeth were spaced clumsily apart. Brown polka-dot freckles trickled across his cheeks, but in the corners of his eyes deep wrinkles dwelled, like those of an old man who has spent his entire life reading the fine print. His eyes were unusual, to say the least. She looked away.

"Aunt Sarah?"

"Grab a knife and start cutting up the onions."

He did so.

When the soup was ready they sat down and closed their eyes. He knew she would not reach for his hand as she did with others, as others did with others when saying grace.

"We ask you bless this food and trust this table which was built for your purity, wood from your forest, labor from our lungs, and a knowledge of the good it would serve. This table has served us well. May we serve you well. May the signs bless us."

"May the signs bless us," Corvus repeated.

The air in the house was still. They did not speak as they ate their soup. She rarely spoke to her nephew except when asking him to do something, and she never had to ask twice because he never disobeyed her. She thought often of the boy's father, her brother, and the promise she had made to look after Corvus. She wanted to help him find his way, for she could only imagine how lost he felt inside. If only the crows would leave him alone.

When they were halfway done with dinner Corvus asked, "When was this table built, Aunt Sarah?"

"It was built by your father twenty years ago," she said quietly.

He rubbed the wood thoughtfully, thinking of his father whom he had never met. "The crack is much deeper here now."

She looked where his hand was. "Yes. We should have been more careful last week. We were careless and moved the table too quickly and dropped it on a stone. The table tells us much about who we are and who we are waiting for. Perhaps we are breaking apart."

"But the wood is thick," Corvus said. "Perhaps there is still life in it yet."

"It will last a while longer. Regardless, it is time for a new table. The Elders will soon be leaving into the woods for this year's Cut." Sarah looked at Corvus thoughtfully. "The Festival of The Ax is the most important festival of the year, and it approaches. In less than a week the men along with the young initiates will travel deep into the woods to cut down the thickest trees. Today is your thirteenth birthday, Corvus. You are now old enough to join the men and set light to the darkness. If you were to go with them you could return with a tabletop for us." She paused again. "Tomorrow I will approach the Elders and question on your behalf."

Corvus was elated. "Oh Sarah, thank you!"

She looked at her nephew and returned his smile, but quickly dismissed herself from the table and began cleaning the dishes.

"Aunt Sarah?" he asked.

"Yes?" she said without looking at him.

"Have you ever gone into the forest?"

She lifted her eyes from the sink and looked out the window. "No," she said quietly. "Women are not allowed in the forest. But it is rare for even the Elders to enter the forest without a good reason."

"Like what?"

"Perhaps to trade with a faraway village or arrange a ceremony of marriage for a young man or woman of age. But let me assure you, absolutely *no one* goes into the illusion by themselves."

He stroked the feather unconsciously. "How come?" he asked quietly.

She turned around and looked at him as she thought of the story that her father had told her. "Years ago, before the village was nearly destroyed, a group of travelers emerged out of the forest like lost fawns. On the verge of starvation they babbled like maniacs. The men spoke of a place far from The White Village where thousands of people lived together in a sea of struggle, though the men insisted that this place, their home, was a paradise compared to the demons and darkness of the forest. Not long after their arrival, the men's madness consumed them and they died." Sarah sighed, shaking away the loom of symbols from her mind. "It was because of this event that The Festival of the Ax was born into existence. Ever since, a small group of initiates have gone into the forest to cut down a clearing of trees to bring light into the forest of darkness, thus giving the community a sense of power in a vast and overpowering universe."

Corvus held the feather on the palm of his hand and stroked it softly with his fingers. "What would happen if someone went into the forest on their own?" he asked her.

Sarah looked at her nephew carefully. "Nothing would happen because no one would be ignorant enough to do such a thing. Now help me clean up these dishes, please," she said over her shoulder, and then turning around she said sternly, "and put away that cursed feather of yours."

That night as Corvus lay in bed, he watched the moonlight cast shadows upon the far wall of his room. He couldn't stop thinking about The Cut. Perhaps tomorrow Elder Mallory would come by and show him how to hold an ax!

Corvus lit a candle and pulled out The Book of Signs. Despite what his aunt thought, Corvus spent a great deal of his time secretly studying the meanings of the symbols. He scrolled his finger down the page until he came to the word he was looking for.

Feather – Depending on the conditions, a feather can be a message of hope or a sign to take flight. The color of the feather can help to distinguish the difference.

Corvus shook his head in frustration. He knew what the color black was supposed to mean. He should never have picked up this stupid book in the first place.

Hearing a scratch at his window he turned and looked over his shoulder. In the dim darkness he could see the outline of a figure behind the glass – a crow was standing at his windowsill. Corvus sat up in his bed and squinted his eyes. The crow was just a silhouette and its features could not be clearly distinguished. Corvus let out a soft whistle and the crow tapped its beak against the glass. This was the first time any crow had done this before. "Oritus?" the boy asked. He softly whistled the Song of Oritus but the crow did not respond. He whistled the song of another bird. No reaction.

Corvus heard the sound of his aunt coming for his room. He quickly blew out the candle, threw the covers over his body, and pretended to be sleep. "Corvus!" his aunt hissed in whisper. He didn't move. "Corvus," she said again, this time more quietly. She had heard him whistling, or at least *thought* she had. His seemingly constant tune trickled through her mind like a forgotten faucet and at times she found herself holding a hand to her ear even when she knew for a fact that he was far away. Sarah wished that the crows would leave her nephew alone but remembering the prophecy that Elder Mallory had foretold, she knew that they would not. She feared for the boy...

Stepping closer she inspected him, but his breathing was that of a sleeper. Sarah glanced up at the window, which to her relief, was vacant. She was glad to see that the boy was asleep, but she could have *sworn* that she had heard his familiar tune. Perhaps she had dreamt the whole thing. She looked down at her nephew and thought to kiss him upon the forehead, but still not fully convinced that he was asleep, she departed to her room.

When Corvus was sure that his aunt had left, he returned his gaze to the window. The crow returned almost immediately. Corvus sat up and inched slowly forward until his nose was less than a foot away from the window. No crow had allowed him to get so close.

The moon hit his eyes and he smiled in realization. It was the same crow which had given him the feather. He placed his hand against the cold glass of the window. Corvus tilted his head and the moonlight hit the glass in a way that his reflection was projected onto the face of the crow. The boy's eyes twinkled. "You look like the rest, but there is a uniqueness about you that I cannot define," he whispered. "I shall call you, 'Korbin'."

And with that, Korbin hopped off the windowsill and flew away.

Chapter Two

The next morning Corvus walked with his aunt down the cobblestone steps of the street until they came to a tall wooden door. The upper half of the door was open, allowing them to see inside. A column of light climbed through the clutter of furniture from the back of the room and dust mingled with the light in the air. Sarah knocked on the door, but no one answered.

"Elder Mallory!" she called. Heavy sounds like wood on wood answered her from behind the house. "He must be in back," she said more to herself than to Corvus. They walked around to the back of the white house. Five men could be seen working together over a workbench. "Stay here," Sarah told her nephew quietly. "I will go speak with Elder Mallory," she said, avoiding his eyes, leaving him to approach the men.

One of the men looked up from his work. He elbowed his adjacent companion who murmured to the others. Elder Mallory looked up and took several steps away from the other men toward Sarah.

"Hello, Sarah," Elder Mallory said with a soft voice of feigned invitation.

"Hello, Elder Mallory," she responded. They held each other's gaze for a moment and Sarah felt a whirlpool of emotions stirring inside of her. She knew Elder Mallory distrusted her nephew, and for good reason. It was Mallory's job to protect his community from harm, but what harm Corvus was to the community, no one yet knew.

She nodded her head to the others who stared at her silently. Sarah knew she was no more accepted by the village than her nephew. She was rarely visited and hardly spoken to.

"Elder Mallory," she said softly but assertively. "I come to ask your permission to allow my nephew to cut wood with the Elders. Yesterday was his thirteenth birthday and he is now of age to participate in The Cut. I wish to ask not only for permission but also for help, as there is not a man in my home to show him how to carve his own ax."

The men exchanged glances. Two exchanged mumbled words and laughed.

"Sarah," Elder Mallory said with a sigh. "You are correct that Corvus is of age." He paused and then looked at the sky. "However, all things considered, I think it would be best if the boy did not join us this year. As of now there are already nine boys who will be cutting for the first time. I believe that inviting your nephew would be inviting trouble."

"But he has as much right as the rest of the boys in the village."

Mallory dropped his voice an octave and took a step toward Sarah with a friendly and honest approach. The smell of her hair pervaded his nostrils, but he shook the temptation away. "To be honest, Sarah, I do not know if the other boys' parents would feel comfortable if they knew your nephew was with their children in the forest…with an ax."

"Forgive me," Sarah said, taking a step back, an edge to her voice, "but my nephew has never raised a hand in anger. He is an obedient boy with good in his heart."

"Then why does he not come to church?" another man asked.

"He does not come because *you* asked him not to come," she said pointing at Elder Mallory. "Because he is *shunned!*" she said in exasperation. "Ever since the child was born he has been looked upon with nothing but suspicion and fear."

"Because of his father…"

"Yes because of his father. But what fault is that of the boy's? What claim do we have to the madness of our parents? Elder Townsend, your mother lost her memory many years ago, but the villagers do not *blame* you for it."

"That is because a flock of crows do not follow me wherever I go."

They fell silent.

"The crows have affected nothing in this village except for the villagers," she said.

Elder Mallory stepped forward again. "Corvus is a good boy, I would agree. Never have I heard him bad-mouth another villager and never have I seen him do ill will. But there *is* a darkness within him. Anyone who looks into his eyes can see that for themselves." A contemplative look came over his face and he looked at Sarah thoughtfully. The signs were coming in stronger and stronger and Mallory knew that something big was on the horizon, headed right for the village. If the boy was what he thought he was, then there was no doubt that the boy must be banished. But if he was wrong, if he banished an innocent person, then he wouldn't be able to forgive himself. For now it was too early to tell. Mallory smiled. "Perhaps there is light within him yet and perhaps the right person can help to bring that out." He set down his mallet and faced Sarah directly. "I will discuss the matter with the other councilmen and we will have a decision for you by the end of the week."

Sarah nodded her head gratefully and walked the path back to the front of the house where Corvus was waiting for her. He looked up at her with his deep black eyes, but Sarah did not meet them and she did not respond. Above them, a line of crows sat on the bridge of the roof and watched the two walk home.

*   *   *   *   *   *

The following day he spent at school, sitting in the back of the classroom as usual. Very rarely did he speak or raise his hand, and very rarely was he called on to do so. A small circle of empty chairs surrounded Corvus and he liked it that way. The less interaction he had with others, the better. He did not like his schoolmates and he did not like his teacher, so while his teacher gave the lesson of the day, Corvus spent his time gazing out the window.

Elder Loyal, as usual, stood in the front of the classroom while he lectured. Loyal was a tall and thin man and at least seventy years old. He had no family and few friends, and so The Book of Signs had become his true passion. He spent most of his days teaching from the text and today was no exception.

"A statue will never fall unless it is pushed," said Elder Loyal. "Can someone tell me why it is wrong to push a statue? Vanessa?"

"Because statues are the tangible representations of the values they stand for."

"And what happens when you push them down?"

"Our values break apart."

"Very good," said Elder Loyal. "We do not want to break the meanings of the signs because the meanings are set and eternal." Elder Loyal walked to the center of the classroom and pointed at one of the boys. "Markus, would you stand up please?" Markus stood. "I want you to come stand by me." Markus did so. "Now," Elder Loyal said, "turn and face the class. I want you to put one arm out in front of you. Straighten your finger as if you are pointing to something. Now place your other hand by your head and extend your finger so that it points to the sky. Very good. Now be still. Do not move a muscle and make not a peep."

"Markus the Statue," a boy said with a smile.

"Can we push him down?" a girl laughed.

"But then you would break me," said Markus laughing, looking slightly ridiculous.

"I said not a peep," said Loyal. "Good. Now tell me, students. If you came upon this statue, looking as he does, what would you think?"

"What an ugly statue," said a boy, and they all laughed.

Loyal quieted them. "What would you make of it? What could it possibly mean? Remember, you are taking a walk and you come upon a statue. Clearly, this is a sign."

"Is there writing on the statue?" a girl asked.

"There is none. There is nothing to tell you what the statue is meant to represent."

"He looks like he sees something."

"Or like he has discovered something."

"What has he discovered? What does he see?" Elder Loyal encouraged.

The children turned around to follow the boy statue's gaze which went to the far end of the classroom. "He looks like he is pointing at Corvus," a student said.

Corvus raised his eyes but not his head. He could see Markus's finger pointing at him, and he didn't like it one bit. He wanted to tell them all to keep ignoring him as they always had. He preferred the shadows of his solitude. Markus's finger was just another example everyone's judgment. No one in this community accepted him. There was no "collective" as far as he could tell, and if there was, he certainly wasn't a part of it. His crows made him different. He *felt* different, too. He wasn't like the other villagers. He didn't want to be.

"Corvus!" a boy laughed. "Someone has finally discovered you."

"Not much of a discovery," said another.

"Alright, alright, let us stay on task." Loyal said. His eyes brightened as an idea came to him. "For you boys about to make your first cut, who *knows* what you will find in the weeks to come? For the sake of argument, let us assume that this statue *is* pointing at Corvus. You and your party have been walking through the forest only to find Markus the Statue. The statue is obviously trying to get your attention; otherwise you would not have discovered it. One hand is pointing at the sky, while the other is pointing past you. When you turn to look at what the statue is pointing at you see Corvus in the back, lazily following the group. Now everyone agrees that the statue is pointing at Corvus. Every sign is a signpost at a specific location in time. Everything was arranged just so. Now we must solve the other half of the equation: what is the significance? Some of you suggest that it is a sign that you should leave Corvus behind, that he is too slow and slowing the party down. Others believe that it is a sign to move at the pace of Corvus, that the statue is pointing to the virtue of patience rather than haste. The mission of the party is to get to The White Village before dark. The statue obviously means something - but what?"

"Leave him behind," a girl said.

"Yeah. He can always catch a lift from his friends. Caw, caw!" a boy said.

Corvus looked at the surface of his desk and said nothing. He didn't care if they left him behind.

"What if he has something you need?" Loyal asked.

"Then search him and take it," someone said.

"What if it is a value you cannot take? Like patience? Perhaps pushing him would break his patience, preventing the party from arriving at the village before dark."

"Alone in the forest with Corvus? At night?" a girl said. "No thank-you."

"Keep pushing," said a redheaded boy with a mischievous smile. "I bet if you pushed him hard enough he would break into a crow...and *peck your eyes out!*"

"Jeremy!" Loyal said firmly, but the Elder eyed Corvus carefully. He did not know how the strange loner might react to being bullied.

"But Markus *is* pointing at Corvus," said a girl. Corvus looked up from the back of the classroom. The girl who had spoken was blond and pretty, and Corvus considered her to be the smartest student in the class. Her name was Celina.

"I know he is now, but I mean this as a strictly hypothetical example. Imagine you are walking through a forest and you find a statue..."

"But Elder Loyal, you said that all events line up for a reason. How is the result of this event different from any other? The forest example is not real, but this one *is*. You asked Markus to extend his hand and become a statue. Well, right now there is a statue with an outstretched hand pointing at Corvus. Right here there is a tangible representation standing for a value, and that value is apparently Corvus."

The classroom went quiet. Corvus lifted his eyes and saw that everyone was staring at him. He looked at Markus who was still pointing directly at him, his other hand raised into the air. There was a strange expression on his face, but Corvus did not think the expression was one of discovery. Instead, he felt like *he* was being given a sign.

Very quietly Corvus said, "If I am the value, then am I not the one to determine my own meaning?"

"The value is for the group, not the individual."

"But what if the individual does not agree with the meaning that the group has assigned it?"

"It is irrelevant," Loyal said. "The individual is not important, only the collective is. Remember, the language of the universe is universal. The fact of the matter is, you could *all* misinterpret the sign. That is why we are here, so that we may learn the true language of the universe."

"How do we know that we are interpreting the universe correctly?" Celina asked.

"Because another sign will always follow to state its correct translation."

"So what do *you* make of this sign?" Celina asked Elder Loyal.

"You mean the fact that Markus has pointed at Corvus?"

Celina nodded.

Elder Loyal looked at Corvus. Even from the back of the room the boy seemed to emit a black light from his eyes, like shadows mixing with the reflection of water. His eyes were evidence enough that there was more to him than just a simple meaning, but Elder Loyal didn't dare venture into *that* unknown realm. "Well, the way I see it," Elder Loyal said slowly, "Markus has, without meaning to do so, found an unlikely value surrounded by empty desks."

One by one, the children turned around to face the front of the classroom. Markus returned to his desk and Elder Loyal began to teach another lesson. Looking out the window, Corvus watched thirteen crows fly across the sky in the shape of a snake.

*   *   *   *   *   *

Corvus walked out the school building and kicked a small stone with his feet as he wandered home. He watched the pebble bounce across the cracks in the road. He looked up at the sky and saw that it was empty. He followed the rocks again, replaying the drama of the statue in his mind.

Sometimes, Corvus pretended that the rocks were houses and the sticks mighty trees and that he was a giant. He smiled to himself, speaking in whispers to the invisible villagers who lived inside the rocks. " 'Watch out,'" he cried in mock alarm. " 'A giant is coming! A giant is coming, help!'" He imagined the tiny people running out of their houses, scattering in the street. He made big exaggerated steps, pretending to crush the fleeing people.

"Someone disturbed my sleep!" he said. "I've come to destroy the dream wreckers!" He kicked a rock and watched it sail through the air and land in a creek.

" 'My house! My house is ruined! Hurry, get out of here!'"

He leaned over and picked up a bigger rock and raised it over his head, preparing to destroy the imaginary village. "Look out, Elder Mallory!"

"What have you got planned for that rock, Corvus?" It was Jeremy.

Corvus turned around and saw a group of three boys staring at him. He lowered the rock slowly. "Nothing," he said, not making eye contact.

"Doesn't look like nothing," said a boy.

"I think you were going to throw that rock on a house, just like you ruined that *other* house," Jeremy teased.

Corvus blushed. "I was just pretending."

"You know, Corvus, people don't *really* live in rocks."

"I know that."

"I don't think you do."

"Do not make fun of me," he said, and raised the stone in his hand.

Jeremy laughed. "Are you going to throw that rock at me?"

Corvus lowered the rock and let it fall out of his hands. "No. I just want you to leave me alone."

The redheaded boy took a step closer. He was at least a head taller than Corvus, but his frame was thin and wiry. Jeremy was not a good-looking boy by any means. He was missing a front tooth and his red freckles made him look feminine. Still, he was one of the more popular kids in The White Village, probably, Corvus figured, because most of the other kids were afraid of him. "Why leave when we just arrived? Besides, maybe we want to play with rocks, too."

"Hey, look!" one of the boys said. In the near distance, two crows flew in their direction. Corvus smiled. It was Korbin and Oritus. They must have felt his tension and come, Corvus figured. It wasn't unusual for the crows to react to Corvus's emotions. They often appeared when he was under stress, almost as if they were protecting him.

The two crows landed on the opposite house, facing the four boys. The boys gazed up at the birds and the birds gazed down at the boys.

Jeremy shrugged. "It's just a couple of birds."

"They're crows," said another.

"They're Corvus's crows," said the third.

"They will not hurt you," Corvus said. "They are actually very smart. I can call more in," he said, excitement rising in his voice, hoping to impress the boys.

"No you can't," said Jeremy. "No one can communicate with the animals." Corvus noticed that Jeremy seemed to shiver at the idea.

"I can too," said Corvus with a smile. "I do not know how they understand me, they just do."

"Do it then. Call in some more."

"I don't know, Jeremy," one of the boys said. "It is not a good idea to play with the signs."

"Says who?"

"Says *who*? Don't you pay attention to *anything*? You're not supposed to play with the signs, *period*."

"That's just to scare people. Besides, it's not like Corvus here could actually manifest. Only the Elders of the council can do that. And only a few of them," Jeremy added.

"The Elders say that it's dangerous to attempt to manifest."

But Jeremy put up his hand and taunted, "Do it, Corvus. Call in your crows."

Corvus looked at them questioningly, waiting for someone to object, but no one did. He thought of his aunt who had once warned him about calling in the signs. A part of him knew that he shouldn't, but he couldn't resist the opportunity to impress Jeremy.

Corvus cupped his hands to his mouth and whistled a short staccato. The whistle was dark and toneless and overall unpleasant to listen to. Corvus turned his eyes skyward as he whistled softly into the air. His song was so soft that the boys wondered what could possibly hear it, though internally, they feared that a blanket of crows would cover the sky and smother the sun. But for now, the heavens were empty. Corvus continued whistling for about five minutes, but to his dismay, nothing happened.

"See, I *told* you he couldn't do it," Jeremy said smugly.

Corvus looked at the sky in desperation. He saw nothing. He lowered his hands from his mouth and stopped whistling. He felt ridiculous and knew he was going to get made fun of for failing to manifest, when suddenly the two crows on the roof began to caw. The boys looked up. The crows were mimicking the pattern of the boy's staccato. Moments later, on the edge of the forest, a crow could be seen flying towards them. The boys watched in silent amazement.

The crow came quickly. It circled over the rooftop and gently landed beside the two crows. When it was settled it began to caw in cadence with the others' rhythm. It was in this manner that crow after crow began to appear on the horizon, the caws calling in the next unseen manifestation.

Corvus watched the spectacle with the rest of the boys, but unlike the others, he was smiling. He whistled softly to each of the crows as they joined the group, and the crows would look down at him and continue the call.

After almost twenty minutes all thirteen crows had come. During this time, none of the boys spoke. Their stares shifted from the crows to Corvus and back to the crows. At last, the crows were silent and only the wind could be heard passing through the empty alley.

Finally, Jeremy spoke. His words revealed a soft tremble in his voice. "The council should know about this. If anyone else were to find out -"

A caw from the rooftop cut him off. The boy gasped and took a step backwards.

"They will not hurt you," Corvus said quickly, giving the crow an annoyed look. "They will not hurt anyone," he said, though a part of him could not help wishing they would give Jeremy a good scare. He deserved it.

"But they're *crows*," said a boy. "The Book of Signs says that crows are messengers of death."

Corvus shook his head. He wanted to light that stupid book on fire. But knowing how holy it was in the eyes of the villagers, he said carefully, softly, "Perhaps The Book of Signs is wrong."

A boy pointed his finger at Corvus. Almost shrieking he said, "You say The Book is false!"

"I did *not* say it is false," said Corvus. "I just think we should question what we are taught. I mean, it is not like all the world's knowledge has been attained and written down. How can we say that we know everything for certain?"

"It is certain that to manifest is to corrupt and you have just manifested a flock of crows," said a boy.

"I have not," Corvus said. "I have called them from their hiding places in the forest. It was not I that wanted to see them. *You* have manifested them through me."

"My uncle was right," said Jeremy with a sneer. "You *are* crazy, just like your father was."

Never taking their eyes off the crows, the group of boys slowly backed away. "You better watch the signs carefully, Corvus," Jeremy said before he slipped around the corner. "They might just turn on you before we do."

Chapter Three

Several days later Corvus was in his house when there was a knock at the door. He opened the door and standing outside was his neighbor Elder Moore. Elder Moore was a short but strong man, and also the youngest member on the council. Moore took a step backwards to stand in the sunlight. "Hello, Corvus," he said.

"Hello, Elder Moore," Corvus replied. "How may I help you?"

"I have come with news, Corvus. Just last night I had a talk with the other council members, and together, we have come to a decision regarding your participation in the upcoming Cut." Corvus held his breath. "Several of the members believe that you are not yet ready or mature enough, and the fact that you are followed by crows doesn't help." Moore sighed and looked into Corvus's deep black eyes. The truth was, Moore rather liked Corvus and admired his intelligence. He had seen the boy grow up over the years and had watched him adapt to the ever-growing number of crows. Like the rest of the villagers, Elder Moore was apprehensive of the crows' presence in the village, but it also fascinated him to observe Corvus interact with the birds in his careful loving way. It was clear to Moore that Corvus had a good heart, albeit a lonely one. Moore believed that if Corvus could spend more time with other members of the community, they would soon see he wasn't so bad after all, and The Cut was a perfect opportunity.

"Corvus, I spoke up on your behalf, saying that since I have known you, you have been a hard worker and an honest member of the village." A crow landed on the roof above them. Moore continued speaking, but kept his eyes trained on the crow. "Corvus, we have agreed to allow you to begin the preparations for this year's Cut, under the condition that we will watch the signs and follow their guidance."

Corvus wanted to hug Elder Moore. "Thank you, sir, for sticking up for me. Truly, I want to do the best job that I can. I really believe that I am ready for this."

Elder Moore smiled dimly. "We shall see."

"What happens next, sir?"

"Well, whenever you are ready, I will be the one to show you how to carve your first ax."

"I am ready now," he almost shouted and then composed himself.

"That is, if *you* are ready."

Elder Moore laughed softly. "I thought you might say that. Gather whatever you need and come next door."

"I can follow you over this instant," he said. "Oh, wait! Wait just a second." Corvus darted inside. He ran to the back of the house and went into his room, took out the crow feather that he kept in his pocket, and hid it under a blanket. Returning, he beamed up at Elder Moore and said, "OK, I am ready."

Corvus followed Elder Moore to his home. Inside, Moore's wife was preparing lunch in the kitchen. Her body stiffened as she eyed the boy walking through their home. "Marguerite, we will be in the shop if you need us," her husband said.

Sunlight penetrated nearly every corner of Moore's workshop. Piles of sawdust were scattered about the room, remnants of past projects.

"The first thing a man needs when making an ax is a good piece of wood. In the corner you will find five different types - Oak, Pine, Redwood, Alder, and Maple. Choose whichever one calls to you."

Corvus knew about each kind of wood. During the last few days he had studied them all very carefully. Redwood represented strength. Maple symbolized beauty. Oak was the symbol of eternity and patience. Corvus chose a beautiful length of pine.

Elder Moore took the next hour to show Corvus how to carve off the bark with a knife. When Corvus was finished, Elder Moore helped him with the cutting of the handle. "It is no accident that an ax resembles the body of a man. Right now we are carving the body of the ax, just as the body of the earth carves each of us to its will. We have no choice in what we look like when we are born, but we have a choice with how we choose to be used. Since everything comes from everything else, we must submit to our humble place in this world. The Book of Signs teaches us that we only have one life in this world, so we must choose a life that means something. Some of us are born as singers, some as seers and council members, and others..." he said looking at Corvus, "well, we all come to represent something or another."

They finished the body of the ax and set to sharpen a metal head that had already been forged. As they did so, Elder Moore continued his catechism. "The head of your ax represents your own conscious judgment and the force of reason. We humans were given a head and a mind so that we may discern what is truth and what is not. When we determine what is false, we cut it down. This is why we go into the forest. The forest represents the darkness, the obscurity, the chaos of the universe. The festival is not only about cutting out the darkness, but a representation of our duty to the village. We must cut out the falseness of the world to let light in."

Corvus was fascinated by the symbolism of The Cut. He greatly enjoyed the physical act of creation, of turning one thing into something else. For him, the idea of turning something dark into something light was compelling. "Who knows?" he thought to himself "Maybe the village is ready for a new symbol."

*   *   *   *   *   *

The sun was approaching its zenith as Corvus ran down the street to meet the others. When he got to the plaza he could see Elder Mallory standing beneath the Tree of Truth. Nine boys were circled around him. Not wanting to look too eager, Corvus slowed his pace to a steady walk. He took a few quick breaths to calm his nerves - his fingers were so tightly wrapped around his new ax that his hands were beginning to ache.

"OK," he said to himself. "Everyone knows you're coming. Just be yourself and they'll see there's nothing to be afraid of. " He slackened his grip on the ax and looked nonchalantly up at the empty sky, pleased to see that for now his crows were absent. His shoes moved softly over the white stones and he approached the group so quietly that a boy named Thomas gasped when Corvus brushed against his shoulder. The boy on the other side of him shied out of the way and Corvus joined the circle.

"Thank you for joining us, Corvus," Elder Mallory said with toned impatience. He looked at the other boys and nodded his head as if answering their question. "Now that we all are here we can leave for the forest. But before we do so, it is important to understand why we are going in the first place, for after all, it is not an outing to take lightly."

Mallory gazed up at the Tree of Truth and smiled as speckles of shade and sunlight washed over his face. He rested his hands on the bark of the old olive tree and mumbled a few indistinguishable words. The boys were watching him closely.

"This tree is the truth of our village. It knows more than your young minds could possibly comprehend. This very tree," he said slowly, "holds the wisdom of our past. When The White Village was nearly annihilated, long before any of you were born, all of our history was lost. Besides a few buildings, it was only this tree that remained."

"What happened?" a boy asked.

Mallory looked off into the distance, remembering the events that had taken place during that fateful night. He remembered the storm that had washed over the village like a thundering omen. Everyone had been so afraid, certain the end of the world had come at last. So much had been lost that night, but some things were best buried in the past.

His gaze, which contained both a mixture of wonder and nostalgia, fell upon the old twisted tree. "The old-timers will tell you it was the Storm of the Century. It destroyed our homes, our crops, *everything*," he said with widening eyes. "A storm, you see, is a symbol of violent change, a sign of the times to come. When the wind begins to blow we will either bend like the willow or snap like a branch. A keen reader of the signs, I was able to convince the people that it was time to bend to the ways of the Creator - it was time to purify our village. Following the storm, we decided that a church must be built, for only when a village has a church does it have a moral compass to steer society. Once the church had been completed, we tried those responsible for the storm...and we banished them."

"But how can someone be responsible for a natural event?" someone asked.

"Nothing comes from nothing," Mallory said. "Everything is connected. The destruction of the village came from the impure thoughts and actions of the villagers. Remember, this happened during the days when people freely shared their dreams, and let me tell you, back then people's dreams were anything but pure. I heard them myself," he said with a look of alarm. "People discussed their desires like drunkards looking for a fight. It is a truth that our thoughts and our dreams create our reality, children. A beautiful thought shared with the collective will build a beautiful village. But a nightmare...to share a dream of destruction is a terrible thing indeed."

Mallory glanced at Corvus out of the corner of his eye. He dreamt often about the darkness of the boy, a darkness that had revealed itself during the boy's birth. A barrage of symbols had come to the village that night and had woven their meaning into a powerful prophecy, though Mallory had been the only one to read it as such. Corvus, of course, along with the rest of the villagers, knew nothing of it. It was imperative, Mallory believed, that the prophecy be kept hidden from others. If the villagers knew what was coming it would manifest all the sooner. Mallory *had* to protect his flock, but for now all he could do was keep a close eye on Corvus and follow the wisdom of the signs.

"We will not be using our axes today, though it is important that we carry them with us. It is important because they are symbols of our external power. Human beings are inherently powerless. We are insig*nifi*cant," he said with emphasis, "in comparison to the vastness of the universe. It is the signs *within* the universe that gives us power, and if we know the meanings of the signs then we can use them to our advantage. In the forest, a place where meaning is mere illusion, our axes are the only power we have."

Mallory picked up his ax, and signaling for the group to do the same, led the way to the edge of the forest. After a thirty-minute walk they had arrived. A small trail protruded out of the woods indicating the entrance into the forest. Many of the boys were visibly nervous. Corvus, on the other hand, could barely contain his excitement. Beyond these trees another world awaited. He, like the rest of the boys, had never entered the forest before. It was forbidden. No one went into the forest unless they had to, or unless they were banished. Corvus had never really given the banished much thought, but standing at the threshold of the forest, he couldn't help but wonder if once inside he would spot one of their skeletons. The Elders said the forest was so dense with illusion that no one could survive inside for long…yet that's where they were going! His palms were caked with sweat.

Corvus looked over his shoulder. In the distance, he could see the old tree at the top of the hill. The crows were most likely watching him from its upper branches. He knew better than to call them in, though part of him wished they would join him. He felt more confident when they were around, even if no one else did. He wanted desperately to change their meaning. Though he would never admit it, a part of him was growing tired of being an outcast.

Mallory leaned on his ax as he addressed the small group. "This will be your first entrance into the forest. That which lies before us is full of illusion and deception. The signs of the universe still exist within these woods, but they are permeated in a language difficult to understand. The purpose of today's journey is to acquaint ourselves with the illusion. It is not something to take lightly. There is much that exists within that even *I* do not fully comprehend." Mallory looked at the boys. At least two of them were visibly shaking. "It is OK to be afraid," he said with affection. "Fear reminds us that we are alive. The purpose of The Cut, however, is not to prove to ourselves that we can go into the darkness, but rather to know that we can cut out the darkness if we need to."

Jeremy rolled his eyes. This was all a bit too dramatic for him. "Can we just go already?"

Mallory faced him. "Let me assure you. There is a madness waiting to be unleashed in there. Woe to the person who it is unleashed upon." With that, Mallory picked up his ax and stepped across the boundary. Jeremy rolled his eyes again and nudged one of the smaller boys. "Geez, Thomas. Get a grip, would you?"

Corvus followed at the end of the line. Stepping across the threshold he began to understand what Mallory was talking about. The forest severed the sunlight almost immediately and though Corvus was not afraid, he was most certainly on edge. The boys were silent as they walked along the thin dirt path, the denseness of the forest only increasing as they continued onward. Corvus was amazed by the variety of trees and plants that he saw along the way. Everything about this place was incredible and far more interesting than anything in The White Village. In the village, the symbols had all been decided, but here life took on new meaning.

Up ahead, someone was complaining. "Hey, you stepped on my shoe. Watch where you're going." It was Jeremy.

"I can't help it. It's dark," Corvus heard Thomas say.

Mallory stopped walking. "Be quiet. I hear something."

Even from the back of the line Corvus could hear it too. An unsettling sound was approaching them. Whatever it was, it was big.

"I want to go back," Thomas said.

"Oh, come off it," Jeremy remarked. "It's probably a squirrel."

Elder Mallory hushed them again and motioned for everyone to duck down. The group didn't have to be told twice because the sound was coming at them like a rolling boulder. Even Mallory looked concerned. He put his finger to his lips, demanding silence from the group. He observed every detail of the forest in hopes of discerning the event's outcome. The noise was all around them now. Bushes and branches shook violently and among it all, Corvus thought he could hear voices. He wondered if it could be one of the banished trying to scare them, though he remembered Mallory once saying that the forest killed all lone travelers. So what could it be? His fingers tightened around his ax.

All at once the sound stopped. The group waited in suspenseful silence. At last, Mallory stood, and after a moment, signaled for the group to keep moving.

They walked quickly and quietly through the forest without encountering any more strange noises. Several of the boys kept looking nervously over their shoulders, but all they saw was Corvus at the end of the line looking back at them.

Finally, the group arrived at a small clearing. Large tree stumps sat in an open glade and sunlight poured into the grassy meadow. Mallory told everyone to sit down and they happily did so.

"This is as far as we will go today. This is the sight of last year's Cut. I know this clearing doesn't seem that large, but it took us three days to clear it. Perhaps now you can appreciate the depth and necessity of our work. In a land so dark and so dangerous, even the smallest amount of light can make all the difference." Mallory looked around at the boys. Many of them were still shaken. Others looked proud that they had made it to the clearing.

Corvus on the other hand, barely seemed affected. Mallory took notice that the frightening event in the forest had hardly fazed him. Corvus was more like his father than Mallory gave him credit for. He was calm and observant. Even now, Corvus looked like he was waiting for something else to happen. Mallory had interpreted the sign in the forest and knew that something hidden was coming, but he wondered if Corvus knew the same.

While Mallory lectured the boys about the madness of the forest, Corvus brushed his hands along the wood of his ax. In three days he would use this ax to cut away the darkness with the rest of the boys. Still, something lingered in his mind. He thought about the noise they had heard. Corvus couldn't help but acknowledge the sign for what it was - the collective fear of something harmless.

Elder Mallory lectured the group for over an hour and then told the boys it was time to return. The boys collected their axes and Mallory led the group back single file. This time the pace was much faster. The forest was now noticeably darker than when they had entered. Corvus figured they only had an hour or two until the sun dipped behind the horizon. He stayed in the back of the line as usual, though his spirits were high as he thought about the upcoming Cut. Thomas walked in front of him and kept looking over his shoulder, the slightest sound practically sending him into a panic.

"There is nothing to be afraid of," Corvus said softly. "It is just the breeze moving the trees." But either Thomas didn't hear him or didn't want to believe him. His pace had slowed considerably, and now the rest of the boys were around the corner and out of sight. Corvus was beginning to get nervous. The last thing he wanted to do was get lost in the forest with Thomas. Corvus was not afraid of the forest but he knew that Thomas's fears could easily manifest something very unpleasant.

The forest darkened and Corvus pleaded with Thomas to get going. Thomas obeyed and went slightly faster until fear took over, slowing him back down again. The trail was becoming harder to distinguish. Corvus was now worried that they would lose their way back to The White Village.

A sharp caw cut through the darkness and Thomas nearly leapt into Corvus's arms. Corvus looked up into the branches and saw a crow. It was Korbin. "Don't worry, Thomas. It is one of my crows. I think it is trying to guide us home."

"But it is a bad omen," Thomas said.

Corvus shook his head, a bit annoyed. "Stop it. That is nonsense," Corvus said. "Come on." He stepped lightly around Thomas and trotted down the trail. He whistled happily up at the crow as he jogged past it. He was certain he was on the right path.

He had gone only a hundred meters down the trail when he heard a scream. Thomas was nowhere in sight. Nervous, he darted back in the boy's direction. When Corvus found him, Thomas was standing against a tree and his ax was at his feet. Corvus couldn't believe his eyes. Standing in front of Thomas was a large creature over eight feet tall. Its legs were gray and hairy. Instead of feet it had hooves and at the waist its body transformed into a man's. From behind, Corvus could see the long horns of a goat protruding out of the man's shaggy hair. Sensing someone else, the creature turned around and faced Corvus. Its eyes were large and yellow and its expression conveyed an ancient anger. Corvus gripped his ax tightly and raised it. "Leave him alone!" he shouted.

The creature stepped toward Corvus. *"You attack with your ax when your mind is at stake. This forest will swallow you along with the illusions you make. Ignorant boy, facing a shadow you think you can see, but one day when you know, you will be unable to lay two eyes onto me. Too blind to care of the truth within. Your kind no longer belongs. Go now and I will spare you, before your destruction begins."*

Corvus lowered the ax halfway. "We mean you no harm. It is our custom to come into the forest and cut out the darkness."

"Your custom *is to destroy what you do not understand. I demand that you leave. This nature is no longer your nature. Your kind has become blinded, your mind but a mirror of the land far away - that sea of endless disease."* The creature stepped aggressively toward Corvus.

Corvus took a step back but then opened his eyes wide with realization. "The Elders were right. You are nothing but illusion!" Without thinking, he raised his hand to his lips and whistled as loud as he could. From Thomas's perspective it was hard to determine which was more terrifying – the half-man half-creature who would murder them both, or the murder of crows which had suddenly descended into the dim darkness of the forest. Corvus raised his ax over his head and yelled at the top of his lungs while his flock of crows flew over his shoulders, their talons trained on the monstrous creature.

"You can only fight what you understand," the creature said, and then vanished before Corvus's eyes.

Thomas screamed. He stood up and ran through the flock of crows that had landed on the ground in front of him. He ran past Corvus who still held the ax over his head, and into the arms of Elder Mallory. Mallory and the rest of the group had returned. Having heard the screams, they rushed back. But when they arrived all they saw was Corvus with an ax over his head and thirteen crows at his feet. The signs were not in Corvus's favor.

Chapter Four

The evening after the incident, Corvus returned home to tell his aunt that he would not be allowed to participate in The Cut this year. Elder Mallory had quietly taken Corvus aside and had told the boy what Corvus already knew. No amount of arguing would change the Elder's mind. Thomas had mentioned nothing to the Elders about the creature in the woods. In fact, he hardly said anything to anyone. It was obvious that he was traumatized by the event, and the next day, Thomas informed the Elders that he would not be going back into the forest.

Corvus looked down the hill. The air of the festival had roused him out of bed and he had followed the cutters to the edge of the forest, just as he had in the years before. He wanted more than anything to join the boys, to prove that he was worthy, but he knew that opportunity had been lost. Instead, he climbed by himself to the hill to be with his crows.

He sighed and pulled his eyes away from the village and lifted them to the tree which stood behind him. He let out a whistle and Korbin fluttered down from the cracked branches and stood before the boy.

"Everyone is so terrified of you," he said distantly, "and of me." Corvus sighed and shook his head, holding back tears. He felt stupid for thinking that the villagers would ever accept him and angry for believing he could change the crows' meaning. "They don't even know *why* they are afraid," he thought to himself. A red coal of resentment burned in the bottom of his stomach. "They are afraid because they are *conditioned* to be afraid. They don't know what I know about the crows. They don't *want* to know what I know," he thought arrogantly. But as he watched Korbin pacing back and forth in front of him, a whirlwind of doubt overtook him and the sadness replaced his anger. Crows had followed him for thirteen years yet he still didn't have the faintest idea as to why such a bad omen watched over him. Maybe the villagers were right to fear him. Maybe the crows really were evil, and maybe, so was he.

"*You* do not have to be afraid, Korbin," he said affectionately. "No one here will hurt you, not in *this* village," he said, shaking his head. "They say it's a bad idea to harm a crow. I think that is why my father named me Corvus…to protect me."

Corvus looked off into the distance thinking about the many strange customs in The White Village, practically all of them designed and implemented by Elder Mallory. Some of the traditions made sense to Corvus, but others seemed superstitious. For example, the council proclaimed that it was wrong to see a snake. It is said that if a person sees a snake it must be kept a secret or else a terrible accident will occur. It is the same reason why no one is allowed to discuss their dreams. Even The Cut seemed a bit strange to Corvus. He thought the trees were beautiful, much more beautiful than the stumps that were left in their places. Still, he would have given anything to cut one down with the rest of the boys in the forest.

Corvus sat under the pine tree for the rest of the day. The sun was about an hour from falling over the horizon when a shout rang out from the edge of the meadow. "They are back!" Corvus exclaimed. He jumped up and bounded down the hill to meet the cutters who were loading the cut wood into piles and returning into the forest for more.

Corvus could hear the sounds of young boys pouring out of the village, eager to help carry the wood from the forest to the plaza. If Corvus ran fast, he could beat them. He was halfway down the hill when he looked over his shoulder to see several of the crows following above. He stopped running and looked up at them helplessly.

"Please do not follow me," he said. "If the men see that you are with me then they might not let me carry the wood." He let out a sharp whistle to scatter the crows away. "I am sorry," he said, and watched them drift slowly back to the hill.

There were several piles of wood stacked near the edge of the forest. When Corvus arrived another boy was already gathering pieces to carry back to the village. It was Thomas.

"Corvus?" Thomas asked with surprise. "What are *you* doing here?"

"Carrying wood to the village," Corvus said shortly, still angry with Thomas.

"But the Elders forbade it. You could get…banished," Thomas said softly, not wanting to have this conversation. It was evident that he felt bad about the way things had turned out.

Corvus glared at Thomas. "Just *say* it, Thomas," he said, his eyes flashing with anger. "Say that you don't want me in the village! Keep isolating me. Everyone else does!"

"It's not like that at all, Corvus," Thomas said. "This morning I heard several of the boys say they felt sorry for you that you weren't allowed back into the forest."

"I don't need anyone's sympathy," Corvus said through gritted teeth. "I can take care of myself."

Thomas looked at Corvus, not knowing what to say. He wanted to apologize, but didn't know if it would help. "No one *hates* you, you know? Maybe Jeremy does, but he hates everything." Thomas grabbed another piece of wood. "I only mentioned Elder Mallory's warning because I didn't want you to get in any more trouble."

"You don't know what you're talking about, as usual. Elder Mallory said I could not cut this year," Corvus said. "He did not say that I am not allowed to carry the wood to the village, as I have done in the past." Corvus began to pick up some wood.

They heard a rustling coming out of the forest. Jeremy emerged with a pile of wood in his arms. When Jeremy saw Corvus he balked. "I'll tell you, Corvus. You don't give up easily." Jeremy looked at Thomas. "He's come to finish you off, Thomas," he said grinning with fingers outstretched. "Quick, run!" Thomas kept quiet.

Elder Moore came out next. He let the wood fall heavily to the ground and he wiped his brow. "Corvus!" Moore exclaimed, looking at Corvus in wonder. The fact that the boy had come to carry the wood knowing he had not been allowed to cut impressed Moore. "That is a heavy load Corvus has got," he said to Jeremy. "How long are you going to keep him standing with your chatter?" Corvus smiled at Elder Moore and then trotted off toward the plaza.

That day Corvus made a total of thirty trips to the woodpile, carrying more than twice the amount as the other boys. Each time he reached the plaza with an armload of wood the more the women stared. "He does not even seem winded," they said to each other.

He had made nearly twenty trips without stopping when his aunt urged him to rest. "Come, Corvus," she said from the shadow of her bonnet. Take a small drink before you collapse."

"But there is still wood to be carried," he called off over his shoulder as he ran out of the village again.

The woodcutters sat at the edge of the forest. Their shirts were off and they watched the young boys carry the wood back to The White Village. Tradition and Law held that once all the wood had been carried back to the village the woodcutters could return and the festivities could begin. The process often took many hours and usually wasn't over until the moon was high in the sky. The festival was carefully planned to correlate with celestial alignments, because the Elders wanted to take full advantage of the cyclical symbols that transpired each year.

"I do believe we will be walking home early this year," Elder Moore laughed.

The others said nothing. They watched Corvus run through the meadow in their direction. Most of the younger boys were now resting with their mothers or slowly walking with a piece of wood under an arm.

"I don't remember him carrying this much wood last year," said a boy.

"I do not remember you carrying that much *ever*," said a man, and they all laughed.

When Corvus returned, the men stopped talking. Corvus was breathing hard. The wood was almost gone, but there were still six large pieces left.

"Two trips to go, Corvus," said Elder Sight.

Corvus eyed the pile. He could easily make two more trips, but he wanted to be the boy to carry the last piece of wood to the village. He knew there was a boy behind him that would take what Corvus couldn't carry.

"I can carry it all," he said, still panting, "but I will need someone to load them for me."

"The Law says that the cutters cannot touch the wood again," Elder Mallory said. "If you'd like, you can try to convince another boy to help you."

"But I doubt you can persuade someone not to take the last log," someone said.

Corvus looked at the pile. They were right. He wouldn't be able to convince anyone to help him. To carry the last log into the plaza was an honor. Traditionally, the cutters followed the last log into the village, singing behind the wood runner, swinging their axes in dance. If he could be that boy, then perhaps he could redeem himself in the eyes of the villagers, but from where he stood, it looked hopeless.

He sighed heavily and began to pick up the logs one by one. With five in his arms he leaned over to pick up the sixth, but dropped his burden. He tried once more, but again, dropped the logs.

"Too bad your crows aren't around," said Jeremy. "Maybe they would carry that extra log." Elder Mallory shushed him.

"Just take the five, Corvus," Elder Moore said softly. "Everyone knows how much you have carried. It is no shame not being able to carry them all."

Corvus looked over his shoulder and saw an approaching boy who would claim the last log. Corvus looked at the wood frantically, trying to come up with a solution. Suddenly, he had an idea.

He took off his trousers and set them on the ground with the legs facing opposite directions. The woodcutters stared at him in amazement, but Corvus ignored them. He placed the wood at the crotch of the pants and made a small pyramid until all six were neatly stacked. He pulled the legs over the pile and tied them in two. Then, with a heavy grunt, he hoisted the wood over his shoulder.

The Elders began to laugh.

"Ingenious!" one said.

"If he were any shorter his pants..." one man laughed, but couldn't finish his sentence.

Standing there in his underwear, with six pieces of wood over his shoulder, Corvus had never felt prouder.

"Well now," Elder Moore said. "We cannot let the last wood runner walk into The White Village without pants. Jeremy," he said to the redheaded boy. "Take off your trousers."

"*What!*"

"You heard me. Maybe this will teach you not to taunt the wood runners."

"Hurry up," said another man. "He cannot hold all that wood forever."

"You are going to have to put them on for him," one of the men said. Jeremy took off his pants, and with a silent red hatred, helped Corvus to slip into them.

"OK, Corvus," Elder Moore said. "Make your walk."

With the wood over his shoulder, the boy with grandfather eyes marched into town like a triumphant soldier. The woodcutters formed a line and fell into chorus:

"Carry the woods in, merry the woodsmen.
Carry the woods in, merry the woodsmen.
Cut them and call them the trees have all fallen,
Carry the woods in, merry the woodsmen."

The youngsters ran at the edges of the line as the group of men approached the town. At last, the woodcutters arrived at the plaza. Sarah could not believe what she was seeing. Corvus was at the front of the line - he was the last wood runner!

The village plaza had been built into the shape of a circle. In the center of the circle was a black stone where the wood had been ritually burned for decades. It was the only black stone in the village and it gave the round plaza the semblance of an eye. Atop the ash eye was the enormous pile of wood that the children had carried from the forest's edge. The pile easily stood over fifteen feet high.

Corvus reached the outer rim of the plaza and the line broke into two parts, tracing the outside of the circle until the center was surrounded. Corvus set down his wood, untied the pants, and one by one threw the wood onto the pile.

"Into the circle of Wisdom and Light
Relax your ax! Relax your ax!
Bury the black to cover the sight.
Relax your ax! Relax your ax!"

The sky was silver gray as the beginning of night took form. A full moon crested over the hilltops in the distance and a milky glow spread out over the white plaza. The singing stopped and a hush fell among the villagers as Corvus picked up the last piece of wood. He looked at the eyes of those who watched him. Did they still shun him? Had he proven himself? The hush grew deeper like a looming thunderstorm in the distance.

Corvus turned to face the giant stack of wood. No one was allowed to speak until he tossed the last piece onto the pile. In this moment he held the fate of both the crowd and the wood. His action would determine it all. Should he fulfill his role in the ritual, or should he burn the past and recreate his own meaning? If he could sacrifice his own life, in this moment, he would save both the wood and the villagers - the wood from the fire, the villagers from their own superstitions. He wondered if the crows still sat in the tree at the top of the hill. He wondered if they observed any of this, and if so, what judgments they came to.

He tossed the wood high into the air and watched it land at the top of the pile. The villagers cheered. Corvus bowed his head and walked to the perimeter of the circle and stood alongside his aunt. Everyone joined hands and the men began to chant. As the men sang, the villagers walked around the plaza, facing the giant pile of wood.

"Now the sins of the darkness will burn with the best
While the light will ignite this symbolic jest.
Capture the meaning
That the fire is gleaning,
And follow the symbolism of this human test."

The villagers circled the woodpile three times as they sang. Finally, Elder Mallory broke from the circle and entered the center. With his hands clasped behind his back, Mallory slowly walked around the pile. The villagers looked at him intently, anxious to hear their leader speak.

Elder Mallory stretched out his arms and looked at his people one at a time. "Villagers!" he said with a smile. "The wood has been cut, carried, and piled over the ash eye. We came here today as both a celebration and reminder. We celebrate the beginning of the year and the first day of the planting which begins on the morrow. We celebrate our lives and our living. How fortunate are we to have men, strong men to provide for our village. We are fortunate to have women, strong-willed women to make use of our men's labor. We celebrate this day of new men. Today many children have participated in their first Cut and have returned from the forest as men. We honor you today, my young cutters."

Elder Mallory took a deep breath. Cautiously raising his eyes to the sky, he proceeded. "And we celebrate in the vigor of young Corvus. Never have I ever seen a boy carry as much wood as you did today, son; nor in such a manner." He laughed and many around the circle agreed and joined in his laughter.

Corvus smiled. He became overcome with emotion and for a moment feared that he might cry. "Do *not* cry, Corvus," he whispered to himself. "You are finally getting some of the acceptance you wanted. Do not blow it all by being a baby!" Corvus looked up and saw that his aunt was watching him and that she was smiling. Sarah shifted her weight and scratched his side with her hand affectionately. Corvus wanted to break from the circle and hug Elder Mallory. He immediately forgave him for not allowing him to cut. He could wait another year. He could wait another *ten* years. He arched his back and listened attentively as Mallory continued his speech.

"Remember that the festival is a symbolic reminder. Though the village was once cleansed of all offense, purification is an ongoing process. We must constantly be aware of our thoughts and actions, because our thoughts and actions lead to our collective fate. We are a community and everything we do affects everyone around us," Mallory said, making eye contact with each of the villagers, "All of us are responsible for the well-being of our home. If one of us is unwell, then we are all unwell.

"The universe speaks to us constantly. Pay attention to the signs and study them carefully." Mallory had reached the Tree of Truth and he closed his eyes as he spoke as if channeling his message from the ancient tree. His voice was deep and resounded off of the white walls that surrounded the plaza. "Years ago a great evil pervaded our village. It was a time when the symbols were not understood. Since those days we Elders have worked hard to create a life with meaning, one full with purpose and direction, peace and service. Many of you have allowed this meaning to seep into your lives, and in doing so, have shared in the abundance of the symbols. Others in the past, however, have resisted. They saw our ways of life as a challenge to their own moral code, a code not in harmony with the universe. Over the years, some who have not conformed to our wisdom have rebelled and they paid the consequences. To be an outcast is a terrible thing. Away from the collective beliefs of well-being, one soon finds themselves in the madness of individualism, the illusion that we are independent and sovereign. That madness will consume you whole. An outcast in the forest will not survive for a week."

Corvus noticed that Mallory's expression danced between judgment and love, power and promise. He thought of the Elder's words and what it would be like to be banished. Now, with his hands linked with the other villagers', Corvus began to think that being a part of the collective might not be as bad as he had thought.

"Look!" a young boy shouted, pointing at the moon. The others followed his gaze. Slowly, the edge of the moon began to disappear. The villagers watched the phenomenon in silence, knowing that the sign they had been waiting for was commencing. It held their attention entirely. Elder Mallory's words had settled into the silence as he too embraced the meaning of the lunar eclipse.

"We need all of you," Mallory said carefully. "Each one of us conveys a meaning that is unique and essential to our way of life. We must strive to be better each day. We must live to be stronger and wiser and practice the efforts of cutting out the darkness in our hearts. Choose your thoughts and actions wisely," he said looking at the villagers. As he spanned the eyes of the people, he stopped on those of Corvus's and softly said, "Or the signs of the universe will fail you."

A log was set aflame and thrown onto the woodpile. The eclipse transformed the moon into a dark red while the people of The White Village danced around the woodpile, singing in celebration of purity until the rays of dawn severed the tethers of darkness.

Chapter Five

Two mornings later Corvus was eating porridge at the table when there was a knock on the door.

"Elder Mallory," Sarah said with obvious surprise. "What are you doing here?"

"Hello, Sarah. I was wondering if I might speak with young Corvus?"

"He is right over there," she said. "Please, come in."

Elder Mallory approached Corvus and smiled. "Hello, Corvus. How are you doing this morning?"

The boy shrugged. This was the first time Elder Mallory had ever dropped by their home. "Fine. Thank you."

"May I sit down?"

Corvus shrugged again. "OK."

Elder Mallory sat down and looked across the table at Corvus. The boy's eyes were full of questions. It was obvious he had no idea why Mallory was here and so Mallory offered another smile. "I apologize for the unannounced visit," he said. "I have been wanting to come by, but did not know how to say what I need to say." He placed his hands flat on the table and sighed. For the last two nights, crows had flown into Mallory's dreams. He had never dreamt of a crow before. The dream symbol could only mean what he had suspected since the very beginning. He studied the boy carefully. He felt bad for Corvus. In a perfect world Mallory would tell Corvus the truth, but of course he could not. If he did he would be putting his village in danger.

"Your wood running caught my attention, Corvus. In all my years I have never seen a boy carry so much. In fact, none of us have. You have run wood before, Corvus, but you have never carried without quitting. It was...unnatural. Many of the villagers were astounded. They said you ran as if you were possessed," Mallory lied, trying to prove his point. The boy's dark black eyes reflected back Mallory's concern, but it was hard for the Elder to identify just what that concern was. With each passing moment Mallory became more convinced that Corvus was hiding something. "My question to you is, well, how did you do it all without...collapsing?"

The expression on Elder Mallory's face was hard for Corvus to discern, but Corvus almost thought that he saw the dimmest hint of contempt. He looked at Sarah whose hard stance and expression had not changed.

"I cannot say," Corvus stammered. "I was just trying to gather as much wood as I could."

"Corvus, try as much as we want, one person cannot do the work of one hundred, without taking a break, that is. Now please, all genuflections aside, tell me, as one friend to another, the source of your stamina the day of The Cut?"

Corvus looked at his hands.

"Embarrassment."

Elder Mallory turned around. "Excuse me?"

"Embarrassment," Sarah said again. "Corvus was the oldest boy not to participate in The Cut this year. How would that make *you* feel? He was doing everything in his power to make things right."

Elder Mallory's eyes gleamed as if Sarah's words had revealed the answer he was looking for.

At that moment, a crow landed on the windowsill. Elder Mallory looked up, his senses fully alert now. "In his power," he said quietly to himself but loud enough for them both to hear. He looked at Corvus and then at Sarah. "Do you know the meaning of a crow on a windowsill? *Do* you? Because I do." Sarah shook her head and held out her hand to prevent him from finishing, but he did so anyway. "It means death."

"Or transmigration," Corvus said almost immediately.

Elder Mallory squinted his eyes. "You have studied the Book of Signs?"

Corvus nodded. "Yes. I read it often."

Mallory was quiet and Corvus could see that he was thinking. "That is good. And what do you think of The Book?"

Corvus chose his words carefully. "I think it is interesting."

"How so?"

"I like to look at the meanings of things. There are so many."

"A meaning for every creature and creation," Mallory said.

"For example," continued Corvus, "a window is a transparent veil and a windowsill is a place for an observer to rest. Since the crow is on the opposite side of the window we can assume it is observing us. That makes sense because the crow is often seen as a judge which is why I believe that it is confused with the symbol of death. The crow is merely an observer and its qualities of observation would naturally make it a good guide. It is *possible* that the crow is here to guide us through the veil."

Elder Mallory threw up his hand in dismissal. "A *guide*? The *veil*?" he laughed to himself, unaware that his tone was mocking. "The Book of Signs speaks nothing of this. This is *speculation*. You have nothing to base your reasoning on. Corvus, you have done well to study the meanings, but do not go and give meanings of your own. The Book of Signs is not a constitution. It cannot be amended. I have read signs long before you have, long before your father for that matter." The Elder immediately regretted saying that last part. Any mention of the boy's father was too much, in his opinion. Mallory had banished him for a reason.

The Elder stood up and walked toward the crow, but the crow flew away. This bothered him. Why could only Corvus call the crows? He had to know. Mallory realized that if he could appeal to Corvus's desire to fit in, then perhaps Corvus would be more willing to share his secrets. He knew he had to be more delicate with the boy, but he didn't know how. He just stared at the empty window where the crow had been. "The villagers are growing restless, Corvus. Every day they ask me why we allow the crows to stay. Some even ask why we allow *you* to stay," Mallory said with a strange look. "It is becoming hard for me to provide reasons for them. Your crows possess a powerful symbolism. They reflect an impurity in the village, and the villagers want to know why. Why are the crows here? Why do they surround you?"

"I do not know," Corvus said. He could feel the muscles in his stomach tighten.

Mallory looked over at Sarah, hoping she could speak some sense to her nephew, but Sarah didn't budge. Mallory had a way of taking her favors the wrong way.

"You have obviously not read the entire Book of Signs, because if you had, you would know that denial is one of the worst."

"I do not know!" Corvus cried in anger. "I swear. All I know is that the crows follow me and that they are my friends. Who else do I have to share company with? It is because of the crows that I am an outcast. Do you think I cradle my life as an outcast? Well I do not!" he yelled in a fiery moment of vulnerability. His hands were balled into fists. He so desperately wanted people to trust his crows. "I do not know why they follow me, *alright*? They just do."

"Nothing just *does*," Mallory said in a flash of violent arrogance. "Everything bleeds because of a scratch and the village will suffer from the same disease no matter who is infected first. Just remember that we are all sign readers, Corvus. The universe speaks to us every moment of the day. We read it like a nursery rhyme," Mallory said condescendingly.

Corvus could feel a familiar anger building up inside of him, but he did his best to suppress it. If only Sarah would get Mallory out of their house before Corvus lost his senses. Luckily, Mallory was beginning to leave.

"We will make sense of this soon," he said. "What happens with you and your crows will determine the length of your days in The White Village."

The dam burst. "I too am a sign reader!" Corvus shouted after him. "And my eyes see a hidden meaning buried under the rules of the council. Do you suggest that the council is infallible? Do they know everything that the universe conveys to them? Have they been to the stars and experienced what the world cannot comprehend? The Book of Signs wasn't created by the universe – it was created by men, yet we villagers are discouraged from creating anything ourselves! We individuals live in a collective, but we are still individuals, each with our own perception of the world around us. Is it not possible that we all create universal meaning in our own individual universe?"

Closing the door behind him, Elder Mallory said, "Your universe is right here in this one."

When Mallory was gone Sarah marched up to Corvus and slapped him across the chest with a hand towel. "Now why did you say *that* to him!? You are in enough trouble as it is."

"I *had* to, Aunt Sarah," Corvus said. "He thinks I am a magician or something. Who knows, maybe he thinks I will turn *him* into a crow. If that happened I imagine the crow's meaning would change like *that*," he said snapping his fingers. "*They* have decided what means what. *They* have chosen our lives for us and *we* have allowed it! Well *I* cannot allow it, Aunt Sarah, because if I do, then my own inaction will be my ending."

Sarah stared at her nephew. He spoke with a confidence that surprised her. He was often so shy and soft-spoken. Now he was beyond himself, speaking wisdom from some other realm. He was like his father. She looked at Corvus and felt sympathy for him. It was evident that he did not know why the crows followed him. Only she and Elder Mallory were the keepers of *that* secret, but Sarah had been sworn to secrecy, forbidden to reveal any of their true meaning to Corvus. In time it would not matter. Looking into the deep blackness of her nephew's eyes, she knew that he would figure it out on his own soon enough.

Chapter Six

Later that evening Corvus walked down from the top of the hill to the center of the village, his crows following behind him like a cape in the sky. He called to them individually as he walked and they dropped down like an indigo pendulum only to swing back up to the flock in the air. The streets in the village were empty. The villagers were in church. Corvus marched across the plaza and sat arrogantly underneath the Tree of Truth. His crows rested on its branches like olives.

He whistled Korbin's song and the bird dropped from its perch and landed at his feet. The enormous crow looked up at him. "Go to the church and listen to what they are saying. Bring me news." Corvus whistled. "Go on, then!"

Korbin took flight toward the church. The bird circled the roof for a moment and then dropped down and sat upon the steeple. Corvus watched it and smiled. He had gotten better at training his birds. He could get them to go places now. If only they could communicate back to him. Perhaps in a dream...

The front door of the church squeaked open. A young girl stepped outside and carefully closed the door behind her. She looked over her shoulder and then calmly walked across the plaza towards Corvus. It was Celina.

At first Corvus thought he was hallucinating, but sure enough, she was approaching him. He looked around frantically at anything and everything to avoid making eye contact, hoping that his blatant disinterest would dissuade her from talking to him. Celina noticed that the crows became more agitated the closer she came. She stopped several meters from the boy on the bench and looked at him thoughtfully. After a moment she said, "I knew you would be here."

Corvus avoided her gaze, still trying to figure out why she was talking to him. He thought she was very pretty and he knew that she was popular among the other students. He also knew that people who talked to him were *not* considered popular. "Why are you not in the church?" he asked, only looking at her feet.

"My parents do not know I have left. They think I am still inside, listening to the teachings," she said, rolling her eyes.

Corvus looked at her face for the first time. "You're skipping? But why?"

She looked over his shoulder at the crows sitting in the tree. "I came to see the crows, for myself. It would be foolish to look at them when the villagers are about. They would think I have some sort of affliction. I don't, though," she said shaking her head. "I just think it is silly to ignore them out of our world." She shrugged. "I *know* they exist. Why deny it?" She took a delicate step forward. "Will they hurt me?"

He watched her, thinking she was rather brave for a girl. "They won't hurt anything. They are friendly birds."

"That isn't what most people say."

"Most people do not know their butts from their hats," he said without amusement.

She laughed and looked at him. Her eyes were crystal blue. "Maybe so." Celina traced her finger over her palm. "Can I touch one of them?"

"Probably not," he said, hoping it made him sound important. "They won't even let *me* touch them. I can call them, but that is all."

"I saw the crow on top of the steeple through the stained glass," she said. "I saw it as a sign, that I should come out, I mean." She looked at him. "I had a dream about them, Corvus."

His heart skipped a beat. "Are you not afraid to talk of your dreams?" he asked quietly.

"I am not afraid of much," Celina said, puffing up her chest a little. "And I am *not* afraid that I am going to manifest my dreams. *That* nonsense is for the Elders."

"Don't be so sure," Corvus said with interest. "Some nonsense is wrapped in truth." He thought about his latest encounter with Mallory.

She looked at him strangely. "What is it that you know?"

"*Know?*"

"I see you each day, Corvus. You walk alone, and I watch you think. You look up at the sky, to your crows, and you watch them and you think. What is it that you think about?"

He shook his head. "I know that talking about our dreams can cause one to dream."

"And you believe it is dangerous?"

"To talk about our dreams?" he asked.

Celina nodded.

"That is what the Elders say and I believe it is true, but I wouldn't know because I don't talk with anyone." He looked at his shoes.

She said nothing for a moment. "Well, what about your daydreams? Daydreams aren't dangerous. You can tell me about those if you would like."

He looked at her strangely, though Corvus could not help smiling. Celina was persistent. He turned over his shoulder and looked up at the Tree of Truth. "I dream that I can understand what the crows are saying to me," he said.

"You mean you don't?" she asked.

He shook his head. "Hard to believe, I know."

"Well maybe you just need to talk to them more," she said.

"I *do*," he insisted.

"And what do they say to you?"

Corvus shrugged. "Usually *caw*, or *squawk*, maybe."

Celina grinned and paced around the bench and walked beneath the tree. The crows were motionless as they studied her. She peered up at them, observing them closely. "How about asking them something?" she asked.

"I do, but they have no answers."

"Maybe you just need to ask better questions. Ask something important. Have you tried that before?"

He shrugged again. "Not much."

"Why not?"

"I guess because I don't even understand what they're supposed to represent in the *first* place."

"I doubt that," she said with a smile. "You can read the signs," she said, remembering his response in the classroom. "Better than most people, I'd say."

He looked up at her and smiled. "Thanks," he said softly.

"So are you going to ask them?" she said, her impatience growing.

"*Now?*" he asked. His hands were sweating.

"Why not?"

He looked at her. "Well, I'd feel weird doing it...in front of you, I mean."

Celina crossed her arms.

Corvus sighed and stood up and faced his crows. The last thing he wanted to say was something stupid. He didn't want Celina not to like him if his crows didn't respond, and he didn't want to ask a dumb question, but his unconscious desire for acceptance rejected his fears.

Corvus whistled softly in his staccato and the crows turned and faced him. Corvus whistled again. When he was certain that he had their attention he addressed them. "She wants to know...or rather, *I* want to know, why, why you all," he looked at them blankly,"...are here."

The crows just stared at him.

He hadn't expected that they would react at all, but it *had* felt good to ask them. Suddenly a barrage of questions poured out of his mouth. "Why do you follow me? Are you trying to help me? Do you want me to do something? What do you want me to do? How can I understand you better? How can I understand *myself* better?"

The crows revealed nothing.

Celina took a step forward. "You can't ask them all those questions at once," she said. "Just ask them one question or else they'll get confused."

A million questions raced through his mind. Finally, he said, "How can I identify my truth?"

All at once the crows on the Tree of Truth took flight, leaving it bare and behind them. In an instant they were out of sight completely.

Celina's eyes were wide. "They left! Where did they go?"

"To the forest," Corvus said softly. He looked at Celina from the corner of his eye. Her gaze still followed the crows' path; her face was fixed with thought. He hoped they hadn't scared her.

"What does it mean?" she asked quietly.

He looked into the distance. "It means my truth is not under this tree."

"Or maybe it means it's in the forest," she said. Her lips revealed a smile. Celina pressed the toe of her shoe against a white stone and then shyly stepped forward. "My name is Celina."

"I know."

She scrunched her eyes. "How do you know?"

"Because we live in the same village. We both go to the same class. I see you all the time."

She blushed. "Oh, right. I was just trying to be formal." She scratched her arm. "I thought it was odd that we have not spoken before. It must be hard. Not having any friends, I mean." He met her gaze. Celina looked over her shoulder. The crow on the steeple was gone. "I should return before they know I have left." She turned around, but then stopped and looked at Corvus. "In my dream I was surrounded by crows," she said reliving the vision. "They carried me out of the church and into the sky."

"And then what happened?" he asked, his eyes brimming with curiosity. No one had ever shared their dream with him before.

"And then I met you." Celina smiled. "Goodbye. Corvus." She walked quickly and quietly across the plaza and disappeared back into the church.

Chapter Seven

Corvus went to bed that night and noticed that his palms were tingling. He thought about his talk with Celina in the plaza and he thought about the sign they had both witnessed. Had she interpreted the sign correctly? Was his truth in the forest of illusions?

When Corvus fell asleep he had a dream that he was lost in the forest. He ran through the trees along a narrow trail only to lose it shortly thereafter. Corvus shouted into the darkness but his cries went unanswered. Occasionally he could hear laughter scatter through the sea of black pines and at times he got the feeling that someone was watching him, as if the dream were not his own.

A flickering light near his feet grabbed his attention. A sliver of moonlight shined up from a piece of glass lying on the ground. Corvus leaned down and picked it up. It was a monocle. Corvus wiped the monocle clean with his shirt and put it to his eye. Now he could see light play about the forest like a silent symphony of new color. A thin feathery trail of light weaved through the trees like a strand of silk and he took to his heels and followed it.

At last, he came to a clearing in the forest and in the center of the clearing was a statue of a crow. Corvus could only see the crow through the monocled eye. In the other eye he only saw the dark shapes of the forest. The statue was nearly ten feet tall and its wings were outstretched, ready for flight. Its eyes were dark and dangerous. Corvus stepped near the statue and put his hand against the cold stone and his fingers brushed across an epigram etched into the rock. In strange script it read:

HokFeerus Edicus sten, Corvus.

Corvus had no idea what it meant, but he whispered the words as he read them aloud. The stone crow looked down at Corvus and flapped its wings and began to caw. The noise was terrifying and Corvus covered his ears with his hands. The crow's talons broke free from the stone and with three flaps it rose into the air. Corvus took several steps backwards, still watching the crow, and backed into a tree, dropping his monocle. He was now unable to see the crow, but the sound of its cawing roused him out of his sleep.

*   *   *   *   *   *

Corvus awoke with a start. His sheets were soaked with sweat.

HokFeerus Edicus sten. HokFeerus Edicus sten. HokFeerus Edicus sten.

The words clung to his thoughts like spider webs. He could still hear the cawing of the crow echo through his mind.

A tap at his bedroom window brought him back to reality. Corvus crawled over to the window and peeked up. Korbin was standing on the windowsill softly clicking the glass with his beak. The crow looked at Corvus with one eye. "Go away!" Corvus whispered, worried that the crow would wake his aunt. But Corvus could not bring himself to leave the window. He watched the bird closely, admiring the black details of the crow against the blackness of the night.

The crow tapped the glass two times. Corvus put his hand against the cold glass and the crow opened its wings and spread them to the edge of the window. The bird looked just like the statue in his dream. *This is too weird,* Corvus thought. The crow opened its mouth to squawk, but Corvus quickly raised his finger to his lips.

"You want me to go outside, don't you, Korbin?" Corvus whispered. He knew that if his aunt or anyone else caught him wandering at night he would be in big trouble. It would be better to stay inside, though Corvus knew he wouldn't be able to fall back asleep. With the dream still flashing through his mind Corvus put on his shoes and tiptoed out of the house.

The streets were empty and a full moon hung below the hilltop. Above him, the stars were radiant. Corvus looked up into the night sky and traced his eyes over the constellations until he spotted the constellation Corvus. Four stars formed the shape of a giant quadrilateral. Corvus thought it looked nothing like a crow.

The villagers were taught that the constellations were the origins of the symbols. The stars and their stories remained fixed in the sky, signaling that their meanings were set and eternal.

Corvus turned and saw Korbin sitting behind him on the roof of his home. "Now what is it you want?" Corvus asked. With little interest in conversation, Korbin left his perch and flew slowly in the direction of the woods. The boy looked up to the quadrilateral constellation in the heavens, and with a reluctant sigh, followed his crow.

The flying crow guided the boy to the edge of the forest and the full moon flooded the fields with plenty of light to see. When he arrived at the entrance, Corvus looked up and saw the faint outline of Korbin in the branches of a tree. Corvus peered into the blackness, his mind spinning with ideas. Was it coincidence that he had had a dream about a statue of a crow in the forest, and now he was being led into the forest by a crow? Could there really be a statue somewhere inside?

Korbin let out a single caw and flew off the branch and hovered over Corvus's head.

"You want me to go in there, don't you?" Corvus asked, bouncing on his heals to keep warm. "Well it's too dark. I could easily get lost."

Korbin cawed again and then dipped through the entranceway and disappeared. Corvus looked over his shoulder at the village behind him bathed in moonlight. Maybe he would go into the forest for just a bit, follow the crow until it decided to return. With a nervous sigh, he stepped into the forest.

Corvus followed the thin dark trail with cautious steps, a trail he had only traveled once before during the day. The forest was pitch-black, forcing Corvus to hold his hands out in front of him as he walked. Even light from the full moon refused to shine through the cracks in the canopy. A root wrapped around his ankle and he nearly fell. Barely one hundred feet into the woods, Corvus couldn't even see where he was going, let alone where he had come from. His heart began to race. What was he *doing* out here?

He put his hands on his legs and took several deep breaths, trying to calm down. After a few minutes he continued. He whistled while he walked and followed the sounds of Korbin deeper into the forest. He walked like this for over an hour. At times, he heard strange sounds that distracted his focus, but convincing himself that these were just the rustlings of small mammals, he continued onward. He could not allow himself to fall into fear.

A crashing sound stopped him in his tracks and he threw himself down on the ground and held his breath. The sound toppled toward him like a falling tree and then stopped several meters from where he lay. Corvus waited anxiously, biting his upper lip to keep from breathing too hard. After a few minutes, the sound moved onward and away, and eventually faded into the black noise of the forest. "So much for not being afraid," he thought. Corvus picked himself up and continued through the darkness.

He hadn't gone far when his shoe slipped under an exposed root and he fell face-first into the mud. His knee hit something hard and Corvus cried out in pain. It was miserably dark, too dark to see what he had fallen on, so he spread out his hands as if sanding a floor until his fingers brushed against something solid – a smooth rock the size of his fist. He rubbed the rock thoughtfully with his fingers in the darkness, noticing that it was not only smooth but also flawless, as if it had been born in a river. "If only I could see into the night," he thought.

At that moment, the moon broke through the canopy and a wide shaft of light pierced through the darkness. The light passed through the trees, over his hands, and onto the ground upon an object where the rock had been.

At first he could barely see the object illuminated by the moonlight, so entranced was he by the carpet of mist which drifted over the ground like water. The mist was receding from something, he saw, and he sat staring at the object like a day dweller seeing the moon for the first time. As the mist pooled away, a flower appeared. For a moment Corvus thought that the flower was moving, spinning even, as it rose through the intangible vapor like a living island coming out of the ocean. The moonbeam bathed it completely in light, though Corvus could swear that the flower was glowing. He leaned over and examined it. Ten large white petals surrounded a yellow center as brilliant as the sun. He noticed that the petals moved subtly in the night air, as if stretching themselves after awakening from a deep rest. Corvus extended his hand, and with the utmost of care, caressed the white petals of the flower.

An electrical surge ran through his arm, up his neck, and into his mind. All at once hundreds of voices burst through his thoughts like a breaking dam and Corvus lifted his hand off the flower and fell over backwards onto the ground. He stared at the lotus in awe as he rubbed his finger. The voices in his mind had tapered away, but a persistent one remained at the edge of his awareness.

"The black in light cannot be seen, though in the darkness exists the dream. The dreamer's truth can be seen with sight, but even truth shall have its price."

Corvus shook his head, shaking the last of the voices out of his conscious mind. What kind of flower *was* this, he wondered? Very carefully, Corvus reached out with both hands and pulled the lotus out of the ground. Cupping it like water, he lifted the flower to his face and examined it. This was the most beautiful flower he had ever seen. He moved it slowly and circularly under the moonlight, but suddenly, the moonlight disappeared. Corvus looked over his shoulder. Behind him, a crow was perched on the branch of a tree blocking the moonlight, transforming the bird into a powerful silhouette.

Corvus whistled into the air and waited for Korbin to return his call. The crow was silent. Corvus whistled again, but the crow remained motionless. Behind it, the clouds passed over the moon, and when the moon reappeared, the crow was gone.

Corvus placed the lotus delicately into his pocket. The clouds had covered the moon again and already it was pitch black. With the slightest tinge of panic, Corvus whistled into the air, praying that Korbin would answer his call. Korbin didn't. Had Korbin left him alone in the forest? Beads of sweat collected on his forehead. He would never be able to find his way back without his crow.

He stretched his hands out in front of him and walked blindly into the darkness. After five minutes he stopped and squinted his eyes. Was he *seeing* something? The boy craned his neck forward and looked at the faint light in the distance. It looked like a fire. His pulse quickened and a curious excitement overtook him. For the very first time tonight he knew where he was going.

When Corvus got closer to the fire he could see a structure of some kind hidden behind the trees. He walked silently among the shadows as he approached what appeared to be a house, but the house was so old it barely resembled anything anymore. Around it, trees thousands of years old climbed into the ceiling of the forest. The shadows of the trees danced against the walls of the home in the firelight. The structure's sides were made out of old massive logs, some of which had collapsed and now rested at odd angles against themselves. The roof, what remained of it at least, was nothing more than pine branches laid out across the foundation. Inside, a wide wooden table, cracked in multiple places, aged away by the countless eons of forest time, stood in the center of a dirt floor.

Delicately, he stepped through the open walls. There was no one in sight and all he could hear was the crackle of the flames.

"Hello?" Corvus whispered into the darkness. He waited. Would someone reply? Who had started the fire, he wondered?

The home was less of a home and more of a relic. The floor was covered in pine needles and the smoke of countless fires smothered the walls. Corvus walked along these walls and noticed that strange symbols had been carved into them. There were drawings of animals, people, and he also noticed the shapes of familiar constellations. How was it possible that someone was living alone in the forest?

A gruff voice cut through the darkness. "What are you doing here?"

The voice surprised him and Corvus jumped. Spinning around he saw the silhouette of a man. The man's shoulders were more than twice the width of Corvus's and the figure brandished a long pole with a knife tied at the end. The knife was the only thing that penetrated the darkness, catching the light of the flame in the shiny metal.

"I came here when I saw the light," Corvus said nervously, backing away from the table.

"There is no light, only darkness," came a raspy reply. "For what have you come?!"

Corvus's palms were sweating. He tried to speak but his words were stolen from him. He didn't know what to say. "I - I was lost in the forest."

"Impossible!" the man said, jutting out his staff. "There is no such thing. There is only placement, nothing more. Enough with your tongues. Be gone or be had."

"Wait!" Corvus said desperately. He could feel the madness pouring off of the man in waves. Corvus knew that he must speak carefully, because his next words could very well be his last. "Really, I am lost, or rather - I am not placed where I wish to be."

"What is wrong with the place where you now find yourself?" the man asked, offended and angry.

"Nothing!" Corvus said, looking around at the dilapidated building.

"I am from a village not far from here. I wandered into the forest and the darkness overtook me. I saw your fire and..."

The silhouette shifted. A bony hand reached out of the shadows and pointed at Corvus. "Take your hand out of your pocket. What do you have there? What have you stolen?"

Corvus reached into his pant pocket and pulled out the smooth stone. "Nothing, nothing, just a rock."

"The *other* pocket!" the figure said in frustration. "Take it out at once." The man held his weapon out and stepped into the light. The flame light glimmered across his face. The man was older than any person Corvus had ever seen before. Long gray strands of hair hung off the man's freckled scalp, and his large eyes bulged out of his head like white tomatoes. Around his shoulders he wore the thick skin of a wolf.

Corvus carefully reached into his pocket and removed the flower. The man took a delicate step forward and peered at the object in Corvus's hand.

"Where did you get that?" the man said, his voice just above a whisper.

"It found me," Corvus replied honestly.

The man reached out and plucked the flower out of the boy's hand. He examined the flower and mumbled to himself while turning the lotus over with his fingers. Corvus got the impression that the man had forgotten about Corvus's presence altogether. The man continued to mutter to himself while he walked to the corner of the building. He reached down behind a large piece of bark and pulled out a small wooden container no larger than a cigar box.

"I have been collecting these flowers," the man said absently, though Corvus did not know if he was talking to Corvus or himself. He set the box on the table and opened it to reveal a dozen lotuses. Corvus unconsciously took a step toward them. They seemed to glow from within the box. They were calling him, it seemed, and the man watched their effect on the young boy with fixed interest. The man placed the thirteenth lotus into the box and then pushed the box across the table to Corvus. "These flowers are very rare and only appear when scratched by the light of the moon."

Corvus sat down at the table and lifted the lid off the box and gazed inside. He felt like he was looking inside of a secret. "What are they called?" Corvus asked in a whisper.

The man's eye seemed to twinkle. "They are known as the Dreamer's Lotus. They are very special. The petals are safe and delicious to eat, but the center is deadly," he said with a serious look. "The poison can kill ten men in one instant. That is why one must eat only the petals which are more powerful than ten dead men combined." The man's voice sounded ancient, older than his skin, Corvus thought. "The Dreamer's Lotus aids us in the work because they are a part of the work."

"What work is that?" Corvus asked.

The man looked surprised. "What work?" he asked. "Why, the work of this world! Did you think we were just brought to this planet by chance? To sit in the forest and fart in the wind? I do not know about you, but I have big plans in this world," the man said, raising his hand dramatically. Corvus looked at the crumbling building and wondered what plans this recluse had in mind.

"Yes, big work in the days to come. Always a pleasure receiving these gifts," he said, pointing at the flowers. "Each of them came to me in a way more unique than the first. Malevolent, benevolent, the universe speaks so many tongues, wouldn't you agree?" The man eyed Corvus carefully. "Can you guess how I found my twelfth?"

Corvus shook his head. "How?"

The old man looked directly into Corvus's eyes. "A crow dropped it onto this table." They stared at each other for a long moment, and only the crackle of fire tickled the silence. The man's eyes widened with interest and he leaned back into his chair. "Now why do you suppose it would do that?"

Corvus thought about the statue in his dream. He had found the statue all right. "One can only guess," he said carefully.

The man smiled wildly, revealing half a mouthful of teeth. "That is all *any* of us can do! Though some think they are better at it than others. The world is full of profiteers disguised as prophets, selling their ideas to mindless panhandlers, hoping for a belief to hold onto. Bah!" he said, waving his hand in front of him.

"But you know," he said, and looked up, "thirteen is a lucky number!" It took Corvus a moment to realize that the man was talking about the lotuses again. "Many people believe that thirteen is an unlucky number but it is quite the contrary. All good things come in thirteens. Why, the light of the full moon reflects back to us thirteen times a year." The man looked up at the heavens and cast out his arm. "Ah, Great Father Sky, how your mystery enthralls us and how the universe beckons us out there. All is external in this internal reality, wouldn't you say?" he said looking at Corvus. "You must forgive me," he said, looking at the uneasy boy in front of him. "I have not even introduced myself." The man stood up gallantly. Casting the head of the wolf skin over his shoulders, he held out his arms with great pride and said, "My name is Obiticus. I am a resident of this planet and a member of this forest and I exist before you now." Obiticus paused, thinking about the rest of his introduction. After a moment of awkwardness, he continued, "My existence is about all I can claim for certain." He smiled at Corvus, pleased with himself. It took him a moment to find his seat again.

Obiticus put his hand on his head and scratched his scalp absently as if trying to remember something. He looked under the table and then up at Corvus. For a moment, Corvus thought Obiticus was going to ask him something, until the old man looked over his shoulder and into the blackness of the forest. Corvus could see nothing, but it was evident that Obiticus did. The old man squinted his eyes as he scanned the illusion, until finally, he turned around to Corvus and said, "Is that crow in the tree with you?"

Corvus couldn't see it, but he wasn't surprised. "Yes. It is." He looked at Obiticus for a long time sizing him up and then pursed his lips and whistled into the darkness. A thin gray silhouette appeared out of the blackness and transfigured into feather and form. The bird landed in the center of the table and hobbled over to Corvus. It came to the edge of the table, but the boy did not try to touch it.

Obiticus clasped his hands together and smiled. "Oh my," he said, almost in song. "You are the crow's caller. That is a very good sign indeed, for the crow is regarded as *the meaning of life*." Obiticus gazed at the crow in awe and Corvus eyed him carefully. "The crow deserves respect, for it sees everything, just as life sees everything. Can you imagine if I could see and remember everything I have done in my existence...in all my existences? Why I would have the vision of a crow! Such merciless vision..." he said, his voice trailing off. Obiticus scampered over to Corvus and pulled a lotus out of the box and then returned to his place at the table.

Corvus stared at the old man. "How long have you *been* here?" he asked slowly.

Obiticus sighed. He leaned back and looked up to the stars, as if asking them for answers. "Many *many* years," he said. "Let me simply say that I cannot remember if I built this building or not. What I can say is that I once lived in a proper home, and after that, a proper luxurious home. But many things are different now than the faraway days," he said, fingering the lotus petals in his hands. "I used to see things differently. I was out there among the people once. Long ago, *long* before The Cut, before The Festival of the Ax."

Corvus put his hands on the table. "The Festival of the Ax?" he exclaimed. "Then you once lived in The White Village!"

"If that is what it is now called, then yes. So much has changed since I lived there generations ago. Even the name of the village has changed."

"Obiticus," Corvus said slowly, not wanting to break apart this reality with thoughtless conversation. "Does that mean that you lived in the village before it was destroyed?" He looked up at the man in wonder.

"Long before, and up until. But I left soon after. I am an outcast!" Obiticus said, putting up his hand, a prideful smile escaping his stoic air. I knew of their lies and deceptions. I knew of the deceit and I spoke of it freely...too freely," he said, wagging his finger. "Others too knew, but unlike me they feared their own banishment. Few can survive outside the collective. The collective is strong. It is everything that we know. It shapes our values, our beliefs, our identity. Without it, we are unidentifiable, most of all, to ourselves. Those who cannot see themselves shall perish in the great illusion. But isn't life the greatest illusion of all? We think we are one thing, until we become the next thing, only to realize that we have been working to become the beginning at last!"

Obiticus stood up and placed one hand behind his back and the other on his chest. Like a lost scholar who had finally found a disciple, Obiticus began his story. "Long *long* ago, the many used to live like we are living now. There were communities all over the planet that lived and thrived in the forests. Back then, people did not fear the natural world because they knew that they were a part of it. Life was simple and easy for most.

"Change is inevitable, however. Eventually, all meanings will merge and dissolve so that new signs can grow. This is exactly what happened. One day, the chaos of the cosmos decided it was time for a change. Many say that they know how the change happened, but I will not pretend that I do. All I know is that when the chaos came, the earth, along with everyone living upon her, nearly perished. Great Civilizations fell. In the end, which was also the beginning, those who were left to create, carried with them a primal distrust of the natural world. The concept of competition fueled man's quest for survival. He believed it was necessary to compete with the earth as well as with his fellow man.

"This leads me to the purpose of my story. The village you know now is not what it once was. For countless years, men were entirely cut off from their connection with the earth. They saw themselves as separate and independent from each other and everything around them. Life was about survival. In those days, society had no standards. Wrong came before right, might came before meek, and the individual came before the collective. In my era, the farmers would farm more than they needed and would share their surplus with no one. The woodsmen would cut down the trees and leave them because they were too lazy to make use of the wood. Sometimes, people would even *kill* one another because of something they coveted." Obiticus shook his head. "It was a strange world to learn from, yet it was everything that I knew." He looked across the table at Corvus and the firelight flickered in his eyes and his mouth opened into a wide smile. "But then, something happened. One day, an organized chaos careened onto the earth to balance the imbalance that the men had created."

Obiticus sat down again and placed his palms upon the tabletop. "In the village a sleeping boy awoke inside his mind. From up above, he could see below that his friends and neighbors were sleeping in the fields. He wanted them to wake up and see that their suffering was perpetuated by old beliefs, but for some reason, they could not. The boy knew that he could use the villagers' fear and distrust to rouse them from their stupor, and so he dreamt a dream that was his and also theirs. The boy dreamt that his village would be visited by a flock of crows, and that the crows would come to show the village the boundary between the individual and the collective. You see, the crow borders the line. It is very individualistic, but it also flies with the flock - a murder to be exact," he said with a sideways smile.

"The young dreamer told the people that an enormous flock of crows would cover the village and remain there for twenty-eight days. He said that the crows needed a sacrifice and he warned the villagers that the crows were not to be harmed. The villagers became very afraid and asked him, 'What will the sacrifice be?' and 'When will the crows come?' But the dreamer only answered them by saying, 'They will come.'

"The boy was right. Three days later the crows came. They flew in from the forest and covered the village like the night. They ate all of the crops until there was hardly any food remaining. The villagers became very nervous. They fell into their programs of fear and victimhood and they pleaded with the boy to dream up another reality for them, but the boy only reminded them that their current reality was being sacrificed for another one. The boy said that after twenty-eight days the crows would go away. He reminded them again not to harm the crows, but they protested and said that the crow was evil because it was doing evil things. What they did *not* understand was that the crow was a reflection of their own greed and selfishness.

"One day, a hungry farmer watched as a flock of crows fought over the last tomato in his field. Distraught, he hurled a stone into the air and knocked a crow to the ground, killing it. I remember the sky turning black that day. There were hundreds of them, thousands maybe. They dropped down two by two and four by four and their talons tore the man to pieces. The other villagers ran to his aid but the crows turned on their attackers and killed them as well. Everyone fled to the safety of their homes and waited until the crows finally left, after twenty eight days." Obiticus had a faraway look as he relived the event, and Corvus noticed a strange expression of nostalgia in his eyes.

"It was my very first experience in dreaming," he said with a lucid remembrance.

"*You* were the boy?" Corvus asked.

"Even though my dream had been horrible, it was celebrated by those left alive. The village was *changed*, the old reality altered forever. The people could no longer deny that the events which transpired around them had meaning. The crows had taught the villagers that they must observe and interpret their reality, or they would become subjects to their reality. It was a powerful lesson for the people to learn but my suspicion is that the lesson is not complete, that the people do not yet *know*, for you see, to learn and to know are two different things entirely."

Corvus was staring at Obiticus in awe. He felt as if he were dangling on the edge of a cliff suspended over absolute knowledge. He wanted to know more about the truth of this reality that Obiticus spoke of, but his mind held tight to his doubt. Corvus fingered the stone in his pocket. "Obiticus, I came into the forest because I was led by a dream, but finding you here fills me with confusion – it goes against everything I have been taught. I cannot help but wonder if I am currently sleeping back at home. I can still see the words in my mind as if they were written in the air before me...*Hokfeerus Edicus sten.*"

Obiticus looked at Corvus and squinted. He leaned forward into the table and inspected Corvus's face. It made the boy uncomfortable. "There is something about the lines in your face. Your eyes describe a remindable story. Perhaps I brought you here after all..." The old man set the lotus onto the table and carefully removed two of the white petals, making sure to trim off a small section near the bottom that touched the deadly yellow center. He handed Corvus a single petal. The other petal Obiticus placed into his mouth and motioned for Corvus to do the same. "Go on. It is delicious, you'll see."

With a bit of hesitation, Corvus placed the lotus into his mouth. A blueberry pulse passed over his taste buds like gentle electricity. It caused his cheeks to flush. He smiled as he chewed it. "It is good."

"Of course it is," Obiticus said. "It was dreamt to be that way." The old man's eyes had glossed over a bit. He cocked his head and looked at Corvus. "I have seen you long ago, back in a time when dreamers were still being born, dangling in waiting from the Great Beyond. And I see you now again, *there*, deep in the black ripples of your eyes, boy with *grandfather* eyes," Obiticus said with a cackle. "Symbolic eyes for a boy your age," he said thoughtfully. He leaned back and folded his hands. "The petals we ate are powerful narcotics. They will soon induce sleep on us both. They will heighten your sense of awareness when you dream, and your dreams will begin to complexity. There is no limit to your potential. After you learn how to dream, you learn how to fly, so to speak."

Obiticus sighed heavily and looked at his hands. "*Hokfeerus Edicus sten.* This is from long ago," he said matter-of-factly, "when the animal-men spoke." Corvus thought of the creature he had seen in the forest. Was that what Obiticus was referring to?

"They are speaking to you now," he continued. "Heed their words, but do not confuse them with the voices of the village, that madness which percolates out of the pores of the collective and into your dreams." He looked directly into Corvus's eyes. "*Hokfeerus Edicus sten.* It is the archetypical language of the body chaos speaking through the dreamer."

"What does it mean?" he asked.

"*Dash their fears upon themselves. Dissolve their dreams and fly.*"

The boy looked at his hands. He knew what the villagers feared. His dark eyes looked up at Obiticus. "My name is Corvus," Corvus said softly.

Obiticus looked at him without emotion. "And what do you see, young Corvus? Do you see with the ash eye as the Elders would like you to? Do you pick and ponder? Have you ever thought to scrape your eye out with a stick to see if you could see what you look like from the stick's point of view?" Obiticus took another heavy sigh. "Forgive my fits. Old men have much to say and few to say it to. If you would just be kind enough to listen to what I tell you before we drop into our dreams, for it is very important: beware the village and beware the villagers. Do not allow their fear to become your own. You must dream a new reality, Corvus. The village is rotting from the inside out. Its bloated body grows behind the false facade and only those with vision and wings shall be saved. You can save them from themselves, you know? As I once did? Oh, if only I could return one day with this dream that I still carry, but first the signs, always the signs."

Obiticus looked in the direction of the crow behind him. "I was once a crow," he said, the madness returning to his eyes, glossy and far away. "We flew over the mountains and into the snow fog. We met with great machines in the sky and they swallowed us whole in their propeller engines. They were made of metal and synthetic light." He yawned. Looking down, he saw Corvus was already asleep. Obiticus rested down on a straw mat, and looking up at the sky he thought of where else he had seen the metal birds.

Chapter Eight

The sky was combing the fingers of dawn and Korbin cawed in the distance. Corvus woke up and looked around. Slowly, the events of the previous night returned to him. Groggily, he got up from the table and saw that Obiticus was still asleep. Eight petals of the lotus remained on the table, but even looking at them filled the boy with confusion and doubt. Silently, he left the shelter. With him, he carried the smooth stone.

Last night's dream bled through his awareness as he followed the trail back home. Never had he dreamt like that before. Never. In the past, the majority of his dreams were nothing more than a bombardment of the day's events. This time it was different. The Dreamer's Lotus had taken him through a silvery veil and strange and powerful archetypes had approached him like long lost friends. He remembered seeing creatures of all shapes and sizes – eagle, fox, fish, and bear – more than he could count. He even remembered being surrounded by the earth, air, wind, and water, and somehow, he was *also* an element. Which element, however, he could not say.

The dream transformed when he encountered the element of fire. He felt the heat speaking to him from the pit of his belly and the fire crawled up his sides and down his arms. It was blissful and ecstatic to transform from one meaning to another. Corvus escaped the forest and soared through the air, high above the world, fire crackling through every cell. The White Village glowed below him and he sailed down like a shredded veil aflame. The village beckoned him down to raze it all in a blaze of light. He was the fire embodied and he watched as the white buildings of the only place he had ever known transform from fire into ash.

Corvus whistled as he ran through the forest and he followed the sound trail of Korbin until he reached the edge of the illusion. He could see a few villagers in the distance, beginning the work of the day. The sun was already several hours over the horizon. Corvus stepped onto the compacted dirt at the edge of the forest when a large gray owl, bigger than any he had ever seen before, burst out of the forest behind him and into the sky. He stared at the owl for a long time as it flew higher and higher toward the sun. Corvus raised his hand to shield the sun's glare as he followed the bird's path. He had seen plenty of owls in the evening, just after dusk, but never had he seen one in broad daylight. The meaning of this incident eluded him. In fact,

Corvus felt for certain that not even the Book of Signs had an answer to what he had just seen. Still perplexed, he trotted off toward home.

When Corvus walked quietly through his front door he saw that his Aunt was waiting for him. She was sewing at the table and she looked up at him when he entered. Sarah set down her work. "Where have you been?" Her tone was measured.

"Hello, Aunt Sarah," he said, hoping to start a casual dialogue. What could he possibly tell her that she would believe? Anything he said would be punishable. But to tell the truth? "I went for a walk. I could not sleep."

"Neither could I," she said evenly. "Corvus, you have never lied to me before. Do not start now. Trust me."

"*Beware the villagers*," Obiticus had said. Was that just madness speaking or was there some truth? "I cannot tell you, Aunt Sarah," he said, looking at the floor.

"I will cut you down with your own ax if you will not! I will banish you from this very table," she said standing up. "You may not find another one. Now tell me where you were last night."

His gaze sank deeper into the floorboards. Finally, he looked up to meet her eyes. "I was in the forest." Sarah waited. "I wanted to find where they cut the wood. I wanted to see the stumps."

He watched her exhale. She turned away from her nephew and picked up her work. Distressed, she set it down again. She faced him. "Something is coming, Corvus. Something dark." She took a deep breath, and about to speak, she caught herself. She looked out the window and back at Corvus. She could not say what she needed to. "You will be making breakfast this week. Well go on, get started."

He went out the back door to fetch water from the well. He lowered the empty bucket, filled it, and brought it inside.

Sarah took it from him. "Here. I will start the kettle. You get some eggs from the hen house."

He walked outside. Three crows sat over the hen house. They watched him as he entered.

He retrieved five eggs and placed them into the basket, but nearly dropped it when he heard his aunt scream from inside. Corvus grabbed the basket and ran to her aid. Inside, his aunt stood by the counter. On the floor was a puddle of water and in the center of the puddle was a red snake. His aunt did not move. She was staring at the serpent.

Corvus set down the basket of eggs and grabbed a broom and quickly pushed the snake out the door and into the bushes. One could not harm a snake, just as one could not speak of them.

He returned inside and saw that his aunt was still looking at the floor where the snake had been. He walked over and touched his aunt lightly on the shoulder, who upon awakening from her episode, said, "I will clean up the water. You break and stir the eggs."

Corvus opened a cupboard and pulled out a bowl. He took one of the eggs from the basket and cracked it into the bowl. A putrid greenness slipped into the basin and a terrible smell instantly pervaded the room. Sarah walked over and stared into the bowl.

"This egg is rotten." She peered at Corvus. "That is *two* bad signs." She took the container away from him and dumped the contents into a waste bucket and then covered it. "We will both fast until tomorrow evening." She turned and faced him. Her cheeks were red and she had fire in her eyes. "This is your last chance, Corvus. Tell me the truth. *Why* did you go into the forest last night?"

He looked at his aunt. He had no choice but to tell her, but he knew it was going to sound crazy.

"I had a dream..."

Her eyes widened. She put her finger to her lips and shushed him, fearing his visions. She knew he was a manifester, and like his father, his visions would strengthen. The signs would either aid him or destroy him. The finger seemed to come down from her lips on its own, gripped by a tragic curiosity.

"And what did you find...in the forest?"

"I found an old man living in a shelter. He has been living there for years," Corvus reflected. He shook his head. "I think he was too far gone. I did not believe in madness before, but I do now. He was insane."

"That is impossible," she said. "No one lives in the forest."

Now *she* sounded crazy. "What do you think happens to the people who are banished?" he said condescendingly, as if speaking to a child.

"They die," Sarah said simply. "You must have still been dreaming. Or maybe you sleep walked into the forest."

"No, I'm pretty sure," he said, his tone still condescending. "When I woke up a crow was at my window, and it led me into the forest."

Sarah put her hand out to quiet him but he pushed her arm away.

"Why do we not talk about the crows?" he asked her in frustration.

She clapped her hands over her ears and turned to the side. "Corvus," she said, dropping her hands, now conscious of her unconsciousness. She faced him again. "The crows are an *idea*. What they represent is more important than what they are. The crow sees deeper into the world than any other creature or dream, and for some reason it follows you around." She hesitated.

"What *is* it?" he asked in exasperation. His dark eyes widened. "Tell me. Please, Aunt Sarah. Why do they follow me? Why can I call them and move them? What is this thing that no one will speak of?"

She smiled sadly. She covered her heart with her hands, afraid that her love for him would pour out unexpectedly. She needed to be strong for him. "I am not The Great Maker. I do not know what path is more pure, nor do I seek certain signs for my own pacification. Others, however, have let fear enter their hearts. They are controlled by it. Corvus, you must understand that the ideas in our minds create themselves into something tangible. Your crows represent a very real fear in this place. The collective fear is mounting and if you don't find your center soon then it will overtake you."

"Can it be changed?" he asked hopefully.

She fell into his presence. He looked so much like his father, so similar in so many ways. She walked to her sewing kit and sat down at the table and began to sew. After a few minutes she said, "We create the reality in front of us by choosing to see what we want and expect to see. Our thoughts. Our dreams." She looked up as she continued to sew. She was an excellent seamstress and within moments she had fastened a design into the cloth. "All of life is full of choices. You must choose your dreams carefully."

"How?"

"With discipline." She picked up the fabric in her hand and handed it to him. It was a thin black strip of cloth and in the middle she had sown a white circle. "Tie this around your head before you go to bed. Every night before you fall asleep focus on the circle and place something in the center of it. When you fall asleep whatever you placed in it will appear to you in your dreams." She stood up. "I must go to the market to trade some quilts for food." She put her hand on her nephew's shoulder. "Be careful, Corvus. There is no turning back once you start down this path, but I suppose that you already have." Corvus looked up at his aunt, wondering how she could have hidden this side of herself for so long.

Sarah gathered her things. At the door she turned around and said, "It is a thin line between a madman and a prophet. Few exist who dare to walk between the two. People are content reading the signs in their external world, but to read the signs in our mind is another thing entirely."

*   *   *   *   *   *

That night, Corvus did as he was instructed and tied the bandana around his head. His hands tingled with excitement. The Dreamer's Lotus had rearranged something inside of his mind. No longer was he just a boy. He was more than that, and so was the crow. Now all he had to do was find out what.

Corvus closed his eyes and placed a crow in the center of the circle. He held the crow steady and it glowed in his sight and the longer he held it there, the brighter it glowed. After a while, he felt himself slipping through the circle over his third eye. His muscles tightened and slackened as he drifted deeper and deeper into a strange trance until at last the glowing crow dimmed down and disappeared.

When he opened his eyes he was standing on a wooden pedestal thousands of feet over the forest. He could see The White Village far below him, tucked into a cleft in the mountain and beyond the mountains crawled the curve of the earth, and at the top of the curve he could see the outline of a great city. Looking up above him Corvus could see the stars falling from the sky and into the earth.

Corvus heard a caw and he looked down to see an unfamiliar crow traveling along the thermal currents, spiraling upwards like a vertical tunnel of wind, until at last, the crow was hovering in front of his face. In the crow's talon was a Dreamer's Lotus. Corvus looked into the crow's eyes and realized that this crow was actually a projection of his mind's desire for meaning. Corvus had not, however, anticipated the lotus that the crow carried. "Does my mind always conspire in ways I cannot foresee?" he wondered.

Corvus reached out his hand and the crow landed upon it. The Dreamer's Lotus began to drip into a white liquid that covered the crow's feet and climbed up its body. Soon the crow was not black but white, and it spread out its wings and let loose a call into the air. When it was finished it pecked its beak into Corvus's hand. TAP TAP TAP. The sound was strange, ringing through the air like wood on a glass box. Suddenly, a white circle appeared around the crow and before he knew it Corvus was falling into the forest.

*   *   *   *   *   *

He opened his eyes.
TAP TAP TAP.
A crow was standing outside on his windowsill. Corvus scooted over to the window but when he opened it, the crow flew away. In its place, was a single Dreamer's Lotus.

His heart began to race. He clutched the lotus tightly in his hand and shut the window. This couldn't be coincidence. Had he *manifested* it or was he still dreaming? He pinched himself hard and grimaced, now convinced he was fully awake.

But there it was, right there in his hand. The lotus seemed to pulse in his palm like a sentient being and a barrage of emotions flooded his mind as he stared into the center of the lotus – fear, uncertainty, curiosity, *excitement.* Corvus rubbed the silk-like petals between his fingers. He thought about the crow from his dream and the flower it carried. This flower could very well be the key to the crow's meaning. "Obiticus knows more about this lotus than anyone else," he thought. "Maybe he'll have answers to other things, as well."

He pulled off a petal and placed it onto his tongue. The sweetness was intoxicating and the potency of the flower began to affect him almost immediately. His vision had already begun to blur and he knew that he must set his intention quickly before he fell asleep. Corvus secured the bandana around his forehead, and with the last of his mental strength, placed Obiticus in the center of the circle.

Within moments he had drifted out of his body and into the night. Colorful smoke swirled around him as he spun with a graceful glide into the forest. Down below, Corvus could see a soft light among the trees and with the slightest effort he eased himself under the canopy. Inside the forest the trees bent and swayed and the ground ebbed and flowed like the tides of an ocean, until Corvus realized that his consciousness was influencing the reactions of his external reality, and everything froze. His focus had incredible power. He could look at an object and the object would glow. Sometimes things would levitate. He suddenly realized that *he* could levitate.

It was then that Obiticus spoke.

"Come down from there. Abandon the temptations of the dream world. It is all a trap. We seek our dreams not for escape but for truth! Now sit, my dear boy."

The body of Obiticus wavered back and forth like the strands of a torn ribbon under water. "I have consumed the lotus as well," he said, "and I know of your dream because I have dreamt your dream. I have called for you." He gazed at the cloth on Corvus's head. "I see you understand the circle of sight," he said.

Corvus was confused. Should he tell Obiticus that his aunt had given him the scarf? Did Obiticus already know? "I placed you in it after I ate the lotus," was all Corvus said.

Obiticus gave a look of consternation and put his hand to his head. "I do not understand. You have brought me or I have brought you?"

"It seems we have brought each other," Corvus said, the drunkenness of the dream wrapping itself tighter around his head.

Obiticus pinched his eyebrows in frustration. "At times I struggle to identify one reality from the next. There is so much mystery in this world that it is hard for me to keep up with it all."

Corvus had so many questions and he did not know how long the effects of the lotus would last. He quickly got to the point. "Obiticus, something is happening to me. The lotus is changing the symbols somehow. The signs are coming to me stronger, yet their meanings are mixed and I do not understand why. I am starting to wish I had never eaten the flower in the first place." He hesitated, still thinking about his dreams. "I feel like I am riding a wave that is about to break against an unknown shore. I have been having thoughts that I have never had before, feelings that do not make sense to me, like I am carrying a purpose of some kind, as if I am here...for a *reason*."

"It is because you are awakening," Obiticus said simply.

Corvus did not know what to say because he did not know what awakening meant.

"You are beginning to see that your reality is not entirely your own, and you want to know why," Obiticus said with a knowing nod.

Corvus looked into the darkness past the fire. "I have never dreamt like I did the other night, Obiticus!" Corvus said suddenly. "The effects of the flower are becoming entangled with my reality!" he said with a nervous look. "My reality is becoming more lucid. At times I cannot say if I am dreaming or not."

"Then you understand that it is *all* a dream," Obiticus said with an interesting nod. "There is not a moment of waking life when we are not the Grand Creation. Each dream bleeds into the next. How lucid is your dream is how lucid is your circle, is how lucid is your dream, is how lucid, how lucid..." The old man's eyes swirled in their sockets. Corvus watched miniature galaxies spin over Obiticus's head. "Be not afraid for there is nothing to fear. We are infinite, boy. *Death is but a dream, and life is merely the daydream of death.*"

Corvus gazed at Obiticus in wonder.

"Your truth will emerge in time. You have powerful things yet to accomplish." Obiticus rubbed his hands together and looked at Corvus with interest. "You are the last of your kind, for true dreamers are hard to come by. The real problem with dreamers is that some never wake up. The dreams of the mind are often more provocative than the external illusion. Most people never know they are dreaming because most never know when they are awake. To rise out of a false reality takes courage indeed, because behind the veil is where the power lay. There are those who still exist within the walls of The White Village who use their dreams for their own benefit. But the signs will fail them, Corvus. Try as they might, they cannot control the collective forever."

"What are you referring to?" Corvus asked.

Obiticus opened his arms and swirled his hands to create a cauldron of vision and in the vision Corvus could see The White Village. In the center of the village he saw the church, and across from it grew the Tree of Truth. The ash eye spun slowly in circles, and as the cauldron expanded, Corvus and Obiticus found themselves enveloped by the spinning blackness.

"The generator of the fear..." Obiticus said. "The ash eye maintains the inertia of the villagers' progress and keeps them centered in another's reality. The false education controls the minds of the unawakened. The history of the Truth must be reborn. The people have been programmed to fear the natural world. It is a *powerful* program. Eventually, all who refuse to awaken will succumb to it. They will believe their thoughts to be their own, but it is not so. Beware the villagers, Corvus. You are a painful reminder in their existence, a free mind in a land of the imprisoned."

Obiticus leaned back and the vision disappeared. "We have been here for many hours and already the dawn comes." The dreamer yawned. "If I were you, I would find someone you can trust, someone whose free will is a mirror of your own. But do not come looking for it out here. I am too old and too mad for good sense to humor me much longer."

Chapter Nine

The change of season was in full step as the warm winds from the mountains blew through the blossoms that decorated the trees of The White Village. Corvus sat in the back of the classroom and he gazed at Celina who sat several desks in front of him. They had not spoken since that day in the plaza, though Corvus thought about their encounter often. At times, he had visions of taking Celina into the forest and guiding her along the hidden trail that led deeper into the forest. He imagined holding her hand as they ran. She was not like the others, he knew. She was different.

While Corvus daydreamed, Elder Loyal gave a lecture to the class about the symbolism of the moon. Specifically, he was talking about a moon halo which was witnessed several times last year. Corvus knew that the moon represented the reciprocal of the sun, and was thought to be a symbol of inner wisdom. For the village, the halo was known as a symbol of fertility.

As the Elder spoke, Corvus noticed that Celina was working on something at her desk. It was evident that she didn't want Elder Loyal to see. It looked like she was writing something. Every now and then she would look off into the distance and then continue her task in secret.

When class was over, Celina was waiting for him outside. She stood by herself and watched the crows which sat on the roof of the school. The crows perked up when Corvus walked out. When Celina saw him she fiddled with her bag nervously. She walked over. "Hello," she said to him.

He blushed immediately. His stomach was in knots. "Hi. Celina."

She tilted her head to the side slightly and grinned, realizing that she was making him nervous. "I made something," she said. Celina looked over Corvus's shoulder and saw Elder Loyal walk out of the schoolhouse. She took his hand and pulled Corvus away. "Come on!" she whispered. "Let's go somewhere else." The crows left their perch on the arch of the school and followed behind them.

Celina and Corvus ran through the narrow streets until they reached the market and turned down the alley toward the fields. She could see the crows above them as she ran which meant that others would know where they were going. She didn't want anyone else to see what she had. In the distance, she spotted a wide hedge at the edge of town. When they got there, they ducked behind it and the crows flew into its branches, safe and concealed. The crows remained quiet and still, although some sought better branches to overlook the boy. Corvus and Celina were sitting down in the grass and the hedge hid them nicely. Past the fields, they could see the single pine tree at the top of the hill.

"You run fast," Corvus said, still catching his breath.

Her skirt was up to her knees and her legs rested against his. She looked at him with an anxious expression. "I made something," Celina repeated. "I would like you to see it."

"OK?" he attempted.

Celina reached into her bag and pulled out a piece of paper folded in half. She held it out to Corvus, but then pulled it back and said, "You cannot tell anyone you saw this. OK?"

He looked at her and smiled. "Who would I tell?"

She raised her eyebrow. He had a point. She handed Corvus the paper.

He took it from her and looked at it. "Is this what you were working on during class?" he asked, nonchalantly.

"You were watching me?" she asked.

His stomach fluttered. "Only because I am in the back of the classroom and I can see everyone. I noticed that you were writing something. That is all."

"I was drawing," she corrected.

"*Drawing?*" he asked, his eyes widening with the realization of what she had done. No one was allowed to create anything on one's own without the support of the collective. "Why?"

"Because I cannot get an image out of my mind. The drawing is my dream and one I have often." She looked up at him, her eyes wide and vulnerable. "No one else has seen this, Corvus."

He opened the paper apprehensively, fearing the consequences of seeing her dream though thrilled by the danger of doing so. It was like looking into her mind.

Corvus's eyes traced over the paper. In his hands was the drawing of a beautiful black feather. At the top of the drawing several lines of black water dripped over the feather and ran down the feather's vanes and onto the quill. At the base of the quill a clenched fist gripped the feather tightly and the water ran down the quill and over the hand like a waterfall.

"This is *amazing*," he said softly.

"Do you know what it means?" she asked almost immediately.

His gaze fell into the drawing. It could mean a lot of things, but he didn't think he should tell her what he thought it meant. It was a beautiful drawing, but something about it made him uncomfortable. He looked over the grass to see several men working in the fields. "Please, put it away," he told her. "It would be a shame if one of the Elders saw it. They would have it destroyed."

She looked at Corvus and then at her picture. She knew he was right. "I think you should have it," she said.

"Really?" he asked.

"Please," she said, putting her hand on his arm. "There is a part of me that knows you will understand its meaning in time."

"But this meaning is yours," he said. "It is *your* creation."

She said nothing and only encouraged Corvus with her big blue eyes to take the drawing and put it away. "It is only for you," she said with a smile. When he smiled back Celina noticed a light escape from the depths of his eyes, as if it had been trapped in that deep blackness for eternity. She looked over her shoulder. "What will you do now?" she asked. "Are you going to the..." Her gaze finished her sentence. She looked over the hedge to the hill in the distance which overlooked the village.

He nodded.

"Will you take me with you?"

He tried to hide his surprise, but he knew she saw it anyway. He didn't like the idea of taking anyone up there. That was *his* place. "Are you sure?" he asked but then regretted doing so.

She smiled and took his hand and ran ahead. "Come on. Before someone stops us."

They took off and the crows scattered out from the hedge and into the air. Corvus and Celina ran through the fields. The sky was clear and blue. They stopped running when they were out of sight and they continued on at a steady walk. "You come up here a lot, don't you?" she asked.

Corvus nodded.

"How come?"

He looked at her. "I like to look at the village from above."

"Like the crows?"

He said nothing.

"Will they be waiting for us when we get there?" she asked.

"Yes."

The breeze blew against their backs as they walked up the hill. They went up the back way along a small trail of stamped grass, Corvus's trail.

"I have never been up to the top before," she said.

"Why not?"

"Because I am not allowed. My father said it would only invite trouble to our family."

"How come?"

She looked at him and smiled. "Why do *you* think?"

He raised his eyebrow. "Because he is afraid."

His answer surprised her. "Does he have a reason to be?"

He watched his feet as he walked. "People in this village are afraid of their own shadow," he said distastefully.

"And you're not?" she asked defensively.

He rolled his eyes. "People are afraid of things they do not understand. What about you?" he asked, looking at her from the corner of his eye. "You said there are few things that frighten you. Is that true?"

She was quiet for a moment and then said, "I am afraid for the village."

"For the village?" he asked. "Why?"

"Because they are afraid of things they don't understand."

His eyes looked into hers, but they revealed nothing. "We are here."

Their last steps brought them to the top of the hill and gave them a three hundred and sixty degree view. Looking across the valley Celina gasped. The village seemed so tiny from so heigh above. She could see past the village, into the mountains, and fancied that she could see every cleft that existed in the tall folded hills. She saw the tops of trees she had only imagined, and savage faces formed on rock walls tall enough to be mountains themselves. Squinting her eyes she could see the villagers walking through the village. They seemed so insignificant from here at the top of the hill, and she suddenly realized that he had seen her too from up here as a tiny dot, walking along like the rest.

"I understand why you come here," she said, still appreciating the view. "It is beautiful. You can see so much."

But Corvus was not looking at the village. He was watching the wind blow through Celina's hair. He watched her eyes survey the village below her, taking in the symbols, making meaning. He took a step closer to her. He was right behind her now. What would happen if he spun her around and kissed her? Would she reject him like everyone else? He bit the inside of his cheek, knowing she would.

Celina looked over her shoulder and was surprised to see him so close behind her, but her soft lips revealed a smile. "It is very nice on the top of the hill," she said. "I can see -"

The sight of the tree behind Corvus silenced her. Her mouth fell open and she let out a soft gasp. For a moment she thought she had fallen and there was no one to catch her - not Corvus, not the earth, not even time. The branches seemed to billow with the blackness of the tree. The old broken boughs, black with crows, loomed above her like delicate knives wavering in the wind.

Corvus slowly whistled his dark and unpleasant staccato. He did it so softly that the wind stole the notes with ease. The crows did not move and made no sign that they heard his sad lonely tune. Celina, however, was hypnotized by its sound and as she watched the birds above her she saw that they heard him and that they somehow understood.

"What are you saying to them?" she asked finally.

He turned from the crows and looked at her. She was making him uncomfortable. A long strand of blond hair hung over her face and she brushed it away. He had told the crows that she was his friend, but of course he couldn't tell her that. "I am telling them that you are a just another villager," he said somewhat condescendingly, "and that your name is Celina." He hesitated, realizing how he must have sounded to her. "I am telling them not to be afraid of you." She smiled faintly, amused by the thought that the crows were afraid of *her*. "I also asked them not to scare you and make you run away. Do they scare you?"

"A little," she confessed. "But I will not run away," she said quickly.

He smiled and unclenched his nervous hands. He looked up at the tree and pointed to a crow at the top. "That is Korbin," he said with a wide smile. "He has become my favorite." Corvus whistled a low note three short times. Korbin flew from his perch and landed on the ground in front of the children. It cocked its head to the side and looked up at Corvus. Celina saw that Corvus's face lit up almost immediately. He moved his head side-to-side, mimicking the crow. He clucked softly to himself, though Celina could tell that Corvus was unaware he was doing this, as if he did this every day. She watched him with great interest, wondering if anyone else had ever seen this side of him. She did not realize that she was smiling as she watched their interaction.

"Korbin," Corvus said, more to himself than to the bird. He took a step forward but the crow did not move. Corvus stopped a few feet from the crow. "This is as close as he will let me get," he said to Celina with an air of experience. Corvus crouched down on his heels and looked at the bird in wonder. "You are such a beautiful creature," he said, gazing at its features. He whistled this feeling and the crow hopped half a foot in the air and then turned in a circle. Corvus laughed. "And proud, aren't you?" He stood up and spun in a circle as well with his hands tucked beneath his armpits, flapping his elbows like wings. Celina couldn't help laughing out loud, but Corvus did not hear her. "He is a *very* proud bird, Celina. But he is also the smartest and most beautiful of the flock. Each of these crows is very unique. Each has their own personality and, well, each has their own meaning."

He looked up at her and saw that she was watching him closely. Her blue eyes conveyed an understanding that he had not seen in the other villagers.

"My mother died giving birth to me," he said suddenly, still locked in her eyes. He didn't know why he had said that just now. Perhaps because he had never said it before, never had *anyone* to say it to. "I do not know anything about her. It is hard sometimes, not having a mother. But that in itself is quite symbolic." He was quiet for a moment. "Just another reason for people to fear me, I guess."

"What about your father?" she asked carefully, not wanting to break his trust in her.

He looked out over the horizon. "Even my aunt does not speak of my father. She refuses to reveal what she knows. I think it is because she does not want to scare me. I know what the villagers say about him. They think he was crazy."

Celina took a step closer to him. "My mother told me that he was a magician."

Corvus nodded. "I have heard that as well."

"Is he alive?"

He looked at her. "No. He was banished before I ever knew him and the forest is large and unforgiving."

"I have never been," Celina said, meeting his eyes. "You are lucky to have gone. Sometimes I fantasize of escaping into its depth, even for a moment."

Corvus shook his head, shaking any fantasy of hers out of his mind. "It is an incredible place, but even *I* do not fully trust it," he said, unaware of his arrogance. "There are indeed things to be cautious of in there, things we do not understand, and to try and understand them could very well shake apart our foundations of belief." He looked off into the mountains. "No, my father is not alive in the forest. Of that I am sure."

"Do you know why he was banished?" she asked.

"My aunt has told me nothing of his departure. I barely know anything about him at all. All that she has said is that my father detested the council."

Celina looked down at the plaza. From above one could not tell that the church was the tallest building in The White Village. It was in the church that the council met.

"What is it they talk about?" he asked her quietly. "In the church?"

She looked at him. No one had ever asked her that before because everyone knew the answer. "Have you never been inside?"

"When I was younger, but now I am forbidden to enter," he said. "Years ago I decided to sneak in." He thought about the night he had entered the church, wanting to know if he was worthy of the crows which followed him. He wanted to tell Celina that he doubted himself, but Corvus doubted she would understand. *He* saw the crows as something wonderful, but of course he was the only one that thought so. Everyone else in the village seemed so confident about everything. At times he wondered if doubt was a kind of illness that only he had.

"There was something I needed," he said, "something I needed to ask for. I knew that if I got caught inside of the church I would be banished from the village, so I went at night when everyone was asleep. The church was locked but a window had been left open so I crawled through it. The moonlight poured in through the stained glass windows and I could see everything inside. There were benches and places where you could kneel..." He blushed, realizing she knew all this.

"Go ahead," she said. "I want to hear everything."

"I went to a bench in the very front and I sat down in it. Ahead of me was a big altar. I started to imagine what it was like on Sundays, filled with people. I started thinking of the faces of people I knew who would be there. I wondered where my Aunt Sarah usually sat. I wondered what kind of things Elder Mallory talked about.

"Behind the altar there was a great white circle and inside the circle was a large white dove and the wings of the dove touched the edges of the circle." Corvus looked at the horizon, replaying the experience. "I must have looked at the dove for an hour. I was mesmerized by it. It was so similar to the crow only it was white. After an hour, I pulled out the thing that you kneel on and I knelt and I started to pray. I did not know if you are supposed to pray silently or if prayers are spoken aloud, so I did both. I prayed inside my mind and I prayed in the softest whisper so no one but the white bird would hear me."

Celina wanted to reach out and touch him. "What did you pray for?" she asked, almost inaudibly.

He looked at her. "I do not think I should tell you. It is embarrassing."

"Please," she supplicated. "I have never heard anyone else's prayer before. We are not allowed to pray on our own. Elder Mallory says we must pray as a group. He says we are only as powerful as our collective vision. I have never heard another's request."

He looked at his feet. "I do not remember everything because I prayed for so long, but I remember that I prayed that the universe would bring back my mother and father. I prayed that everyone in the village would start to like me. I said even if I was not popular, all I wanted was just one friend who I could talk to and play with. I prayed that my aunt Sarah would touch me, that she would hug me." A tear rolled down his cheek. He gritted his teeth and shook his head. "I prayed that my stupid crows would stop following someone so unworthy and disappear. I wished that they had never come and wished that I could just be a normal boy." He closed his eyes and cried softly and Celina watched him.

Corvus wiped his eyes and his voice hardened. "But it never came true. That was so long ago and none of it has come true. Instead of no crows, I'm followed by *more* crows." He sat up and looked at the tall white building below, that building full of lies and empty promises. He wanted to burn it to the ground. "That is why I sit outside of the church on Sundays, hoping that maybe one day they will allow me back inside and teach me the correct way to pray."

"I do not think they have to teach you how to pray, Corvus," Celina said, "because one of your prayers came true." She reached out her hand and put it on his shoulder. "I want to be your friend. May I be your friend?"

A slow growing smile emerged from his face like the sun cresting from behind the mountains. She grabbed his arm and pulled him up and hugged him tightly. For the first time in his life, Corvus felt something he had never felt before and he wondered if this was how most people felt all the time. Her blond hair brushed against his face and when he inhaled he noticed that somehow it smelled like the petals of The Dreamer's Lotus. "Thank you," he whispered in her ear.

They walked down the hill together hand in hand. From the old tree the crows could see them return to the village. They were not the only ones watching.

Chapter Ten

Corvus rested in his bed and looked up at the ceiling. He held the flat stone that he had found in the forest and he turned it absently as he thought of Celina. He could not get her out of his mind. Every time he closed his eyes he saw her face. He thought about the first time she had spoken to him and the dream she had shared. Perhaps he had a dream for her as well. He thought about the lotus he had manifested and he began to wonder what else was possible. What else could he dream into being?

The lotus seemed to call to him from the nightstand. He traded the stone for the flower and pulled off a petal and placed it into his mouth. Within seconds, currents of energy were surging up and down his body. The corners of the room receded and the softness of his sheets caressed his skin. His heartbeat quickened. His mouth salivated and a growing tightness swam through his loins. Quickly, he wrapped the dream scarf around his head and placed Celina in the center of the circle.

As Corvus fell asleep he felt like he was bringing his body through the circle. It was a sensation he had never experienced. This weighted feeling followed his mind until he found himself hovering over a wheat field at the edge of the village. At the far end of the field he saw Celina standing by herself, looking up at the sky, her hands stretched up toward the moon surrounded by a misty halo.   When he came closer he saw that Celina's body was wrapped in a thin translucent blue veil. Underneath it she was naked. He could see the curves of her body perfectly and they lured him ever closer like the sight of an oasis in a vast desert. She did not see him, though Corvus sensed that she knew he was there, that she wanted him to see her this way. An unfamiliar anxiety was pulling at him from every corner of his being. He had never seen a naked girl before and the sight of her evoked feelings he had never felt. Corvus longed to slip under that veil with her, to touch her flesh with his own, to be held by her soft hands, to know what it meant to be loved by another human being.

By the time he was standing next to her he was overcome with passion.

Celina looked at him for the first time and smiled. Her blond hair waved over her face. "The time is right for physical change," she told him. "Your own rite of passage is upon you. Do what must be done." Suddenly, she was gone.

All at once he was overtaken by a heavy dizziness and his surroundings bobbed up and down like waves in a sea. Corvus walked slowly through the fields towards the village plaza. Entering the village, the moonlight dimmed as clouds covered the sky. In his mind, Corvus called to his crows and soon felt the movement of wings over his back. A low mist hung around the bottoms of the buildings as he entered the plaza. The crows spread into a circle around the village center.

Corvus was compelled to the apex of the plaza. He stood over the black soot stone while the mist pooled around his knees. His back was to the church and he faced the Tree of Truth. All around him the plaza pulsed with a quiet strangeness and the crows guarded the scene like stone sentinels. He felt the world swirl around him, though his feet remained planted and firm, as if he were the spoke, holding the world together with a vision he could not yet see. He had never felt so lucid before in his life.

He was overcome by an incredible feeling of ecstasy. He raised his hands into the air. His palms began to tingle and his feet began to sweat. Somewhere in his mind he could hear Celina's voice circling the currents of the dream like an invisible tapestry. "Do what must be done."

The world spun faster and faster. His clothes began to crackle and his hairs were standing on end. The crows were cawing now. Their cawing increased into a crescendo of chaos until all at once they stopped and everything went silent and black. Corvus held his hands high in the air, waiting...

Light flooded the plaza as if the sun had suddenly fallen from the sky. Corvus watched in astonishment as a bolt of lightning split through the clouds and came into contact with the Tree of Truth. The tree exploded into pieces. The thunder followed. It ripped through the air like a thousand panes of breaking glass and immediately transformed into a low and primal rumble that echoed against every stone in the village. The sound seeped into the deepest recesses of Corvus's mind and his eyelids fluttered like the wings of a bird and he awoke from his dream. He was still standing in the plaza. Pieces of the smoking tree were scattered over the white stones like bits of burning charcoal.

Corvus took a step back and blinked his eyes. It dawned on him finally that he had sleepwalked into the plaza. The heaviness of the dream poured off of him like a bucket of water. When he came to his senses he noticed that the crotch of his pants was damp with semen. Along the rooftops the crows watched him silently. He stared up at them with an overwhelming hopelessness, unable to believe what he had done. One by one, the crows took flight and disappeared into the silence. Corvus understood the sign at once. Gathering his wits and now fully awake, he ran through the shadows of the village until he was home, safe and unnoticed.

*   *   *   *   *   *

When Corvus woke up the next morning he could hear voices outside his window. He quickly put on some clothes and went into the kitchen. Sarah was standing in the doorway. Behind her, Corvus could see people walking down the street. His aunt looked concerned.

"What is going on?" he asked.

"There has been a sign," she said, still looking out the door. "They are saying that the Tree of Truth has been struck by lightning." She turned to her nephew. His eyes looked worried. She wanted to ask her nephew if he knew anything about it, but she was afraid of what he might say. Perhaps he was just reflecting back her own emotional state.

Corvus walked past her and went outside. "Where are you going?" she asked him.

"To see the tree."

When he got to the plaza it looked like everyone in the village had come. People were gathered together in small groups and were talking nervously. Even the children looked worried. Corvus scanned the plaza, hoping to see Celina, but she was nowhere in sight. Corvus walked slowly through the crowd until he was able to see the remains of the tree. The center of the trunk had been split down the middle. What remained bowed together like a Vesica Pisces. Bits of charred bark still littered the white stones.

Elder Mallory was standing next to the tree talking quietly with Elder Loyal. Both men looked very serious. When Mallory looked up to survey the crowd Corvus ducked down so he couldn't be seen. He walked quickly towards the far end of the plaza and stood behind a bench where the Elders wouldn't see him. His legs felt like jelly. How had this *happened*? If they found out that he was the culprit they would banish him from the village without a second thought.

The sound of the school bell rang through the streets. "Alright everyone," one of the Elders said. "All you children get moving to class. There will be plenty of time to analyze the sign later."

Corvus walked quickly to the schoolhouse and was the first person to enter the empty classroom. He took his usual seat in the back. After a few moments, children began to file into the classroom. Elder Loyal had not yet arrived. Corvus fidgeted with his hands nervously. He stared at Celina's empty desk. Where *was* she?

Jeremy approached Corvus. With Jeremy were two of his friends who seated themselves in the vacant chairs around Corvus's desk. Jeremy remained standing. He stared at Corvus with a confident smile that stretched into a sneer. Panic flooded Corvus. Jeremy knew something!

"Corvus," Jeremy said. "How ya doin', pal? You mind if we sit here? These seats aren't taken are they?" The other boys laughed.

"What do you want?" Corvus asked moodily.

"Just to talk. Can't a boy talk to his fellow classmates?" Corvus eyed them. Jeremy looked exceptionally cocky today. He leaned over and put his elbows on Corvus's desk. "I saw you yesterday," he said with a grin.

Corvus's heart skipped a beat. This was it. It was all over now. Jeremy was going to tell the Elders. Corvus was finished.

"I was walking home from class yesterday and I couldn't help but notice that you were walking up to your kingdom. What's the name of your kingdom, by the way?"

"It is *not* my kingdom. It is just a hill. Besides, what do you care?"

"Well, I care about my peers."

"You do not care about me, Jeremy."

"I wasn't talking about *you*, crow head. I was talking about that poor girl you tricked into coming with you."

"We saw you up there with her yesterday," his friend said.

So *that* was what Jeremy was referring to. Jeremy knew nothing about the Tree of Truth, but the fact that they had seen him yesterday with Celina wasn't helpful either.

"He's blushing!" the other boy pointed, laughing. "He's embarrassed!"

"Kind of ironic, really. It's Celina who should be embarrassed. Hanging out with Corvus the Crow. So is she your official girlfriend? Or are you just going to...toss her to the wind, so to speak?" Jeremy smiled at his friends.

"She is *not* my girlfriend," Corvus said, getting angry. "She is just my friend."

"That's not what it looked like. It looked like she was tricked into kissing you. Quite a trickster, this one."

Corvus balled his fists tightly beneath his desk. He wanted to knock Jeremy's teeth out, show him what it felt like to be in pain. "We were not kissing, you half-wit."

"Watch your mouth," Jeremy warned.

"We were hugging. Why don't you knock off your spying. Spying is a serious offense. Maybe *I* should tell someone. Maybe Elder Loyal would be interested to hear that *you* are breaking The Law."

"It's not worse than kissing a crow."

"We were *not* kissing any crows!" he nearly shouted.

"I was talking about her face and your beak," Jeremy taunted and his friends laughed.

Corvus stood up. "I am going to hit you in your face if you do not stop talking about Celina like that."

The other boys stood up and formed a half circle behind Jeremy.

Jeremy was far from intimidated. "I'd like to see you try," he said, standing over Corvus.

"Just get out of here," Corvus said steadily.

Very casually, Jeremy looked over his shoulder at Celina's empty desk. "By the way, where is your girlfriend?" he asked.

Corvus looked. Jeremy was right. Celina was still absent. Corvus hadn't seen her since he walked her home yesterday.

Jeremy looked at Corvus and smiled a contemptuous smile. "She probably got sick from kissing your face. She's probably throwing up feathers right now."

Corvus stepped out from behind his desk, cocked back his arm, and landed his fist square on Jeremy's face. Jeremy toppled over backwards. His friend reached out and grabbed Corvus by the shirt, but Corvus wrenched himself free, and with all his strength, pushed the boy over a desk. The third boy was so dumbstruck that he only stood there.

Before Jeremy could pick himself up, Corvus flung himself on top of Jeremy and straddled him. He took a good look into Jeremy's eyes and the two souls mingled for a short dark moment. Corvus hated Jeremy. He hated everything about him. Most of all, he hated what Jeremy represented – the illusion of fear. He punched Jeremy in the face once, then twice, and then it became a blur and he lost count. Each time he hit Jeremy he felt every pain ever committed against him pulse through his body and burst through his fist. The students in the classroom now stood in a circle around Corvus, a look of horror written over each of their faces.

Tears were streaming down Corvus's cheeks and blood was pouring out of Jeremy's nose as he held up his hands in a pathetic way to ward off the punches. Hearing the screams from down the hall, Elder Loyal rushed into the classroom. Both of Jeremy's eyes were swollen and blood was splattered on his white collared shirt. In one swift motion he pulled Corvus off Jeremy and pushed him to the side and then carefully helped Jeremy up. Loyal asked Jeremy if he was all right, but Jeremy wouldn't answer.

"Outside!" Elder Loyal yelled to Corvus.

Corvus pushed his way out of the classroom and sobbed as he walked down the hallway.

*   *   *   *   *   *

Ten minutes later, Corvus was sitting in a chair in the headmaster's office. The headmaster was a tall barrel-chested man with hair that crawled out of his white sleeves and over his wrists.

Corvus had stopped crying. He felt nothing now. He was not sorry for what he did, but was sorry for what would happen to him. No one had ever been kicked out of school before. If they kicked him out of school then he was as good as banished, which meant he could never talk to Celina again.

"Corvus." It was all the headmaster said. His expression was stiff and serious.

"Sir, they were making fun of my friend -"

The headmaster raised a finger to stop him. "That is enough." His words were measured as he studied the dark eyes in front of him. Corvus's comment had caught him off guard. As far as the headmaster knew, Corvus didn't have *any* friends. He had never seen the loner with other children before. "What an unsightly sign to begin the day. And what with the tree this morning...what on earth were you thinking? I never considered you to be a stupid boy, but boy, that was just plain stupid. Now I know that Jeremy is not the friendliest lad in the village, but you still must learn to live with one another." He looked off into the distance.

"You are not the first boy to come into my office on account of fighting. Disagreements happen and young men often find themselves resolving conflicts in bad ways. I usually send them home with a bit of extra work and a few extra considerations to think about. But you are a bit different, Corvus." Corvus looked at him and the headmaster held his gaze. "I do not have to spell it out for you, Corvus. You *are* different and *you* know why. People are *scared* of you, boy! They watch you walk around the village with your flock of crows and they wonder...well, I don't know *what* they wonder. I suppose they wonder the same thing I wonder. 'What is this boy doing with a flock of crows?' You got any answer for that?"

"No, sir."

He eyed the boy suspiciously. "I guess everyone's just waiting for the other shoe to drop. What in Creator's name is going to happen when...well, it happens?"

"When what happens, sir?"

"You're going to sit there and ask me that after what you did this morning?" Corvus looked at his shoes. "People are waiting for you to *snap*, boy, which is exactly what happened today. You beat the bloody pulp out of Jeremy. What's going to happen the next time?"

"There will not be a next time, sir."

"And why should I believe you? Perhaps you're plotting something this very moment."

"But I am *not!*" Corvus said in exasperation. He stood up, his anger running over him like hot water. He wanted to throw something out of the window. No one believed him. All Corvus wanted was to be left alone, like he had always been.

"That very well may be," he said, "though it is not something I can decide. That can only be determined by the council. They will read the signs and settle what is in store for you." He shook his head. "I do not know what to say, young man. You have always been a good kid. You do exceptionally well in your studies, but there are external influences that I just cannot ignore in good conscious." The headmaster scribbled something on a piece of paper and placed it in his desk. "Run on home, Corvus."

Chapter Eleven

The sun was high in the sky as Corvus walked home. A line of crows watched him from the rooftops. He did not whistle. He walked slowly and without purpose, weaving through the streets, watching his feet as he walked, and passing like a shadow through The White Village.

Why did Jeremy have to make fun of him? It had felt good to hit him, but it wasn't enough. Jeremy needed to pay for what he had said about Celina. Corvus wanted to make *all* of them pay. He wanted the villagers to stop questioning him and the crows, but the only way that would ever happen was if the crows left him alone, which wasn't likely. Their presence was becoming stronger every day.

Corvus stood in front of Celina's home. The crows settled atop the roof. Corvus walked to the door, and reaching up, grabbed the copper knocker and rapped against the wood three times.

A woman came to the door. It was Celina's mother. She stood in the open doorway, her great frame obstructing any view of the home's interior. She was a tall woman and she peered down at Corvus from her considerable height. She showed no fear. If anything, her look was one of contempt.

"Yes?"

"Um, hello Lady Cause. I was wondering if Celina is home?"

Lady Cause looked up at the sky. She was not looking for crows but rather at the sun. "Why are you not in school?" she asked him.

"Well, I *was* in school, but they...sent me home early. Anyway, while I was there I noticed that Celina was not in class this morning, and well, I wondered if she was alright?"

"Celina is menstruating. She cannot be around children today, especially *boys*." She said the last word in a tone that matched her stern expression.

Menstruating? It must be her first, Corvus thought. The Law requires that girls isolate themselves from the rest of the community during their first menstruation. Sometimes they are absent for several weeks.

"Oh," he said. "Well, could you tell her I said hello? My name is Corvus, ma'am. Tell her that if she wants to see me, that I will be at the same place I was yesterday."

Lady Cause eyed the boy suspiciously, mumbled a response, and closed the door without saying good-bye.

Corvus walked home. His mind raced – the tree, the fight. Suddenly, the totality of the dream came back to him. He remembered seeing Celina at the edge of the forest. They had been in a wheat field and she had pointed to a full moon encircled by a halo. His dream had predicted the future, though he had been unable to decipher it. He would need more practice.

Walking through the door of his home he knew Sarah would be gone. She was at the market trading her quilts. On the windowsill, Corvus heard a flutter. Korbin tapped the glass with his long black beak and Corvus pressed his hand against the windowpane. He thought of the forest. It would be nice to tell Obiticus what he had done to Jeremy. Obiticus would be proud. Corvus stared at the crow, thinking. His aunt would not be back until later, and even when she returned she would not expect Corvus home until just before supper. He had six hours to find Obiticus and return before Sarah suspected anything.

Corvus tossed a knapsack with food and water over his shoulder and ran out the door.

*   *   *   *   *   *

He ran briskly knowing he had a good distance to cover and he whistled to his crows to keep up. The forest air was cool. Narrow strips of sunlight trickled through the high branches but did little against the darkness. Though this was only his third trip through the woods, he felt as if he had walked this path many times.

He arrived at the first fork and took the left path. After an hour, he came to a brook and stopped. Corvus knelt down and took a drink. Twelve crows rested above him on the lowest branch of a tree next to the brook. The thirteenth, a small and shy one, joined the rest and began to caw. Corvus looked nervously over his shoulder, but then realized that he was too deep into the forest for anyone to hear. The crows could caw as loud as they liked. But while he drank from the brook, the crow on the tree still cawed. Realizing that he was being given a sign, Corvus stood up and began to unravel the many meanings around him. A river or a brook is a symbol of change and renewal. A crack of light passed through the trees and hit the water in front of him, casting light on the tree's roots. Corvus was interpreting correctly for a new sign had come. He took another deep breath and continued.

The roots of the tree were thick and traveled deep into the earth, signaling the importance of history. Again, the newcomer cawed. Corvus gazed for a while at the crow. It is stated that the crow is a judge, but this was not just any crow, it was a crow unannounced, undetected. Corvus's eyes lit up as the meaning of the sign finally dawned on him. He was not alone!

His eyes followed the water's flow which passed through the trees and disappeared under the brush. Should he follow the water's course? He looked up at the crow and it began to caw and the others joined in. The signs were in his favor. He would follow this brook of change, but he would do so quietly, because whatever lay ahead did not know he was coming.

*   *   *   *   *   *

After only fifteen minutes of following the stream, his feet had become caked with mud. The stream grew louder as he followed it. He wondered how far into the forest it went - he wondered how far he would be able to go, but when he leaned down to get another drink of water he heard voices nearby.

Corvus ducked and peered through the branches of a thick bush. Ahead, he could see a small group of men only twenty feet away. He recognized them all. There were five of them and each was a member of the council. They were standing in a circle around a pile of stones. Elder Mallory was pacing back and forth as he spoke while the other men processed his words. Two of the men held axes defensively, as if to protect themselves from something. A pair of rucksacks and two walking sticks rested on the ground. Corvus sensed that he was the only other living person that knew the Elders were here.

Mallory spoke softly. "It cannot be denied, though I wish it could be. Everything has pointed to this coming. Every moment it draws nearer and before we know it, it will manifest like a terrible black wave and destroy our village and all of its people. Something must be done." The others nodded in agreement.

Mallory pushed down his swelling emotions. "Our beloved tree has been destroyed. It can only mean that more destruction will follow. My dreams have been troubled lately as I seek answers to our future. The seeds of a prophecy were planted long ago and already their roots are firm in the earth. I have kept this prophecy from you all because the stronger its hold on the collective mind, the faster it can manifest. When I awoke this morning to find our Tree of Truth in pieces, I realized that no amount of secrecy can contain what is coming." Mallory stared at the pile of rocks in front of him.

"I called you to the illusion because it is the one safe place to share what I am about to share." He looked at the men carefully, knowing the danger of his words. "Last night I had a dream, a vision if you will. In the dream I was flying in the air and I could see our precious village below. The village walls were not white but black, black from the soot of a terrible fire. On the horizon, beyond the vastness of the forest, I could see the outline of a nightmare rooted in reality. It was The Great City, a place so different that I can only describe it as our symbolic reciprocal, a land without meaning, an eye without vision. I know of only one man who has been to this place, and there he remains. In my dream I sought out this man to make my request. I shall keep this request to myself for the time being. Just know that this man is powerful and that his wisdom of The Great City has the potential to keep the wisdom of The White Village hidden and safe. He is not a warrior, nor a savior. He is only a man, but this man knows much and he uses his knowledge in a clever way, for he is a magician."

Suddenly, a crashing sound came from behind. The men tightened their hands around their axes and opened their eyes wide with fear. Now the sound came from two different directions, closing in on the small group. The noise rose and fell, rose and then fell again until the forest settled into silence. The Elders' eyes twitched nervously. Finally, they lowered their axes, confident that the danger was gone for the time being.

Mallory looked at two of the Elders. "Elder Wise and Elder Sight, you will leave into the forest to seek out The Great City. It is very far, my friends, and it is a perilous journey. The forest is rich with illusion and it will swallow your senses if you do not follow the signs for what they are." He put his hand on Elder Sight's shoulder as a general might do to a soldier headed into the battlefield. "No one must know of your journey. I have chosen you both to go because you are the most cunning of the council. I have faith that somehow you will make it there. But beware, it is believed that the language of the signs will have no meaning and no place within the walls of The Great City. Theirs is a universe removed from our own."

"And what shall we do when we reach The Great City?" Elder Sight asked.

"You will seek out a man by the name of Solomon. Do whatever it takes to find him. Learn from him and help him in any way he needs. My vision and his have aligned and he knows what I request. He knows you are coming and has promised me that he will help us." He looked at his council with concern. "I am sorry for this news, but it is a reality that must be acknowledged. We are on the edge of a terrible precipice. A new wisdom challenges our truth. Left on its own, it will destroy all meaning for good."

"You speak of the boy."

Mallory nodded without words.

Corvus felt the palms of his hands begin to run slick with sweat. He inched closer through the bush that he peered out from. The voices of the men had dropped, almost as if they knew someone was listening.

"The boy is learning fast and his skill as a caller increases by the day. In time, his power will be a danger to everyone around him."

"Then why do we not banish him?" someone asked.

"It is the last thing we would want to do. He is not like the other villagers," Mallory said thoughtfully. "He does not fear the darkness and the creatures of the darkness do not fear him. If he were to return from the forest unharmed then the villagers would begin to question the illusion. If the other villagers were to learn about the hidden meanings of the forest then everything we have done to protect them would be ruined. If we can rid ourselves of him for good, then we shall never see a crow again. Believe me; I do not refer to banishment. I conspire a permanent end to his whistling."

"We *cannot* hurt the boy," an Elder said. "We would only bring about our own demise."

Mallory put up a finger and smiled. "Do not let worry take your heart just yet. The boy's aunt is his only living relative and she cares for the boy more than you would believe. She has been training him in the art of dreaming. I have spies of my own you see, and they have revealed much to me these last weeks. This training of his is coming to its end..."

Fury gripped Corvus. He felt the same rage that he felt when he had rained blows upon Jeremy. It blinded him. Mallory was planning something against him and even worse, against his aunt. If anything happened to her...well, it wouldn't. He would *never* let that happen.

Corvus stood up. His black eyes stared at them with a powerful hatred. He would kill them all with a single whistle! He cared nothing about the signs. He cared nothing about The Law. He cared only for justice.

Corvus leapt from his concealed position, but a sinewy hand clamped over his mouth, and within moments, he felt only darkness.

Chapter Twelve

The darkness lengthened like a tunnel.

He drifted through this darkness for some time until a black forest appeared. Occasionally, he saw the faint outline of a man he knew to be his father. The man walked through the darkness of the forest and drifted between the giant trunks like a subtle mist, disappearing and then reappearing back into vagueness. The man-mist inched closer and swirled around Corvus and an intense dizziness overtook him, until he surrendered and drifted through the black trees of his mind.

The mist carried him to a portal, and on the other side of the portal there was blackness and space. Galaxies and stars could be seen in the distance. Behind him the moon, below him the earth, and within the earth were trillions of creatures with worlds of their own. He could see the earth as a whole and total organism and he noticed that each being contributed to the symbol he saw.

He dropped to the earth and fell to the woods until he reached a lake. The lake was as black as the universe above, but the moon shone down and reflected on dark waters, giving the lake the semblance of an eye. Slowly, a faint glow appeared from the bottom of the lake. The orb of light pulsed faintly like a dim lantern hidden among the reeds on the lakebed. The glow called for him to retrieve it. *"You cannot fly with another's wings,"* said the voice. *"You must take flight on your own."*

He felt himself being released by an invisible hand, and he frantically flailed his arms as he careened downward with incredible speed. All at once, the black lake burst into a flood of light and flame and now the light was just as blinding as the darkness had been. It terrified him. *"This is the eye of your mind,"* the voice said again and Corvus crashed through the water, dissolving the last of the dream.

*   *   *   *   *   *

When Corvus awoke he was lying under a tree. It was dark and the flame of a fire cast shadows against the forest background.

"You are safe, Corvus."

"Obiticus?"

"Yes. I have rescued you. Again."

"Rescued me? From what?"

"From yourself. You were about to execute the greatest error a person can commit."

"What is that?"

"Self-revelation. One must never share with others one's true self unless absolutely prepared to deal with the consequences. You were acting on instinct, not rationality. Those men would have overpowered you in an instant."

Corvus suddenly remembered what had happened and sat up. "Aunt Sarah! They are after my aunt. There is a plan to have her and I both killed. Obiticus, we must stop them! I *tried* to stop them. But *you* stopped *me*. Why did you stop me??" he asked angrily.

"Because you were not prepared. You are so under-prepared, my dear boy. You still have much skill to learn and employ. You were no match for those men. Not in that moment."

"How can you say that? Do you not know that I am followed by a murder of crows that beckon to my call? I could have them killed in an instant!"

Obiticus smiled, intrigued by Corvus's anger. "What good is a crow without a caller? Do not deceive yourself into believing that those men would not hurt you, that they *could* not hurt you. The Elders have hearts darker than any of your crows. You are skilled, young Corvus, but you are also very young. Those men have been trained in the signs for many years. They wield the signs as a cutter wields an ax. You would have disappeared into the roots of the trees...as many have before you."

"They were talking about going to The Great City," Corvus said, reliving what he had seen. "I overheard Elder Mallory discuss it himself. He sent two of the Elders to seek it out. What is it that they hope to find?"

Obiticus sighed. "There are many secrets within the walls of The Great City. It is a place like none can imagine - far from the reality that is The White Village." He chuckled. "The White Village. What there is to learn in a day in The Great City would take a lifetime to understand in The White Village."

"You have *been* there?" Corvus asked in surprise.

Obiticus nodded a knowing nod. "Long ago, when my skin clung tighter to my skeleton. I made a journey through the vast forest, and when I reached the other side I was no longer the same person. A part of me suspects that the scouts Mallory sent will not make it. If they do, The Great City will most likely finish them off."

Corvus looked up at him expectantly. "How can such a place even exist? The Elders have never mentioned it before. Why would they hide it from the villagers? Is it because they are afraid, and if so, why would they seek it out? They practically shuddered at its very mention."

Obiticus eyed him carefully. "Your reality is very small, your scope drastically limited," he said. His tone was neither condescending nor arrogant. It was simple and honest, but Corvus's arms were already crossed in front of his chest. "There is much to tell you, young prophet, but I feel that now is not the time." He grinned a long sly toothless grin. "Let me just say that the lessons will come to you in good time."

"But I do not have good time!" Corvus said in frustration. "Their meaning is sinister. They plot against me and my aunt!"

Obiticus pulled a hand out from his cloak and sealed it over his own mouth. A strange look of panic covered his face, and through his fingers he whispered in a pleading tone, "Not a word of it, Corvus. Not a word. Promise me. Sinister yes, of that I agree. Those Elders hold nothing good for the collective, only for their own self-prolongment. Elder Mallory is using all of his resources to prevent something. He has seen something coming, something that he did not create himself. His own creations he can handle, but the creations of others, well, that is a bit trickier. For years he has cast the shadow of fear upon the village. But his projection is returning full circle, otherwise he would not be sending his Elders to The Great City." Looking off into the distance he rubbed his hands together. "There is hope for us yet."

Corvus thought about the Tree of Truth. "Obiticus…is it possible that the Elders…well, do you think they might ever misinterpret the signs?"

The old man looked so deeply into Corvus's eyes that he startled himself with his own reflection. "Yes. There is no one alive that fully understands the true meanings that the All conveys." He looked into the distance, and even in the darkness Corvus could see Obiticus clench his teeth. "I know Elder Mallory *very* well. Perhaps better than most people who still live in the village, even after all of these years. In his youth, he was considered one of the keenest readers of the signs. I am sure that his skills have only increased since I have seen him. My sense is that he has anticipated something coming for a long time but only now does it knock on his door. Elder Mallory will do everything in his power to stay in power. He is not trustworthy. He is a false leader, an unwelcome omen, a bad seed. Unlike his head, his heart is hollow. He feels no guilt at what he has done, no guilt whatsoever. I *despise* that villain."

Corvus could see the pain on the old man's face as he spoke. "What was it that he did to you, Obiticus?"

Obiticus looked quickly down at Corvus, as though he had entirely forgotten he was there. "People sought my advice to council their dreams. My experience as a boy made it evident that dreams have power, and by understanding them, so do we. Mallory was not born until several years after my dream of the crows. The universe is full of ironic twists, I dare say. Here I had burnt down the forest and already new weeds were growing.

"Since the beginning, Mallory proved himself as a skillful sign reader. He understood that the world had meaning, and he took pleasure in conveying this meaning to others. It soon became evident to him that people were willing to sacrifice their own understandings to someone with more confidence than their own. I saw it myself," Obiticus said. "People are afraid of their own conclusions, because if they are wrong, they have no one to blame but themselves. Mallory saw that my knowledge of the illusion gave me a power and wisdom over others, and it was a wisdom Mallory wanted for himself.

"He was just older than you are when he started his creation. Mallory's lust for power could not allow a conscious collective. If you want control, feed them fear. Mallory brought the fear of the past into the present, using *me* as his example. He reminded everyone how my dream had brought death and chaos. He did not blame me for it, but rather he blamed my *ignorance*. It was because of my ignorance, he said, that my dream manifested as it did. Mallory convinced the council to forbid *anyone's* discussion of their dreams. Before long, the significance of the symbols had been rewritten."

Obiticus looked at the heavens, his face twisted into a sick and tormented anguish. "I would have dreamt Mallory out of existence had I known his plan. All I ever wanted was to create a village of my own!" he cried. "To create the world in our own image is all any of us truly want but Mallory beat me to it. He is a vile and *hideous* man. He has attempted to hide his repulsive perception by white washing his external world, even though his face still reveals the ghastly ghouls of his soul. Did you know, young prophet, that our inner workings are reflected throughout our physical machinery?" He laughed a contemptuous laugh. "Of course you did not know that! It has been removed from the literature. *Many* truths have been removed from the literature." Obiticus looked off into the distance. "You must leave the village at once, Corvus. It only darkens your eyes and smothers your dreams."

"If I leave the village then where would I go?" Corvus asked. "It is known that the forest swallows the minds of men." He shook his head. "Nor do I fully trust the illusions that dwell here," he said, thinking of the satyr.

Obiticus laughed. "Swallow the minds of men," he chortled. "I have lived in this forest for half a lifetime and I am sharp as a stick. The only madness in *these* parts of the woods are the talking trees," he said to Corvus, with the same knowing nod. Corvus, however, did not know how to respond.

"The forest will shape you in a way that is most revealing," Obiticus said with a crazy look in his eyes. "Out here you will become who you are *supposed* to become, not who *they* want you to become. They prefer you to be just like them, asleep and unaware. You say you do not know your destiny, but if you follow my advice you eventually will. You call the crow, Corvus. It came from the forest to find you. It still has secrets to reveal, secrets that dwell across the forest, and once these secrets are revealed to you, *then* you can return, for then you will know your meaning. You and your meaning shall return to the village and you will cast down your crows, slay the unbelievers, and set the world into motion once more!" Obiticus was beyond any sense of collection. He stood and shook his fist into the air, imagining himself as Corvus, leading the black wings of battle into the hearts of the deceivers.

Obiticus looked at Corvus, and with a secretive smile he said, "Some destinies are etched on paper, others are carved in dreams, but trust that our own perceptions are never what they seem." The smile lengthened across his face like a riddle as he continued his rhyme. "In the forest you will find a little key to free your mind. But think you must not before you arrive, or the map inside," he pointed at his head, "will not survive."

With that said, Obiticus handed Corvus a sheet of paper. The paper was so old that Corvus was afraid it would disintegrate in his hands. He opened it up carefully. On the paper were handwritten symbols traced along a dotted line. Corvus recognized the forest and the dotted line weaved through it like a lost drunkard. The line continued from one end of the paper to the other, until it reached an ominous X.

"It is a map, Corvus. It will lead you to new discoveries, ones that will open your world a bit wider."

Corvus was transfixed by what he held. "What will I find?" he asked.

"Perhaps nothing," Obiticus said with a sigh. "Perhaps I wrote that map from a dream that no longer exists. Or perhaps *you* are the one that is not real."

Corvus traced his finger on the ink. "Is it written in blood?" he asked, unable to hide his worry.

He smiled. "Hen's blood; follow it and you will find the hen's egg."

"And what is the hen's egg?"

Obiticus waved his hands in front of his face. "It would not be a secret if I told you, now would it?"

Corvus folded the map and tucked it in his pocket. "Sometimes I wonder if these conversations even happen." He looked at Obiticus, whose expression was lost and far away.

"You will find out soon enough," Obiticus said absently.

"I must be going now," Corvus said. "Twilight comes."

"Yes, on your way then. Much to experience in the days to come."

Corvus eyed him suspiciously. Taking a step away he turned around again and addressed Obiticus one last time.

"Obiticus. You said earlier that our inner workings reflect our outer machinery. Is that true?"

Obiticus nodded.

Corvus sighed and looked up to the stars that could just barely be seen from beneath the pine needles. Even in the darkness of this strange place with a strange man who was perhaps mere fantasy, Corvus asked a question that no one else would answer. "Then why are my eyes so odd?"

"*Odd?*"

"Yes. My eyes are very different from anyone else's."

Obiticus looked at the boy. The firelight waved back and forth casting shadows across his face, but the boy's eyes were as still as the night, never wavering from his own. They held him there with an incredible force that rose from the depths of a child who knew not his own power or worth.

"They say that the eyes are the windows to a person's soul. Do you believe that?" Obiticus asked.

"If that is true then my soul is blacker than the deepest night."

Obiticus smiled. He reached out and handed Corvus a Dreamer's Lotus. "Get going, Corvus. It is going to be daytime soon."

*   *   *   *   *   *

Sarah looked at the sky from inside the house. The sun was well over the hill but Corvus was still gone. That afternoon, Elder Loyal had approached Sarah in the market and told her about Corvus's fight with Jeremy. When she got home she expected to see Corvus waiting for her, but the house was empty. She looked at the mountains past the village. A tightness rippled across her chest.

Over her shoulder she heard a sound in her nephew's room. She marched down the hallway and opened the door to find Corvus with one leg in the house and the other hanging outside.

"Aunt Sarah!" Corvus swung his leg into his room, closed the window behind him, rushed to his aunt and grabbing both of her hands he said, "I saw the Elders in the forest and heard them talking about secret things - they were talking about me – about *us*, Sarah! They are planning something. They say something is coming but no one knows what though they have read the meaning of the signs and they -"

"Woa..." she said. "Slow down, slow down. What are you talking about? What is all this?" she asked. The tightness in her chest was expanding like a balloon.

Corvus looked out the window and lowered his voice. "I saw Elder Mallory with several others. Mallory has sent Elder Sight and Elder Wise to The Great City to find a man named Solomon."

"A meeting in secret? *Solomon*? What does this all mean?"

He shook his head in frustration, wishing his aunt would pay attention. "I heard them myself, Aunt Sarah. They were talking about me. They think that I am a threat to the village. They say they cannot hurt me, but they also say that they can. They are *planning* something."

Sarah grabbed Corvus by both shoulders and faced him. "You are not going to tell a *soul* about this. You hear me?"

He looked at her incredulously. "Who would I tell?"

She bit her lip and turned away. "A growing wave is coming. It was barely a ripple for such a long time, but the ripple is stacking up against itself. The vision is expanding."

"What *vision?*"

She looked down at Corvus. His eyes gazed up at her with all their powerful blackness and within them Sarah saw a soldier, a warrior of sorts wandering the empty battlefields, looking for a sign of war. The tightness moved through her core. There was no more avoiding it. The time had finally come to tell her nephew the truth.

Without emotion she said, "There is a prophecy that you will destroy the village."

"A *what?*"

Sarah took Corvus by the arm and led him out the room. They walked down the hallway to the north end of the house and into a room without windows. Closing the door behind her she told Corvus to sit down.

"There is a prophecy that you will destroy the village," she said again. She exhaled and continued, this time slower, her words pulling Corvus along like a fish with a hook in its mouth.

"When I was a girl, just several years older than you are now, the village was in the midst of a terrible drought." As she spoke Corvus could see the vision in her eyes. "For two years the sun burned the earth into a raging inferno and not a drop of water fell from the sky. All of our crops were lost. All of them. Men were forced to travel to other villages and barter for food. Most did not make it back. Some people starved to death." She shook her head, remembering that time clearly. "It was a strange period for the villagers because the laws and signs were being rewritten. Elder Mallory and his council had been redrafting them for years. My brother was a strong opponent of this movement. He was an adept sign reader and so it was only natural when your father became part of the council. He believed that solidifying the meanings of the signs was a violation to our connection with Source. There was little that he could do about it, however. Remember, this had been going on since he was your age.

"During the drought, the Elders decided to hold a special council designed to help them see what was causing the chaos. Five men, including your father, went out to the fields to perform Ceremony. They gathered all the cornhusks lying in the field, all of the withered vines from the tomato plants and whatever meager remains there were of the year's crop and placed them all into a large pile. Then, the Elders paced around the pile for hours, hoping for a sign.

"I do not know how the pile of debris caught flame, but I have my own inclinations." Her eyes revealed a secret wisdom, a wisdom she rarely shared. "We cannot call for life with a symbol of death. The Elders chose to use their dead crops as a beacon for the signs, but what they didn't realize was that their beacon was actually a symbol of their own helplessness. Can you believe it? Not even the members of the *council* knew how to communicate with the signs! They were using their despair to get the attention of the universe to say something back to them. I cannot imagine that your father was surprised when their dead crops ignited into flame.

Sarah was speaking quickly now. "As the flames rose into the sky, a large bird flew over the burning pyre. Its form was masked by the smoke and only a dim outline could be seen. It was so big that people thought it was a hawk or an owl. More and more birds appeared out of the night and flew through the thickening smoke. The Elders knew they were witnessing a powerful sign and they tried to decipher it, hoping that its meaning held them in favor." Sarah exhaled all at once. "It did not."

"The last of the thirty birds flew through the smokestack and the men looked madly for anything tangible to give them meaning. Suddenly, a wind swept down the mountains and into the valley! It blew through the fields and picked up the flame like a burning matchbox. Giant balls of fire careened over the landscape until they reached the edge of the village. Two houses lit up like stacks of tinder and the fire spread to the church.

"The church was halfway burnt down by the time the Elders finally arrived. Upon the roof of the church was a carpet of crows, black as the night, unconcerned by the fire that blew in their path. When the church fell over the crows took flight. Over the crows, high in the sky but clear as day, a solid white halo surrounded a full moon. I never saw it myself because I was helping your mother give birth to her one and only child. She was young, not much older than I was, and your birth was sudden and unexpected. In one moment she was pregnant and fine and then within under an hour she was bringing a child into the earth. She died moments after your father ran through this very door.

"Elder Mallory was at his side," she said, looking at Corvus with a seriousness that her words could not convey. "You were in your mother's arms and she was in your father's. She passed quickly," Sarah said, wiping a tear from her eye. It was the only time Corvus had ever seen his aunt cry and it made him feel uncomfortable. "All of us were horrified, but it was not your mother's death that troubled Mallory - it was the flock of crows that surrounded her. They came through the open door moments after you were born. As you cried, the crows cawed until all of their calls melded into one and the same. We witnessed this together - myself, your father, and Elder Mallory, and we each took our own meanings. Then, just like that, the crows took flight and flew away, all but one, and every year another returns.

"Your father was banished," Sarah said, her voice hardening. "I knew why and so did your father, but I was helpless to do anything about it. Mallory was acting on fear. The truth is," she said with an ironic smile, "Mallory did not know what the sign meant. All he knew were the stories from the past about a village being destroyed by a flock of crows."

Corvus suddenly thought about Obiticus's dream. "Sarah, how do you *know* all of this?" he asked.

She looked at her nephew. "Because Mallory told me. He came to me one rainy night, full of despair, full of emotions and desires." Corvus saw her shudder. "He needed someone to talk to and I was just as confused as he was. I will never forgive myself for what I did that night. He told me I could help the collective by helping him, and so I gave him what he needed: an ear to hear him and a bed to share. He made me promise not to tell anyone I had slept with him or else he would banish me, though he said it so lovingly I thought he was kidding. Afterwards, Mallory told me everything. It was a moment of weakness and the only one I have ever seen since. Elder Mallory was not afraid of me because he knew he could control me, but he could *not* control your father. Your father spoke to me often in private about Mallory's growing control. He knew that Mallory was manipulating the beliefs of the villagers and Mallory knew that he knew this, and so Mallory began a slander campaign the very day after your mother's death. He told the villagers that your father had knowingly conceived a child with a woman too young to bear. He called him a murderer.

"Now I have no idea what your father's relationship was with your mother," Sarah said, raising her hands to clear her conscious. "They were not married and I do not know if they were in love. I do know however that it wasn't *that* unusual for men to couple with girls of much younger years. It was of course dangerous for the young girl, but kids will take risks when they think they're in love. I remember several girls before her also died in the same way. Using your father as an example, Mallory took this slander as far as he could until the villagers believed his every word.

"When a person disappears into the forest they are forgotten. But how could they forget your father when his only son was followed by crows? Mallory, of course, defamed the crows as much as he could, planting the seed of distrust among the villagers. I heard it myself. 'Do you remember!' he would say. 'This church was burnt to the ground and thirty crows cawed from above. It is a warning. In the past they came to cleanse a village and murder the righteous. Do not let it happen again!'

"It is hard to keep a secret of such magnitude, nephew. I have not a soul to tell it to. My existence balances between fearing the consequences of revealing the truth, and the madness from not doing so. I am an outcast too, you know?" She smiled at her nephew as if to say 'sorry.' "The villagers are confused by your presence, Corvus. They have been brainwashed by Elder Mallory. But they do not hate you, Corvus, so you do not have to hate them in return. No one knows why you are followed by crows, and it is OK if you do not either. Their meaning has been changed and reshaped so many times that they are barely recognizable anymore. Maybe *that* is why you have those dark eyes of yours," she grinned, "because you mean so many things."

Corvus traced the wrinkles near his eye as he gazed at his aunt. She looked totally different to him now. He felt so much love toward her, so much empathy for her struggle. Had he known the burden she had been carrying all of these years he would have opened his heart long ago. He realized that she had been his greatest ally, though he had never seen it for himself, until now. He placed his fingers in the center of his forehead. "I heard them say something about hurting you, Aunt Sarah."

She smiled dimly and shook her head, thinking of Mallory. Elder Mallory resented her, but Sarah doubted he would ever harm her. "No need to worry about me. Just keep your wits about you. You just got kicked out of school for hitting a boy. Please, Corvus, keep your emotions in check. You *must* return to the shadow that you have always been. You must be careful, nephew."

She clasped her hands around his head and held him to her bosom. He had become her child but he was still without a mother. "If only this earth would accept us all," she thought to herself, "then we would not have to guide ourselves through our own misunderstandings." Quickly releasing him, Sarah kissed him on the forehead, turned him around, and led Corvus out of the windowless room.

Chapter Thirteen

Corvus did not return to the forest since he spoke with his aunt. Instead, he returned to school as the same quiet student that he had always been. He isolated himself even further from his community, making an effort to avoid any and all interactions with the other villagers. Corvus was more convinced than ever that his separatism was a value that only he could see. It was a strength, he believed, for while the other villagers spent their time talking about their meaningless lives, he spent his hours in the hallways of his mind, picking apart the barrage of symbols which were intensifying day by day. The Dreamer's Lotus had helped his understandings considerably. He no longer needed the advice of Obiticus. The old man was dangerous and insane and Corvus considered it best to avoid him altogether.

In class, Corvus listened apathetically to Elder Loyal's teachings while he drew pictures of crows at his desk. At times, Corvus felt the arrogance of his teacher to be quite maddening, though the old Elder was oblivious that he often embodied it. At other times, Corvus felt almost sympathetic. Elder Loyal was an old dreamer whose dreams were no longer matching reality. Everything he taught to his students had been falsely taught to him, and though it was obvious to Corvus, Loyal was blind to this fact.

Jeremy still detested Corvus, though ignored him entirely, covering his feelings with proud vanity and a quiet rage. For the most part however, any unkind words or harassment against Corvus were gone. Corvus knew, however, that something remained unsettled. He felt a powerful force emanating between the two boys like sheet lighting at night – soundless, yet all encompassing.

Mallory appeared in public less and less. He remained locked in his chambers and studied the signs obsessively, which he scrawled all over the chamber walls. Only at night was he seen returning home. Corvus suspected that Mallory was up to something sinister but decided that for the time being, there was nothing he could do about it.

Celina remained absent for over two weeks. No one saw her, though everyone knew that she was in physical transition and so her absence was understood. Corvus, however, missed her presence rather dearly. Often while Loyal lectured, Corvus created fantasies that corresponded to his infatuation with Celina. He imagined the two of them running through the trees in the forest at twilight, consumed by the consumption of The Dreamer's Lotus, their bodies entwined in carnal delights. Afterwards, they would drift into powerful reverie and vanish forever into the colors of infinity and imagination.

At the end of most days, Corvus spent his time at the top of the hill overlooking the village. He worked diligently with his crows, perfecting his calls and strengthening his bond with them. On one occasion, Korbin flew down to a low branch and perched just in front of Corvus. Only several inches apart, Corvus could see every detail in the crow's face. He saw a deep intelligence within the bird and understood there was a connection that was so deep between them that he did not yet have the courage to examine it fully. It struck him for the first time that the crow's eyes were incredibly similar to his own. The glossy blackness resembled a clear mirror and he could see himself in their reflection. He was beginning to understand what others must feel like when they looked into his. No wonder the villagers detested him. It was intimidating to see oneself in such profound detail through the eyes of another being.

*   *   *   *   *   *

Corvus waited patiently in the empty plaza. He could hear the muffled catechism of Elder Mallory coming from within the church. Corvus knew she was in there. He had not seen her, but the signs had told him clearly that she was inside. With a short whistle, he sent a crow to sit beside the steeple of the church. Moments later, Celina opened the large wooden doors and stepped outside.

She rushed up to him and hugged him which he enjoyed more than life itself, though he left his arms at his sides, afraid she might judge him if he hugged her back. It had been nearly three weeks since he had last seen her. She looked different, he thought. She was clearly carried by a different wind than before her menstruation. He almost wondered if she were taller somehow.

"I have missed you," he said carefully.

She blushed. "Really?"

He nodded.

"I have missed you, too. It was terrible being locked up inside that house for so long. I almost forgot what the trees in the distance looked like." Her eyes widened. "I saw your sign," she said, referring to the crow. "Where are the others?" she asked, looking around.

"I needed only one," he said with a sly smile. "Can you come with me now?"

She looked over her shoulder at the church. The service was only halfway over. Celina nodded. "Yes, but we must be quick."

He grabbed her by the hand and they rushed down the alley and into the fields. He took her deep into the meadow where the thicket became dense. They settled into a patch of tall grass and sat down.

"There is so much to tell you," he said. "So much has happened since I last saw you."

"I heard about the fight," Celina said.

"Oh that," he rolled his eyes. "That was ages ago, it seems. I had almost forgotten about it."

"Not I," she said in an excited rush. "He deserved it. It is a shame you did not break his nose."

Corvus grinned. "Perhaps. But I did not bring you here to talk about such things." He leaned forward and for a fiery moment Celina thought that Corvus was going to kiss her. Instead, he bucked himself off his heels to reach into his back pocket. Gallantly, he presented her with a piece of paper. "It is a map," he said.

"A *map*? Of what?" she said, her eyes widening.

"Of the forest." He opened it up and laid it flat on the grass. They both leaned over and examined it closely. Her shoulders were touching his.

"That is the forest boundary," he pointed. "We are sitting close to it here."

"It appears the trail begins at the edge of the village," she said, showing interest.

"I think so, too. It is very difficult to tell what is what. Like right here," he said. "I cannot tell if the stream becomes part of the path or if the map is just suggesting to follow the stream."

Celina looked closer. "To me it looks like the stream is part of the path, but it is hard to say for certain. What do you think it is leading to?" she asked.

"To the true meaning of the symbols."

She looked into his eyes and would not release them. "Do you think so?"

"I *know* so. It *has* to be. The meanings have come out of the forest to find me."

"The crows?"

He nodded. "They will lead me to the truth. Why else have they followed me for so long?" Still locked in her gaze he looked at her longingly. "Will you go with me?"

She hesitated. "I cannot leave the village, Corvus. We have no idea how far that trail goes. It could take *weeks* to get to where the map leads. Besides, something tells me the village needs me. I cannot say why, but I feel it in my blood. I feel the same way about you," she said looking at him. "The village needs you too, Corvus. Maybe you have to do this," she said thoughtfully. "And if so, maybe you are supposed to bring back meaning for the rest of the village."

He almost laughed. "I'd rather be banished," he said roughly. He traced the lines of his palm with his finger and said nothing else.

Celina changed the subject. "I can help you prepare, though," she said with a new smile. "I can bring supplies." She looked at the forest behind her. "Maybe I will go in with you for a short distance."

Corvus tried to contain his excitement. "We will have to be careful that we are not seen entering the forest. If they know children have wandered into the woods they will form a search party."

"I am no child," she said brashly. "Not anymore."

He gazed at her in awed wonder. Her mystery seemed all the more provocative. It was true what they said about the transition that girls went through in order to become women. It transformed them fully.

"Nor am I," he said, though part of him knew that according to their culture, he was very much still a child. He had not cut wood with the men which was the village's most critical element regarding his rite of passage.

"Where did you get the map?" she asked, avoiding any embarrassment that the direction of the conversation might take.

"From just another of the forest's illusions." He looked at her and then took her arm. "I have a secret, but you must promise not to tell."

"I promise."

"There is a man who lives in the forest in a roofless house more ancient than the hills. At times I wonder if he is real or not, but the fact that you can confirm the existence of this map proves to me that he is. His name is Obiticus and he has been helping me in the art of dreaming." He held her hand. "One day I will share my dreams with you, Celina. I will include you in my practice..."

"Look!" she said suddenly. She pointed overhead. Looking skyward, Corvus saw a vulture soaring in the air currents above them. "That is not a good sign," she said.

Silently he agreed. It had to be one of Mallory's spies.

"How deep into the forest are you planning to go?" she asked, still watching the vulture.

"The coming full moon will provide enough light to see and we can also bring a torch to guide us the rest of the way. We won't get lost, I *promise*. We will return before the dawn. The new moon has just passed. In several weeks the time will be right." He looked at her longingly. "I do not think it would be a good idea if we spoke to one another until then."

"But..."

"Please. Trust me. There is something much larger at work here."

"What is it?"

"I do not have time to explain."

"Why?" she asked, leaning closer.

"Because you are supposed to be in church."

He started to stand up but Celina held his hand and pulled him back down.

"What is it?"

"I didn't know that this is what you were going to tell me."

He looked at her oddly. "What did you think I was going to say?"

Without warning, Celina took Corvus by the shoulders and pulled him in closely and kissed him. Her lips were warm and soft and he could feel that she was shivering. The sun had just dropped below the horizon, and for a moment, he shared her shiver. She released him and he looked deeply into her eyes doing his best to see himself in her reflection, understanding full well that she could in his.

"Corvus," she said, spinning out of her dream, "I dreamt about you last night. I dreamt that you and I were running through the forest. We had a box. Corvus, I think the map is leading to the box."

He smiled. "You should not share your dreams."

"It did not feel like a dream. It felt like I was really there."

"Were you afraid? In the dream, I mean?"

She stood up. "The service is almost over. I must go." She put her hand on his shoulder and squeezed it softly. "I will be with you when the moon is full, Corvus."

She ran away from him and he looked up into the sky and saw neither crow nor vulture in sight.

Chapter Fourteen

The days passed slowly. Abiding by their decision, Corvus and Celina kept their interactions to a minimum. Corvus spent his days watching Celina from the back of the classroom, wanting her to turn around and smile but hoping that she was wise enough not to. One day after class Celina walked past Corvus and brushed against his arm. She peeked up at him shyly and quickly shoved a note into his hand and walked off.

He took the note to the top of the hill and read it. "I dreamt about you again last night. We were running through the woods only this time the box that you were carrying grew so big that you collapsed under its weight. Why do I keep having this dream?"

Corvus wasn't sure. The content of her dream worried him, but if he could see it for himself, then perhaps he could better understand it. That night, he pulled out his dreaming scarf and the Dreamer's Lotus. He tied the scarf around his forehead and sat for several minutes observing the dark petals of the flower. His breathing quickened with his anxiety. He had never eaten two petals at once before, but he knew it was the only way he could find her in her own dream.

He ate the two petals in one bite and placed Celina and the box from her dream into the circle. The effects of the lotus took effect on him quickly and within moments the room was beginning to spin. Corvus closed his eyes. He felt his awareness slip out of his body and pass through the circle on his forehead. Below him he could see himself sleeping in bed and he drifted through the ceiling and into the sky.

In the distance, at the edge of the forest, a gray mist swirled like a cyclone. When he projected himself closer the outline of a figure materialized within the column of mist. It looked like Celina. The figure's skin was a radiant white and the hair as bright as the sun. The mist disappeared as it poured into her body until at last Celina stood whole and complete before him. The potency of the lotus staggered his thinking, compelling him to embrace all that he saw, yet there was something about Celina that he didn't fully accept.

She held out her hand. "I am not the real Celina," she said, as if reading his thoughts. "I am the symbol of Celina that you have created for yourself." Her words emerged from her throat like white crystal thoughts.

"You have come seeking answers but you are unaware of the peril on your path. To venture consciously into your own dream is one thing, but to enter into the dream realm of another is like hunting tigers with your own flesh for bait. One person's dream can be another's insanity."

Corvus reached out his hand to the apparition when a figure charged through the vision like a gust of wind, transforming it back into mist. This figure was the dreaming Celina who had stopped upon reaching the entrance of the forest. Corvus watched in fascination as a subtle white light appeared on the other side of the arched entrance. With a careful step, Celina crossed over the threshold.

"One person's dream can be another's insanity." The words held him in place. On the other side of the entrance, Celina dreamt a dream about Corvus. He knew that her dreams were affecting his reality and he wanted to know why. The lighted archway was dimming. If he was going to follow her, he must do so now, and so with a heavy sigh he passed through the entrance.

Celina could be seen in the distance walking deeper into the forest. Corvus called out to her but she did not hear him. The glow from the entrance was already gone and he was confronted by a mild panic. He would not be able to leave this dream as easily as he had hoped.

He followed her quickly, barely aware that he had a body again. The forest was dark but pockets of light on the forest floor guided his way – indentations left by Celina's footsteps. Still calling out her name, Corvus trudged along behind her, awkward with his movements in her dream. He followed her for some time until the footsteps disappeared, leaving him standing by himself in the darkness. When something brushed against his neck he gasped in fright and spun around. There, on his shoulder, was a white feather. He pulled it off gently and held the glowing feather in front of his face. Another one brushed against his cheek. Corvus looked above him and saw hundreds of feathers falling from the sky, landing on the trail, indicating the way forward.

He carried the single plume as he ran over the trail of white feathers. His feet moved soundlessly over the path that narrowed the further he ran. At last, he came to a clearing in the shape of a perfect circle. In the center of the circle was an ancient oak tree as thick as any house in The White Village. Its long heavy branches stretched to the edges of the circle and its crown crawled up to the stars in the sky. Thousands of feathers rested on the ground like fresh snow and upon them were hundreds of tiny acorns.

Celina took several steps toward the tree until she reached out her arm and placed her hand on the bark. From the edge of the circle Corvus could hear her whisper something to the old giant, and for a moment, he could hear the tree whispering back.

"He does not know," he heard her say.

"It is because he cannot see," the tree replied.

She took her hand off the tree and stepped back. A thin red line weaved down the bark like a line of water. Its scales glistened in the darkness. When the snake reached the ground it circled Celina three times and then crawled into the dirt. It wiggled its tail back and forth as it struggled to penetrate the hard earth until it disappeared. The ground began to rumble and bulge. The bulge swelled like a bloated volcano until the earth tore in two and a stone statue rose twelve feet out of the ground. Corvus couldn't believe his eyes – it was a statue of him, and in its hands was a wooden box. Celina approached the statue and Corvus knew she was going to open the box, but for some reason the thought terrified him.

Corvus stepped into the clearing. An acorn cracked under his feet. "Wait!" he yelled.

Celina turned around. He felt her gaze upon him like a pair of hands and his back began to tingle. His shoulder blades felt like they were being yanked on. When he reached behind himself he pulled out a fistful of feathers. Looking over his shoulder he was shocked to see a pair of black wings coming out of his shirt.

"Corvus?" Celina said with a look of surprise. "Is that you? Are you alright?"

Corvus stumbled forward. His surroundings pulsed with new life. He was entwined in her dream now. "Celina," he said. "I came to find you."

He watched as the meaning of his presence finally dawned on her. She was lucid now and her face was glowing brighter than the falling feathers. "It's really you!" She rushed to him and wrapped her arms around him. "You never cease to amaze me." She looked at the wings on his shoulders and stroked them. "These are beautiful," she said. "At last you have wings of your own."

"But they did not appear until you looked at me."

"Then perhaps you are too willing to accept my projections." She studied him and then smiled. "Now you can help me discover the meaning of the box," she said. She grabbed his arm and pulled him toward the statue. "I have never seen this statue before," she said looking up at it. "It looks just like you," she said, gazing at it in wonder. "What does it mean?"

Corvus did not answer. Instead he was staring at the box in the statue's hands.

"Corvus?" she asked.

"I heard you tell the tree that I do not know. What did you mean?"

She looked at him with sympathy. "Oh, Corvus," she said sadly. "You really cannot see, can you?" she stroked his wings softly with her hand. "You are followed by a gift you carry within, yet you cannot see it for it is hidden beneath an unknown shadow."

He was standing below the statue now, looking at the box in front of his face. A thin layer of dirt covered the top and he brushed it off with his hand revealing a spider etched into the wood. Its eight legs stretched over the edges of the box and its red eyes beamed out of its head like little coals.

She put her hand on his shoulder. "Are you ready to open it?"

His heart was beating inside of his chest like a drum. He knew he had to look inside of the box, but he was terrified to do so. His fingers touched the rough texture of the wood as he lifted the lid.

Corvus nearly fell down. A thick gray snake of mist pierced the center of the clearing and coiled around his legs. Inside of the box was a crow covered in blood. Its mouth was open, its eyes were white and lifeless. It was Korbin. The forest began to shake. Trees cracked and branches fell. Corvus, however, could not move. The sight of Korbin held him firmly in place.

Above him, a thin fissure appeared around the neck of the statue. Like a falling boulder, the head of the statue rolled off the shoulders. Celina screamed, but it was too late. Entangled in the mist, Corvus fell over backwards and crashed through the ground like a sack of stones as he watched the head fall upon him. Coldness clutched his heart as Celina faded away into the darkness.

*   *   *   *   *   *

Somewhere in the distance a muffled voice was calling his name. "Corvus...You...need... Corvus? Wa-up!" Corvus struggled to open his eyes. The darkness of the dream kept him buried like a grave.

"Corvus!"

Calling upon an unknown strength, he opened his eyes. Blinding colors rushed into his vision. His eyes felt like they were on fire, but through the fire he could see a man's face leaning over him, shouting his name, shaking him violently.

Corvus sat up with a start and pushed the man away with a strong shove. The man stumbled backwards and into a wall. The colors of the room melted together like a water painting and the four walls bended and blended as if alive. He squinted his eyes, trying to regain his composure, but attempting to stand up he fell back down onto the bed. The man across the room was panting heavily and held out a hand to ward off the boy in case he attacked him.

"Corvus," the man said in-between gasps of breath. "Calm down, Corvus. Everything is all right. Everything is fine."

"E-Elder Moore?" Corvus stammered. The room and the man were coming into view. "W-What are you doing here? Where am I?"

"Why in your room, Corvus, in your room."

At that moment, Sarah walked through the door carrying a pot of water. "Corvus!" she gasped. "My stars, you're OK!" She rushed to her nephew and hugged him. Pulling him away from herself, she examined him closely. "Are you alright?"

He thought so. It took him a moment for the experience to fully register. "I appear to be. When I woke up I was being shaken. By Elder Moore." He looked at the man suspiciously and the Elder mirrored the boy's expression.

"Elder Moore came to your rescue," she said. "Oh my. Corvus, you gave me such a scare. I came in this morning to check on you, for normally you are up by this hour, but when I entered you were fast asleep. My word, I thought you were dead!" She put her hand to her head, clearly troubled. "You did not move and I could scarcely see you breathe. I called your name but you were unconscious. Not knowing what to do I ran next door and summoned Elder Moore for help."

"The moment I saw you I feared the worst," Elder Moore said, rubbing the arm which had made impact with the wall. "Your eyes were rolled into the back of your head and your tongue was halfway out of your mouth. I thought for certain you had died in your sleep. You were not even breathing! But just as I had given up hope you gasped ever so subtly. I told your aunt to quickly fetch some hot water. It was at that time that I began to shake you, hoping to rouse you from your stupor."

Corvus felt somewhat embarrassed. He was certain that their panic was not unfounded. In his heart he knew he had come close to dying.

"Thank you, Elder Moore," he said, looking him in the eye. He was lucky that Elder Moore had helped him. He felt bad for pushing him and wanted to apologize, but he could only stare at the Elder.

Elder Moore straightened his posture. He bowed his head slightly to Corvus, acknowledging his gratitude. Then turning to Sarah he said, "It looks like everything turned out alright."

"Thank you so much for your assistance, good neighbor," she said. "I am so grateful for your help."

He nodded again and departed.

Sarah closed the door behind Elder Moore and looked intently at her nephew. "What happened, Corvus?"

"Please, Aunt Sarah. I cannot talk about it right now. The images are too intense. Let me just say that I had a nightmare."

She widened her eyes. "Your dreams are taking a turn for the worse. Oh had I never given you that scarf you would not be on the brink of inner madness."

"Aunt Sarah, I will be fine," he said, with a bit of annoyance. "You must not worry yourself."

"You give me plenty of reason to worry. I worry when you do not wake out of sleep like a normal person. These dreams of yours, Corvus. Please be careful with them. You are still very young, and young men can be quite foolish."

Corvus rubbed the back of his neck. "I will be careful," he said, but his mind was still entranced by the memory of the dream. Though he had almost died, the experience had left him with an odd sensation of power that no advice could tempt away.

Chapter Fifteen

The next day he went to school. When Celina walked into class she gave him a worried look and Corvus knew she wanted to talk to him, but now was certainly not the time. Last night's dream rolled through his mind like an endless reel. Fascinated by the dream's symbolism, Corvus was determined to understand what it meant.

Elder Loyal left the students alone for the day to work on their assignments, telling them he would return at the end of the hour. Corvus pulled out some paper and scribbled down a list of the dominant symbols:

-Oak tree
-Feather
-Spider
-Statue
-Snake

He winced as he thought about the crow in the box. He would avoid looking into that meaning for now. He worked quickly and diligently, occasionally using The Book of Signs as a reference. Writing down the last of his notes, he shoved them into his pocket just as Elder Loyal entered the classroom. With the remaining formalities of the day, the lector dismissed his students.

Corvus and Celina walked out of the schoolhouse side-by-side and Celina brushed her pinky finger against Corvus's hand. Looking over his shoulder to make sure no one was watching them, Corvus passed her a note. She read it immediately.

"The symbolism within our shared dream was profound. The veil between this world and that one is so thin that at times it drives me mad. You will understand what I mean in a few days. I look forward to exploring the forest with you. I cannot imagine not doing so."

They walked down the steps of the schoolhouse. "I was worried about you," she said softly. "I thought the statue had crushed you. I remained alone in the forest, just staring at the stone head. It took me forever to wake up. I needed your help, Corvus, but you were gone, as if you had just seeped out of my dream."

"Talking about dreams?" they heard a voice say. It was Jeremy. "Talking about your dreams is not allowed," he said, taking a step forward.

"Why if anyone else heard you doing such things you could get baaaaaniiiiiished." He said with a spooky tone while wiggling his fingers.

"Oh knock it off, Jeremy," Celina said. "We were not talking about dreams. You obviously misheard us. I said something had seeped through our stream. We have a stream that runs past our house. Last night I saw a sign that suggested flooding."

Jeremy laughed. "You must take me for a real fool. That isn't at all what you said. I know what I heard. You told Corvus you were worried about him. Well, you should be. He might just get you banished."

Corvus stepped forward. "Mind your own business, Jeremy."

Jeremy took a step away and put his hands up. "No need to get violent, Corvus. I was just worried about the integrity of the community. You know good and well that it is a violation to discuss our dreams."

"Then why are you discussing them?" Corvus asked.

"Elder Loyal!" Celina gasped.

"Still outside the school house?" he asked. "Usually you are as far away as you can possibly get by now."

"We were just talking," Jeremy said, giving a sly look to Corvus.

Elder Loyal tightened his brow. "What is so fascinating to keep you on the steps of the school?"

Before Corvus could reply, Elder Loyal pointed at Corvus's feet. "Do you mind picking up that piece of paper?" Lying between Corvus's feet was the note he had written. He reached down and placed the paper nonchalantly into his pocket, but Elder Loyal held out his hand. "Let me see that."

Corvus felt a wave of defeat come over him as he handed Loyal the paper. Loyal put on his glasses and began to read it. Celina and Corvus stared at their shoes while Jeremy looked up at Loyal with a perverted sense of excitement.

"Is this what you were doing while you were supposed to be studying?" Loyal asked.

"I – I…"

"This isn't at all what we have been working on. We have been preparing for the fall semester. Yet I open this up and in Corvus's handwriting I see the drawings of certain symbols, and next to them an advanced handwritten description of each of their meanings. An *oak* tree? When have you even *seen* an oak tree?"

"Maybe in his dreams?" Jeremy offered.

Blinding rage coursed through Corvus's blood. He knew instantly that the presence of Elder Loyal was the only thing protecting Jeremy's health. Loyal took off his glasses and widened his eyes. "Is this true? Is this dream imagery?" he said, shaking the paper.

"I heard them talking about their dreams, Elder Loyal. Celina said something about Corvus's dream. He was probably telling her all about *his* dreams. He probably tells her every dream he-"

"That's enough, Jeremy. Thank you. Go home."

Jeremy looked at Corvus and widened his eyes mischievously, silently saying, "*I got you!*" Turning on his heels, Jeremy trotted off down the road.

"He is lying, Elder Loyal," Celina said. "We would never discuss our dreams. We *know* it is forbidden. And besides, it is dangerous. I was merely asking Corvus if he spent all his time in class daydreaming. All he does is look out the window."

"Well, he apparently does a lot more than that, none of which is actually assigned. You should go home too, Celina. Corvus, come with me." Celina looked over her shoulder as she walked away, watching Corvus until he was out of sight. She hoped he would be OK.

Corvus followed Elder Loyal down the hallway and into the classroom. Loyal shut the door behind them and told Corvus to take a seat.

"A snake, a spider, a statue...I might almost believe you were just studying up on your symbols, but I haven't the faintest amount of confidence that you have seen an oak tree before, Corvus." He took off his glasses and studied him carefully. "*Have* you?" Loyal asked, ready to accept that Corvus had spent plenty of his time alone in the forest.

"No, Elder Loyal. I promise. I have never seen an oak."

"Then why the reference?"

Corvus looked at his hands. "I cannot tell you because if I did I would break The Law."

Loyal squinted at Corvus as if staring at a mirage. "You *dreamt* it," Loyal said, almost inaudibly.

"Yes, sir," he said quietly. Loyal waited. "It is just, well, I had a very strange dream, and the oak was in it. We never discuss the oak; hardly anyone does, so I had no idea what it meant. I figured I would look in The Book. I merely wanted to gain clarity, sir, that is all."

Loyal eyed him carefully. "Describe to me your dream, Corvus."

"Sir?"

"You can tell me. It is safe." The Elder's look was menacing, though it was evident that he was trying to hide it. Elder Loyal considered himself a master sign reader and a skilled dreamer. Corvus felt like he was being psychoanalyzed.

"I feel it not to be," Corvus said. "Besides, The Law forbids it. Something might happen." He could hear Obiticus clearly. "*Beware the villagers.*"

"I am an Elder, Corvus, and a master in dream imagery. I believe that your dreams might very well be prophetic. You are unlike the other children. There is magic in your vision, but without proper council, it could be wasted, or worse...not understood." He said the last part slowly. The Elder's look had become more intense, almost pleading. To Corvus, the Elder looked like a starving man encountering food just out of reach. "Tell me your dream, Corvus."

Corvus had no choice, but he would leave Celina out of it. To divulge that kind of information would mean banishment for her. He decided it would be best to make Celina's dream his own. He described how he walked through the forest until he came to a clearing. He told Loyal about the oak tree in the center of the clearing and the statue which rose out of the earth.

"And the statue was holding something," Loyal continued.

Corvus was impressed. "Yes. It was holding a box, and etched on the box was a spider."

"What was in the box?" Elder Loyal asked quietly.

Corvus winced noticeably. "A symbol I did not recognize."

Loyal was sitting on the edge of his seat now. "Was it...a crow?"

Corvus hesitated and then shook his head. Loyal wanted something that he could create for himself. Corvus decided to give Loyal a new creation to ponder.

"It was my school teacher," Corvus said quietly, not meeting the Elder's eyes. "He was afraid and confused because he was floating in water."

They sat in stillness for a long while.

"You will not mention this to anyone," Loyal said finally. "I will consult with the rest of the Elders."

"No!" Corvus shouted. "You cannot! It is *my* dream."

"*Is* it?" Loyal asked, his face a contortion of unanswered questions.

"You cannot share my dream," Corvus repeated. "If you do, then perhaps it will manifest, as The Elders suggest."

Loyal eyed the boy carefully. The boy's eyes were wide and pleading and for a moment the Elder was contained within them.

"You are correct, young master. We will keep it to ourselves. I shall not tell a soul, you have my word. But promise me this: no more dream work, and certainly not in my classroom. If you fear your dreams manifesting through others' intentions then you would be wise to spend your evenings in a dark and dreamless state."

Corvus nodded and gave an unintelligible agreement. Still transfixed in Corvus's eyes, the rector dismissed the boy and bade him good day.

*   *   *   *   *   *

The clouds covered the sun as he walked home. Furious, he kicked the stones on the ground as he scoured the empty streets for his enemy. "This is all Jeremy's fault!" Corvus thought. "There wouldn't have been any problem at all if Jeremy had just kept his mouth shut. Jeremy got me in trouble. *Jeremy* did this to me," he said to himself over and over again. He was going to find Jeremy, and he was going to make him pay.

He saw Jeremy now who was sitting on the front steps of his house playing with a deck of cards, fiddling with the arrangements of the suits. Corvus scoffed, marching toward him without fear.

The redhead gave a short gasp when he saw Corvus standing over him and he dropped the cards he was playing with. Regaining his composure he stood up straight and arched his neck. "What do *you* want?"

"You tried to get me into trouble," Corvus said. "You *deliberately* tried to get me in trouble."

"Like I told you, I was just trying to preserve the integrity of the community. The last thing we want are people discussing their dreams with one another. Why something terrible could manifest," he said innocently.

"You do not even know what we were talking about!" Corvus accused.

"You mean to tell me you *weren't* talking about your dreams?"

"It is none of your business!"

"It is when the safety of the village is at risk."

"The only person's safety at risk is your own," Corvus said menacingly.

Jeremy eyed him carefully, but then grinned. "What are you going to do? Hit me with another cheap shot? You are such a pathetic outcast that you have to hit someone that doesn't even want to fight."

Corvus considered hitting him right then. He wanted to see the blood rush over Jeremy's face like it had in the classroom. He wanted the satisfaction of shifting that mocking expression with his fist. He felt the rage pulse within him. It felt good. Even Jeremy could feel the rage and he unconsciously took a step backwards. Corvus wanted revenge, desperately. He wanted to give this mongrel a taste of the hatred that he had given Corvus all of these years. For an instant he thought of calling his crows and tasking them against this vermin, chasing him out of the village, over a cliff perhaps. But there would be consequences. He was on thin ice as it was.

"There is nothing you can do to me," Jeremy mocked. "You are just a bastard child in a purified village. To me, you represent noth-"

"Shut up," Corvus said sharply. The edge in his tone cut Jeremy off at once. "I am smarter than you are. Deep down you know this. Your disgusting innards sense your own self-distaste. I may be a bastard, but at least I am not you. I do not have friends because I am followed by a flock of crows. What is *your* excuse?"

"I have friends!" Jeremy retorted.

Corvus laughed heartily. "You call those boys *friends*? They are your friends only because they fear you. They fear your mockery. But what a senseless thing to fear, to be mocked by a weasel. Better a crow than a weasel, I say. No, Jeremy. You are nothing more than a boy wrapped up in the illusion of something important."

With an angry shout, Jeremy lunged at Corvus. Corvus witnessed the attack in a kind of slow motion and he easily stepped to the side, dodging Jeremy's blow. Jeremy skidded across the dirt, scraping his leg. He stood up quickly, however, and prepared to charge again, but Corvus thrust up an open palm, and with an intense force in his voice he said, "I would not do that." It was as if he held Jeremy in place with his words, or perhaps it was the energetic power of his hand. He couldn't tell. Regardless, Jeremy stood stock-still.

Breathing heavily, his shoulders lurching up and down, Jeremy looked like he was about to cry, but Corvus knew that he wouldn't. Voices could be heard coming around the corner and the two boys knew that their encounter had come to a close.

"I'll get you, Corvus. Believe me, I'll get you."

"Not if I get you first, weasel."

*   *   *   *   *   *

That night, Corvus pulled out the Dreamer's Lotus and placed two of the petals into his mouth. Anger swam through his mind as he thought about Jeremy. It seemed that no matter what Corvus did Jeremy was determined to make Corvus's life miserable. He had been lucky that Jeremy hadn't gotten him banished today. Corvus knew that eventually his luck would run out if he didn't do something. Securing the bandana around his forehead, he placed Jeremy inside. He was going to pay him a visit.

Within moments of falling asleep he came to the familiar misty environment of his subconscious. Corvus waited as he held his intention. Soon, dark wings could be seen flying through the mist.

"*You have called for me,*" Korbin said.

"The other night I learned a valuable lesson," Corvus said to the crow. "I do not yet have the ability to safely merge my awareness into the dream of a friend, much less an enemy. This is why I have summoned you. I set before you an important task. My enemy haunts my waking days with projections of fear. I seek retaliation to send the fear back to its source."

"*You ask me to haunt the haunter.*"

"Correct."

"*All actions have repercussions. What you do to another you do to yourself.*"

"That is untrue," Corvus said. "I am not a part of this collective. I never have been. I have *my* ideas and they have *theirs*. It is not my fault we are separate. They have separated themselves from *me*. But that is not the point. I have called for you because I seek balance to an injustice."

"*Who are you to decide what is just and what is unjust?*"

"I am merely a boy," Corvus said innocently. "Though I am a boy that knows that something must be done. I cannot stand idly by and allow another person to damage my name."

"*A name is just a title, and without the owner it has no meaning. All that* you

107

know about yourself has come from the judgment of others," the crow said condescendingly. *"If you do not enjoy another's judgment, surrender it. But if you fear for your health and safety then action must of course be taken."*

"My fear is not in question. I fear less every day."

"You seek power then."

"Go, Korbin," Corvus said with impatience. "Enough nonsense. I seek not power nor judgment. I simply seek a price unpaid. Now fly into his mind and settle this once and for all."

"As you wish."

Corvus watched the phantom crow fly off into the realm of another's dream. Corvus intended a nightmare so great that Jeremy would never bother him again.

*   *   *   *   *   *

The next day Jeremy did not show up to class. Corvus saw the vacant seat as a wonderful sign. Whatever message Korbin had carried to Jeremy had had its intentioned effect. A growing confidence spread over Corvus's stomach like warm water. He sat in the back of the room and watched the empty desk while a new sense of power dug its talons into his ego. He raised his hands to the back of his head and thought about his accomplishment with pride. With more practice he would have no one to fear - he would answer only to himself.

After school, Corvus walked past Jeremy's house, but the front door was closed and the windows were shut and shaded. Whistling softly to himself, Corvus walked home.

The following day Jeremy was still absent. A thin trickle of nervousness wrapped around Corvus's conscience, but his ego pushed it away, still enjoying the look of the empty desk and what it represented. Corvus figured the desk would be occupied soon enough and he just as well enjoy a few days in class without the redheaded nuisance. But by the third day Jeremy had still not returned. Elder Loyal inquired if any of the students knew anything about Jeremy's prolonged departure, but of course no one did. A lurking fear crept into Corvus's stomach. Something was very wrong.

After school that day, Corvus hid behind the corner of the schoolhouse and waited for Celina. The full moon was only one day away, but Corvus's mind was racing like a whirlwind. He had to talk to Celina. He called out to her when he saw her and Celina trotted up to him with a smile, but his expression stalled her approach. Corvus grabbed her strongly by the arm and pulled her rather violently into the shadows.

"Something is wrong," he said.

"What is it?"

"I have done something. I fear that I have created another drama."

108

The other night I sent out -" His chest ached. He looked at Celina and his old sense of humility returned to him. She was so pure, so innocent. Did she *have* to know? Would she even understand? If he revealed his mistake he could very well lose his only human friend. She could never understand. No one would understand him if he told them the truth.

"I – I," he stammered. He looked into her eyes. They reflected his worry. Already he could see he was doing more harm than good. "Nothing," he said. "It is just, well, I have been thinking about the full moon, and, I wanted to know if you would not mind setting out earlier than we had discussed. If we leave when the moon is already high in the sky then we might be seen, but if we leave just before it comes over the horizon then we have a better chance of going in undetected."

"I think that is a good idea," she whispered. She looked into his eyes. "Maybe before that we can meet up in our dreams again."

He held up his hand and looked away. "Please, Celina. No more talk about dreams. No more dreaming. It is best if we do not talk until tomorrow night."

"Is everything OK?" she asked with a confused look. She saw that Corvus was noticeably troubled. She wanted to help him, but did not know how. She was worried about him. Even his eyes looked different. She held onto his hand, hoping to coax out the truth.

Had Corvus looked into her eyes for a moment longer he would have told her everything. He trusted them more than he trusted himself. Corvus shook his head no but then said, "Yes. Everything is as it is." He squeezed her hand gently and stood up. "I will see you tomorrow then?" She looked up at him with those big soft questioning eyes, but before she could say anything he turned and walked away.

He walked restlessly through the streets. He felt terribly responsible for Jeremy's absence. He was worried that something bad was going to happen, but to whom he could not discern. He quickened his pace, thinking to walk past Jeremy's house one last time to see if he could gather any information about Jeremy's health. He was in luck! The door was open and someone was standing in the doorway, but Corvus could not tell who because the person was more in the house than in the street.

Corvus clung to the shadow of the alley. Leaning forward he could barely make out what was being said.

"…will be enough to accomplish it."

"But will it allow enough time for…?"

Corvus craned his neck forward but then ducked back when the person stepped away from the door and into the street. It was Elder Mallory. Mallory was carrying a heavy looking handbag in his left hand. It appeared he was talking with Jeremy's father. His father looked nervous.

"I do not know if he will go through with it. After what happened."

"I understand, but if he wants them to go away, then he has no choice. It is in benefit for us all," Elder Mallory said, putting a hand on the man's shoulder. "Trust me, there are other ways I would rather do this, though it seems clear to me that our only solution is to take action." Jeremy's father nodded his head to Mallory. Mallory turned to leave, but his heel bumped into an uneven stone in the road. The Elder's arms flailed out to his sides and his large heavy body came down on the white stones. Jeremy's father rushed to Mallory's aid and leaned down to grab the Elder's arm and pulled him to his feet.

"Are you alright, Elder?" the man asked.

Corvus didn't think so. Elder Mallory clearly looked dazed. Corvus had seen him hit his head when he fell.

"What a strange happening," Corvus heard the Elder say. "I have not fallen in…" He cut himself short. It was evident that he understood the meaning of his fall and he did not like it.

"Elder Mallory! Your bag!"

"Oh!"

The Elder's bag had fallen onto its side leaving the top wide open - slithering out was a long red snake. Corvus could not believe his eyes. What on earth could Mallory be doing with a snake? Within moments, Jeremy's father had retrieved a broom and cautiously swept the snake back into the bag. The men looked at each other nervously. Neither of them spoke. Elder Mallory delicately closed his bag. He lifted it up and clutched it carefully against his chest and walked quickly away in the direction of the church.

Corvus sprinted home. He scoured the house for Sarah but she was not there. Where could she be? He waited at the table trying to think, knowing that Elder Mallory was planning something. Corvus wished he could talk to Obiticus. He needed a sign, something to tell him that everything was going to be all right. Hopefully, Jeremy would be back in school tomorrow. That would be a start.

Chapter Sixteen

The next day Jeremy was back in class. Corvus sighed with relief when he heard that Jeremy had returned, but his relief was short-lived when he saw him. Jeremy's eyes were wide and glazed over, and he turned around constantly to look at everything in the room, yet there was no indication that he actually understood what he was seeing. He would not talk to the other students, but several times during Elder Loyal's lecture he interrupted with strange requests.

"Elder Loyal! I'd like to go for a walk."

"Excuse me?" the teacher replied.

"I would really like to go for a walk."

"Well I'm sorry, but you will just have to wait until the end of class."

Ten minutes later Jeremy interrupted again.

"Elder Loyal!"

"Jeremy, please. There is no need to talk so loud. What is it this time?"

"I was wondering if you could see the village from here."

"The village? What village?"

"Why our village, of course. Which village did you think I meant?"

Loyal looked at the boy oddly. "Jeremy, are you *feeling* alright?"

"Why are you avoiding my question?" he asked "You still haven't told me if you can see the village." Elder Loyal mumbled a response and continued teaching.

Corvus watched Jeremy from the back of the room. It was clear that Jeremy was not feeling well. Corvus wondered if his parents made him stay home due to his strange behavior.

"Elder Loyal," Celina said. "Perhaps we could go over yesterday's assignment," she said, trying to calm the energy of the room.

"Yes, good idea. Everyone, if you would please pull out your - Jeremy!" Elder Loyal said. "What are you doing standing on your chair?"

Jeremy was indeed standing on his chair. His arms were out to his sides, his fingers were spread apart, and he was moving his arms up and down in a flapping motion. "I can see the village," Jeremy said. "Elder Loyal, I can see the village. Can you? Can you?"

Elder Loyal cautiously approached the redheaded boy standing on his chair. Loyal took his hand. "Come down from there, Jeremy," he said softly. "Why don't you go on your walk now?"

Jeremy bounded off the chair and darted out the door. The students looked at one another.

"Is he alright?" a girl asked.

The Elder just shook his head in confusion.

"He was acting kind of crazy," said another.

Corvus looked out the window. He could see Jeremy running away in staggered steps, zig- zagging through the street. Silently he assured himself that Jeremy's mental state was temporary, that madness was not permanent, and hopefully, not contagious. But watching Jeremy run Corvus had his doubts. He put his head in his hands. He felt *terrible*! Jeremy was a bad kid, but he didn't deserve this. No one did.

When school was over, Corvus left quickly. Celina wanted to talk with him, but Corvus had other things on his mind. When he saw her he gestured that he would meet her in their designated place that evening.

Suddenly, out of nowhere, Elder Mallory appeared. "Hello, Corvus," he said smartly. "How was class?"

"Good," Corvus said flatly, eager to get going.

"How have things been, young man? I mean, how are your studies treating you? Are they too difficult?"

"My studies are fine, Elder Mallory. They are not too hard."

"I suspected as much. You demonstrate quite a keen sense when it comes to reading the signs."

"We do other things as well, you know?"

"Yes. But the language of the signs is by far the most important subject."

Corvus nodded appeasingly.

"Tell me," Mallory said, motioning for Corvus to walk with him. "How have your dreams been lately?"

Corvus's pulse quickened. "Excuse me?"

"Well, Elder Loyal told me that you were taking down some notes about your dreams the other day. I just wanted to offer my insight if need be."

So Loyal *had* told Mallory. Corvus looked at Elder Mallory, wondering how much he knew.

"I thought we were not allowed to talk about our dreams," he said straightforwardly.

"Very true, but you see, one of the reasons The Law forbids talking about dreams is because they tend to manifest if discussed. This would be OK if we all had pleasant dreams, but as I am sure you know," he said, giving Corvus a peculiar look, "that is far from the case. Often we cannot distinguish what is a pleasant dream and what is a nightmare. Nightmares develop in the mind and can only be purified in the church where dreams are shattered into nonsense and make-believe.

"Now tell me, since you never come to church, why not confess your dreams to me now?" he said, motioning for Corvus to sit down on the sidewalk where they stood. "It is no different than in the church, really. People come in and confess their dreams to me all the time. I merely listen, analyze their dreams, and then we symbolically burn them so they cannot cause trouble. For example, if someone has a dream of a tree, we might burn a piece of wood." Mallory studied Corvus. "Any dreams of yours that need the fire of purification, Corvus?"

"No," he said quietly.

"It is OK if there are. We are simply burning the *illusion*. It is a form of action that we can take against something that we fear. Dreams must be dissolved in *both* realms, the physical and the intangible, otherwise they have the tendency to overtake our awareness. A vivid dream can be a powerful thing for a person's mind, Corvus," he said looking straight at him. "They can take us to fantasy and they can take us to our deepest fears. Look at Jeremy, for example. I have a mind that Jeremy's illness comes from a dream. I think Jeremy had an encounter that has changed him in a powerful way. What do you think about this?"

Corvus caught him in the eye like a wrangler. He buried his deep black eyes straight into Elder Mallory's, sharing a faraway timelessness that was now engaged.

"I know nothing about it. He was shut indoors the entire time."

Mallory nodded. "Yes I know. I visited him." He shifted his weight and looked upwards and smiled to himself. "His mother and father were worried sick, but at least we know what happened to the poor boy. It is quite obvious that he is the victim of an attack." He looked at Corvus with a raised eyebrow, the smile now only halfway gone.

"Attack?"

"When I saw young Jeremy," Mallory said like an old storyteller, "he was living in another reality. He could scarcely sit still. He walked about his home emptying the cupboards and throwing out the contents of his closet. He shouted erratically about this and that as if he were a general of sorts, telling the voices in his head to search and find the real Jeremy. But it was *within* all of this peculiar behavior that was the most revealing. In-between his stints he would stop where he was and raise his arms and flap them up and down, up and down...*tirelessly*! The strangest thing of all was, he squawked like a crow."

Corvus felt a chill run down his spine.

"He was compelled to go on like this for hours despite our efforts. Not even his father could pin him down he was so mad. By the third night he had exhausted himself entirely, and fortunately, he passed out. If you saw him today you would agree that he is far from stable." Elder Mallory looked over his shoulder and then back at Corvus. In a low whisper he said, "Are there any dreams you would like to confess to me, Corvus?"

The words came out of his mouth like water out of a broken dam. "You think I did it!"

"I *know* you did," Mallory said through clenched teeth.

Corvus balled his hands into fists. "And *I* know that *you* were carrying a snake out of Jeremy's house yesterday!" Everything within him told him to stop, told him to bite his tongue, but he couldn't. "I know that you shared a bed with my aunt. An *Elder!*" he cried. "I should tell the rest of the village. The people would be amazed to find out that their leader is a fraud!"

Mallory's expression transformed into worry. He looked over his shoulder again and involuntarily put his finger to his lips. "Hush, you *miscreant!*" he hissed at Corvus. "You are a bastard in this town with nothing for no one."

"And you are a fraud!" Corvus yelled again. He wanted to call his crows. He wanted to see bits and pieces of Mallory's face spread out across the stones, but he knew there would be repercussions if he did so. Besides, the crows deserved better than that. He had already learned his lesson with Jeremy. Corvus tempered his anger and calmed himself down. Mallory had nothing on him, whereas Corvus had seen Mallory with a snake. If he was wise, he would bide his time and wait until the moment was right to expose the old Elder.

Elder Mallory spat. Beads of sweat had collected on his large face. "I know what you did and I know you'll do it again. You leave me no choice. I have to protect my village. The storm is coming, Corvus, and you are about to get blown away. Your crows only quicken its approach." Mallory grabbed Corvus's hand and walked him down the alley toward Corvus's house.

"Hey! Where are you taking me?" Corvus asked, his voice rising in panic.

"There are some things I want to see," Mallory said walking briskly, tugging Corvus behind him. "You know, Corvus, we are in the midst of a unique age, a time when the universe will speak to us in new ways. It will talk to us as clear as we talk to each other. If you were any brighter you would know it is telling you to wake up."

Elder Mallory didn't bother knocking on Corvus's front door and let himself in. "Lady Sarah," he called out. "Might I have a word please?" He paced the living room. "Where is your aunt?" he asked impatiently.

"I do not know," Corvus said. "She was gone when I woke up this morning."

"Lady Sarah?" Mallory called again.

Corvus didn't want Mallory snooping around. He knew what Mallory was after. Mallory was looking for the dream scarf that Sarah had made for Corvus. Corvus was glad she wasn't around so she couldn't be put in the situation of answering Mallory's questions. "I'll check her room," Corvus said. Maybe if he found her the two of them could quickly discuss a solution, maybe even expose Mallory. Corvus walked down the hallway but

Sarah was not in her room. "Maybe she is at the neighbors?" he suggested.

Mallory left and reappeared a moment later with Elder Moore. "She stopped by for a chat while you were at school, Corvus." Moore said. "She went home hours ago. I thought she was still here."

"Sarah?" Elder Mallory called out.

He marched into the back of the house, but it was empty. "Check your room, Corvus."

Corvus opened his bedroom door. His room was a disaster. His possessions were scattered as if a windstorm had come through the window. The covers of his bed were ripped apart and the Book of Signs was lying on top of the mattress, torn to shreds. In the center of the room was the body of his aunt. Her face and her arms and her legs were covered in hideous scratch marks. She was dead. Standing over her, upon the windowsill, was a large and ugly crow. Corvus had never seen it before in his life.

"No!" he yelled. "No! Sarah!" He rushed to his aunt and fell to his knees. He held her lifeless arm in his hand.

"This is horrendous!" Elder Mallory exclaimed. "She has been killed! She has been slain!" he thundered. "Corvus, what have you to *say* for yourself?" Mallory held out his hands revealing his pudgy palms. He wore an expression of utter amazement. His eyes were wide and unbelieving, but behind them, Corvus saw a look of satisfaction, one that asserted Mallory's beliefs, that Corvus was indeed a killer.

Elder Moore walked into the room and yelled in horror. Holding his head in his hands he said, "Corvus, what have you *done*?"

"I did not do this!!" he screamed. "I have no reason to! She is my aunt! I have never seen that crow in my life!" he said, pointing at the black bird on the windowsill. The crow ruffled its wings and hopped into flight. "You cannot blame me for this!"

Mallory's arms were crossed. "This is incredibly serious, Corvus. We are going to have to form a council about this. Immediately." He reached out his arm to take Corvus's, but the boy edged away. He looked around his room frantically. It was a complete disaster. His dreaming scarf was lying on the floor along with the map Obiticus had given him. Sweat ran down his forehead. In a madness, Corvus screamed and ran straight through both men, pushing them out of the way with all of his strength. They called out to him, but he didn't care. People in the streets stopped walking when they saw Corvus running past them at breakneck speed. He ran as fast as he could. His heart pounded in his chest, but he would not stop.

He could hear voices calling to him in the distance, but turning his shoulder he saw that no one was following him, yet. What was *happening*? Was this real? Was he dreaming? It sure felt real.

He ran up the hill, going the back way so as not to be seen. He would go up to the tree and count the crows. He would see if there was a new crow and then he would decide what to do.

When he got to the top of the hill, someone was already there. He could see them standing with their back to him. Corvus recognized the fiery red hair at once.

"Jeremy?" he called out. He walked slowly toward Jeremy, the pinecones cracking under his feet.

Jeremy was facing the tree, watching the crows. He looked over his shoulder. "Corvus? What are *you* doing up here?" he asked, his expression confused.

"This is where I come," Corvus said.

"*Really?*"

"Yes, really." Corvus looked up at the tree full of crows and counted them quickly. There were twelve. "What are *you* doing up here?" he asked Jeremy.

"I came to see the city." His eyes were glazed and wild looking. Jeremy looked mesmerized. "The view is *incredible!*"

"The city? You mean the village?"

"No - *The* City. The Big City. The *Great* City. It's out there, you know?" Jeremy was most certainly not himself. He didn't even seem to really recognize Corvus.

"So I hear."

"I wanted to fly there, but I couldn't," Jeremy said with great intensity. "I knew I would need wings to reach it. I had a dream of a bird the other night," he said absently. "The wings of the bird changed from black to white and white to black. The changing difference made me mad because I wanted it to be one or the other, not both. But it never remained the same – it was always changing.

"I wanted to fly to The Great City because that's where nothing changes, everything remains the same. I knew if I could get there I would never have to change, but that crazy bird in my dream wouldn't leave me alone. Black white white black white black black white. I knew that if I were going to see the entire fractal of my reality I would need a better vantage point. *That's* why I needed the wings! But when I came to this hill," he said looking up at the tree, "I saw all of the birds and I thought, maybe one of *them* could give me wings."

Jeremy turned around. For the first time, Corvus noticed the blood on Jeremy's hands. His eyes were wide but distant, perhaps flying over The Great City now. In his arms was Korbin. Its wings had been ripped from its body.

Corvus fell to his knees and began to moan in horror. Jeremy did not seem to notice and he continued talking. "When I asked for the birds to help, they just sat there, staring at me. Have you ever seen a crow stare at you, Corvus? It is intimidating. They just look at you with those big black eyes like they want to eat the liver out of your living body." He looked at Corvus and squinted. "You know, come to think of it, your eyes are rather similar." He did not say this in an antagonizing way. He said it as if he had recognized it for the first time. "You even have crow's feet at the corners." Jeremy shivered unconsciously.

Corvus's fingers gripped his head like a vice. *Korbin*! How could he have let this happen!? He would never be able to forgive himself. Slowly, he stood up and looked at the old tree before him. Its dead branches cracked audibly in the breeze that now blew over the hill. Corvus could sense a great disapproval from the crows as if they somehow knew what had transpired. Tears streamed down Corvus's face. He watched as the sun slipped behind the northwestern mountains on the horizon. The breeze quickened and it suddenly grew cold. He looked at Jeremy but Jeremy was mumbling to himself now, perhaps unaware of the conversation that had just taken place.

Corvus looked up at his crows with an air of finality. He and the crows had taught each other much over the years, but in the end, they had both caused each other tremendous pain. Hundreds of meanings flashed through his mind as he replayed the death of his thirteenth crow, but none of the meanings made sense. He had never felt more disconnected from himself and his truth.

He could no longer allow himself to get mixed up in the meaning of a bird which had come to define him. Because of the crows he was an outcast, an outcast in a collective community. "What happens in one realm must happen in the other," he thought to himself. "I have no place in this world."

He turned his back on his crows, just as his own community had turned its back on him. He would leave them all behind - the village, the crows, the symbols and all of the meanings he despised. He would leave behind his own meaning as well as the prophecy that he refused to fulfill. Mallory had won. Corvus would find his fate in the forest of illusion.

He looked over his shoulder at the crows one final time, waiting for them to communicate to him, praying that they could forgive him for his own conclusions. Answered only by silence, he set off down the hill. Corvus ran swiftly through the brush to the forest. There he would wait by himself until nightfall, for by now, he had become accustomed to the darkness.

Chapter Seventeen

It was almost pitch black outside, but Corvus could see the faint glow of the moon coming over the eastern hills. He rubbed his hands against his arms. He had no jacket and had not eaten since before noon. He was surprised that a search party had not been sent out for him yet. Perhaps they figured he would return. No one could conceive that anyone would willingly go into the forest alone.

It was likely that Elder Mallory had called an emergency meeting to discuss what had happened to Sarah. After a brief explanation, it would become obvious in the eyes of the rest of the villagers that Corvus had orchestrated her death.

Corvus did not expect Celina to come. He figured that she had been swept up in all the excitement. Right now she was probably huddled in a large group with the rest of the villagers discussing the events that had recently transpired. Besides, even if she did show up, it wouldn't matter because he didn't have the map. Still, he wanted to see her more than anything.

Corvus looked at the dark forest behind him. He would need food and warm clothing, of which he had neither. It would be dangerous to return to the village now. More than likely there were people out patrolling the streets looking for him. In fact, there was a good chance that someone was in his house right now, waiting for him to return, and when he did they would grab him and lock him up. They would try him, find him guilty, and then? They could not banish him, Corvus realized. Someone had been murdered and that sign would have to be purified. By fire.

He saw a movement in the distance. A lone dark figure advanced across the valley. It had to be Celina. He watched as she approached the meeting place. She would never find him where he was hiding unless he revealed himself. With a heavy sigh, Corvus broke his forest cover and dashed across the prairie grass in her direction.

He moved toward her like a shadow and she did not notice him until he touched her arm. She gasped, "Corvus!"

"Hello, Celina," he said solemnly.

"Corvus, what have you *done?*" she asked. "The Elders are saying that you killed your aunt. Is it true?"

He shook his head but then remembered that she could not see him. "No, it is not true."

"Then what happened?"

"It all happened so fast. Right after I saw you this afternoon I ran into Elder Mallory. He accused me of hurting Jeremy and then grabbed me by the arm and took me to my home. When we got there, my aunt was lying in my room. It looked like she had fallen. Maybe she was pushed or something - but she was *dead!*" he said emotionally, reliving the memory. "I couldn't have done it, Celina. I was in school all day. You *know* that."

"Corvus," she said darkly, "I saw the scratches on Lady Sarah's body. The Elders made us all come and look. She had claw marks up and down her arms and wrists, as if she had been fending something off. Elder Moore said that when you opened the door there was a crow on the windowsill."

His head was spinning. He felt sick to his stomach again as he relived the experience. "Celina," he said, regaining his composure, "the other day I was in the forest alone when I saw five of the Elders holding a secret council. Elder Mallory sent Elder Wise and Elder Sight to The Great City!"

"The *what?*" Celina asked.

He shook his head. "It does not matter. What matters is that when I saw the Elders I overheard them talking about me. They were talking about ways to get rid of my aunt and me. And then, just yesterday, I was outside Jeremy's house when I saw Elder Mallory coming out. When he came out he tripped and a *snake* fell out of his bag." Celina looked nervous. "I know I am not supposed to talk about snakes, but what was Elder Mallory doing carrying one around? He looked suspicious, Celina. He was up to something and I think it had to do with my aunt. I think he planned to kill her himself. Or maybe he planted the snake in my room somewhere hoping to kill me but it killed her instead."

"How do you explain the crow?" she asked.

"Magic," he said.

"Oh, come on, Corvus."

"OK, maybe not magic, but whatever he did was the next closest thing." Corvus sighed. "Listen, the reason Elder Mallory came to my house in the first place was because he suspected that I had something to do with what happened to Jeremy."

"Why would he think that?"

"Because I did. I am sorry, Celina, it is true. But it is the only part of it that *is* true. The other night I sent Jeremy a nightmare. I wanted to get him back for getting me in trouble, but the nightmare was too powerful. I just wanted to scare him a bit, not make him *crazy*. I am afraid it has shaken apart his foundation of reality. I am miserable, Celina. I had no idea any of this was going to happen."

They sat silently.

"You believe me, right Celina?"

She did not respond. He sat there again in silence, waiting for her to speak, to tell him that she believed him. Slowly, the moon began to emerge over the hills. Its light bathed the valley in a mystical white glow. The light spread across their faces and Corvus was surprised to see that Celina was crying.

"What is it?"

"It's just that I do not think that I shall ever see you again. Of *course* I believe you! The moment I walked into your room I believed that you had not done it. Everyone was talking and shouting so loud that no one was thinking. Everyone was just scared. Most people were demanding that we form a party to find you and bring you to justice. They want blood, Corvus. They are *terrified* of you now. Mallory has told them that you will call your crows upon the rest of them. They fear your retribution."

He could not meet her eye. He had lost so much in such little time - his aunt, his crows, and now he was about to lose Celina. He would probably never see her again, unless of course he came back for her. The forest loomed over his shoulder like a prison.

She reached behind her. "I brought you something," she said, revealing a small satchel. "I figured if I found you out here I would give it to you."

He opened the bag. Inside were his dreamer's scarf and the map Obiticus had given him. Lying atop them was Celina's drawing of the feather. He smiled for the first time. "How did you get all this?"

"When I was in your room. No one even noticed that I was there because everyone was so worked up. Your map was lying out in the open so I grabbed it before anyone saw it. Next to the map was your dreaming scarf and wrapped inside of it was the stone." Corvus pulled the smooth stone out of the scarf. "The rest I got at my house," she said. "There's some food and also some water here, as well as a light jacket."

He looked at her with affection. "Thank you," he said softly. He unraveled the dream scarf and handed it to her. "I want you to have this," he said.

"But it is yours."

"Please. Perhaps you will find a use for it." He looked out toward the moon. Its light seemed to intensify. He knew that he would be making this journey alone. Neither Celina nor the moon would be joining him into the forest.

He hugged her fiercely. "I will miss you," he said. They sat quietly together for some time, holding one another. He could smell the wind in her hair. He rubbed his hands over her skin and demanded of himself to remember everything about this moment.

Celina took his hand in hers and traced a finger over his palms. "These hands have much to do yet," she said. "There is a new story to write and one to be rewritten."

Voices in the distance broke the silence. He could see figures moving through the shadows in their direction. They were approaching, fast. The moonlight had revealed his location.

"You have got to leave, Corvus," she said. "They are coming for you."

He stood up reluctantly. He gave her his hand and pulled her up and they ran together to the entrance of the forest. Above them the trees bowed together at the top forming a natural archway.

A voice in the distance shouted. Corvus thought he heard his name. Looking closely he could see five individuals running their way.

"Go!" Celina said. "I will do my best to slow them down."

He hugged her one last time and kissed her passionately. He would never forget this moment. She meant so much to him, and just like that, he was leaving her. With a final look, he slipped into the forest like a phantom. "Don't disappear forever, Corvus!" he heard her say behind him. "Promise me you will return one day!"

"I promise," he shouted back. He could only see a silvery outline of her now. It was a promise he wanted to keep, and perhaps someday he would fulfill it, but he knew little about the future in this moment, for the present permeated his breath. First, he would have to survive the night.

Part Two:

Through the Illusion

Chapter Eighteen

The moonlight cut through the trees like a thin knife allowing just enough illumination for Corvus to guide himself. For now he kept on the familiar path. Already he could hear shouts behind him entering the forest. They would follow him until they caught him, he knew. They wanted justice and a trial and they knew this forest far better than he did.

Corvus ran as fast as he could. With each passing moment he could hear them more clearly. They were gaining ground and the sound of their feet on the forest floor echoed through the darkness. He looked over his shoulder and saw the light of two torches. He broke from the trail and crashed into the brush, hoping to lose them, but nesting birds dashed out madly, screeching like sirens, revealing his location. The Elders' voices were crisp and clear, and in his mind's eye Corvus could see their placement in the forest. Elder Moore was in the lead and Elder Loyal was behind him. Far back in the rear Elder Mallory panted to keep up, but Corvus knew that Mallory was too old and too fat to arrive before the others. Mallory would find Corvus eventually, however. He would follow the signs.

"Corvus!" a voice rang out. It was Elder Moore. "Corvus, stop! You *must* stop!"

Corvus's heart was beating so hard in his chest that he thought he was going to collapse. His muscles burned like fire. He could feel blood running down his leg where branches and thorns had scratched him. He was running for his life.

Corvus tripped again. He knew he would not have enough strength to physically hold them off if they caught him. He had no choice but to hide. He looked around desperately for some kind of cover. Surely there must be a nook nearby where he could take shelter. He crawled over to an ancient log which had collapsed over a large boulder. Time had covered a hidden recess with vegetation, making it a perfect hiding spot. Corvus ducked through the plant matter and crawled into the hole. He pulled his legs into his chest, and with all the effort in the world, calmed his breathing and became silent.

Elder Moore was almost immediately behind him and when he approached Corvus's hiding place he stopped. For a moment all Corvus could hear was the sound of insects swirling around Moore's torch. The suspenseful silence lasted only a minute until the raucous sound of approaching footsteps severed the quiet drama.

"Have you lost him?" It was Elder Loyal.

"Shh," Moore said. "He is about. I can feel him."

Time seemed to stretch into an eternity. Elders arrived one after the other and stood only paces away from Corvus, not knowing he was right below them. They strained their hearing into the silence. Corvus feared they could hear his heart beating in his chest. Exercising all of his strength, Corvus inhaled as deeply and silently as he possibly could and exhaled in the same manner. He did this several times until he had sufficiently calmed himself. His twisted body was hunched and uncomfortably curled into the shape of the log. He tempered his racing mind and aching muscles by imagining that the wood and his flesh were one and the same. His heartbeat slowed the more he ignored the presence of the Elders just outside of his hide.

"Let us fan out," one of them said.

"It is possible he is long gone."

"Unlikely," said a new voice. Corvus could hear the heavy panting of Mallory's approach. "I sense his presence," the old man said, trying to catch his breath. Mallory knelt down and traced his finger in the dirt. "He is near."

"Where?" Loyal asked.

Mallory was quiet for a moment. "He is so near I can *smell* his panic."

Corvus held his concentration on absolute stillness. It was a miracle they were unable to hear his thoughts and ticking pulse. He cleared his mind, knowing that if he thought about his capture he would manifest it instantly. All he could do was continue to imagine himself as part of the log, part of the forest.

"Elder Moore," Mallory said. "Would you lower your torch? Show us what is beneath this root."

Elder Moore brought down the light of the flame and waved it in front of Corvus's face. Corvus felt himself falling deeper into his breath and away from the Elders. He would not admit defeat, even if defeat's light were cast upon his eyes.

Mallory spoke quietly. "Hold the light. He is below."

It was as if Corvus were floating now, lost among a strange and unfamiliar configuration of matter and time. It was a place free from worry or ego, and it was during this dance with the present unknown that a remarkable thing happened. The flame light dissolved into the trees and the Elders' retreating footsteps carried away the last of all sound. They were gone. Corvus, however, remained still as the dead.

As he sat there in the darkness, an unfamiliar sensation overcame him, as if his mind were inhabited by another being. A clear and distinct voice broached his awareness. The words were gradual and slow, as if roused into motion by an ancient memory.

"We…welcome…your return. It has been such a…looong time since your kind

has merged with us."

Corvus opened his eyes. He had heard the words so clearly that they could have been whispered into his ear, yet where could they have come from? All around him was darkness. Corvus waited for five minutes until he carefully crawled out of his hide and looked around. There was nothing to see. Who on earth could have *said* that to him?

Corvus took a cautious step onto the trail and looked up. The glow from the moon, barely visible from below the thick canopy, was being covered by clouds. If it hadn't been pitch black before, it would be soon. Corvus leaned down and picked up a long wooden staff and used the end to fend off the obstacles in the darkness and he advanced deeper into the forest.

He made good time and good distance, despite his inability to see well. He could hear nothing now, save the crackling of pine needles as he walked. He was tired and wanted to rest, but he pressed onward knowing he had to get as far from the village as possible. He walked for miles at a careful rhythmic pace, using the staff like the cane of a blind man. The Elders were still searching for him he knew, but for the time being, he had lost them. He wondered if *anything* could see him in this terrible darkness.

Corvus stopped to rest when a soft gust of air blew across the hairs on his neck. The breeze quickly ceased and the forest became still as a corpse. Something was coming...

The next sound crept out of the night like a phantom. "Cooorvus..."

His fear spun his body around. His hands gripped the wooden staff with iron terror and his arms extended the weapon into a large figure standing in front of him. Corvus's shock magnified as he watched the wooden staff pass through the body of Mallory as if the Elder were made out of smoke. Mallory instantly disappeared leaving only the sense of a sinister smile. Now back in the blackness of ignorance and vulnerability, Corvus's head spun like a broken top. He felt like a hunted animal.

"You are not safe here, Corvus."

The voice was behind him again. Corvus turned around only to replay the confusing drama. He watched his staff pass through the air like a practice swing in an empty stadium. He scoured the darkness frantically, brandishing his weapon in a pathetic attempt to fend off the unknown.

After a long and tense silence, Corvus put his hand on his knee while still staring into the abyss. "This has got to be a dream," he said to himself. "This has *got* to be a dream."

"It is *no* dream," he heard the Elder's voice say. Elder Mallory materialized in front of him. His edges were soft and seemed to glow, but Corvus knew that the moon was gone and that the only visible light was a trick of the mind. Mallory stood straight and still. His hands were crossed behind his waist and his eyes never left Corvus's.

"Then why can I not awaken?" Corvus asked, still panting.

Mallory chuckled. "Ignorant boy. Do you know nothing about the place which you have escaped into? Why it is like fleeing from a farm into a den of hungry wolves." Mallory opened his mouth into an ugly smile. "This forest will destroy every last hint of sanity you have hidden within you. Do not fear *me*, Corvus," Mallory said, still smiling. "You have much *darker* things to fear." The Elder sighed in contemplation. "I have seen it happen before and I suppose I shall see it again. The Creator has given mankind free will. Sadly, some individuals choose their own will over that of the collective. I suppose that is where the madness truly begins." His expression changed. "I have come to offer you an escape, Corvus - an escape from your madness, a return to the village. Accept your responsibilities and together we shall purify your sins."

Corvus spat. "I want nothing you have to offer me. Your purification is my death."

"You have taken a life, Corvus. The villagers know this. *I* know this, the *universe* knows this. Things are not right. The symbols must be realigned in order to achieve balance again. It is better that you accept what awaits you in the village than be ambushed by the demons of the forest."

"I have taken no life," Corvus declared boldly. "I did not kill my aunt. I am innocent."

A long smile spread across Mallory's face like a crack in a windowpane. "*Innocent?* Were you not involved in the madness-making of young Jeremy?" Corvus tried to interject but Mallory held up his hand. "Your act against Jeremy is unforgivable and irreversible. There is no cure for madness, as you will discover if you decide to stay. What happens to him will happen to you." Mallory shook his head. "I knew from the beginning that this would end badly for you, Corvus. A caller of crows will call them eventually, much to the dismay of his peers. You had the choice to use you crows for the betterment of the community, but instead you decided to hurl your inner demons at an external reality. Now your demons are out of control. They are here in the forest, waiting for you..."

"I do not fear the forest," Corvus replied.

"Oh, you *will*," said Elder Mallory, his eyes widening. The Elder's apparition grew with ominous intensity that made Corvus huddle against a tree. "The madness of the forest is *your* madness. It is the reflection of the suppression of the savage soul - and there are none more savage than yours!"

"Perhaps then I am just *your* reflection," Corvus retorted.

Mallory's figure grew larger. His arms lengthened and his head expanded into a glowing orb. The eyes bulged out of his head like white lifeless globes. "Then I shall show you just how dangerous this reflection can become! You will not return?" Mallory bellowed. "I will haunt you deeper and deeper into the woods. What you did to Jeremy is only a fraction of what I can do to you. I can prepare your mind as a chef prepares a fine meal set with poison. You will not even know you are eating it until it is too late."

Corvus struggled to understand what was real and what wasn't. His stomach tightened with fear and doubt gripped his mind. Slowly the hideous figure began to shrink until it was even with Corvus. A look of concern returned to Mallory's face and he held out his hand again to the small boy. "I implore you, Corvus. Return with me and all will be forgiven. I will take you home myself. We will fly together as brothers of The White Village, set on the course of higher callings."

Mallory's words propelled Corvus into a new awareness. Behind the taunting face and extravagant black magic, Mallory was hiding something. Mallory knew that if he couldn't get Corvus back to The White Village then he would never know if the boy would one day return unexpectedly.

The symbols of the prophecy flickered through Corvus's mind and thirteen crows crashed through his third eye like dogs of war. The crows were the seers. They had revealed the false reality of life in The White Village, the one Corvus had been duped into accepting. Today, he was no longer deceived. He was aware and he was infuriated. The White Village was a bloated body of lies, its inhabitants, mindless bacterium eating away at whatever deception remained. He felt sorry for them. He did not, however, feel sorry for Mallory. Corvus had been shunned his entire life because of this man.

"I will return," Corvus said softly.

A smile spread across Mallory's face and he extended his hand out further. "You have made a very good decision. You will see that -"

But Corvus stepped brazenly forward, his words cutting through Mallory's like a knife. "I will return when the moment is right, and when I do, I will set fire to The White Village just as it has been foretold. I will lift the veil of illusion that you and the other Keepers have kept hidden from the rest. I will liberate the ignorant from your prison." Mallory could see the black hatred swirl in the boy's eyes like columns of thunderclouds. "And as for you, Elder Mallory," Corvus said with fiery resolve, "when I return, I will peck your eyes out myself."

Elder Mallory glared into the boy's eyes and cursed loudly into the night. "You mean *nothing*!" he yelled. "You are a figment of your own imagination. You are a son of a forgotten outcast and the dream of a whore!" Suddenly, Mallory began to laugh. His laughter transformed into a wave of roaring hilarity, mocking the boy with all his might. Finally, wiping his eyes he said with a smile, "As you wish."

A flash of white light engulfed the sky and a powerful thunderclap followed. Mallory's apparition was gone.

The sky began to leak and the raindrops fell heavy and fat. In the pitch-blackness, Corvus held his arms out in front of him, looking for a tree to hold onto. The sound of the rain was deafening and the torrents of water confused his sense of direction. He waved the staff out at length hoping to gain a sense of place. He needed to find shelter...fast! The staff touched the bark of a tree and Corvus rested beneath it, standing so he didn't have to sit in the mud.

The rain was coming down in sheets and by the time the next flash of lightning illuminated the forest, Corvus could see that his feet were almost entirely submerged by water. It was rising fast. Corvus knew that if it continued to rain like this, the bottom of a canyon was the last place he wanted to be. A flurry of thoughts crashed through his head. Among them, one stood out. *"I am the chaos of consciousness. I flood this canyon just as your ego floods your mind. Best to seek higher ground either way."*

Another flash of lightning revealed that the water had crept up past his ankles. Corvus walked blindly away from the tree, guiding himself along with each violent illumination. He had to find the slope of the canyon so he could climb to safety. Sticks and debris rushed past his legs as he trudged onward. He dropped his staff into the moving water and he clutched at the bag which Celina had given him. Corvus lost his footing at one point and was swept away on his stomach. He reached out in desperation and caught hold of a branch of a young sapling. *"Go,"* it seemed to say to him. *"Get moving!"*

Soaked to the bone, but too frightened to be cold, Corvus stood up and continued moving perpendicular to the current's flow. At last, he felt his feet set into an incline. It did not take him long to get out of the flash flood, but the ascent proved to be equally as treacherous. The slope was steep and the water came down it in cascades. The dirt had transformed into a rocky muddy slush, making it extremely difficult to gain footing on.

The trees and vegetation thinned the higher he climbed. The lightning created a strobe-like effect and everything around him pulsed with eerie irregularity. From where he stood he could see the water's current in the canyon below, rising and falling with the predicable undulations of an organized chaos that only a flood can create. Branches and logs and entire trees could be seen tumbling down the canyon bed creating shapes and ideas as they moved out of sight.

The rain pounded him relentlessly from above, but Corvus watched this scene for nearly ten minutes. He had never seen a flood before in his life and he watched the violent waters with fixed fascination. There was nothing he could compare this to - no sign or reference to tell him what it meant, no book or Elder to shape his perception for him. It was awesome, it was unbelievable, and it was breathtaking. There was no more defining it than that.

He was about to continue uphill when Corvus glimpsed a man in the water. The flooding river spun the man around, under, and over until the man looked up at the hillside and spotted Corvus. Time seemed to stop. The rain no longer fell as fast and the cold had vanished altogether. Corvus was looking at Elder Loyal. Elder loyal stared back. In that moment, neither one of them was a pupil or mentor, a good person or a bad person, or any other definition which they had come to represent in the other's eyes. Elder Loyal would be swept away and he would drown. They did not wave or speak,

Loyal did not call for help, and the young boy did not know what it "meant," but somehow, it meant more than just about any sign he had ever seen.

Loyal disappeared around the corner and Corvus continued his ascent, knowing that he was on his own again.

He hiked uphill for over an hour and the rain gave no sign of ceasing. Instead, the wind had picked up speed and it blew sideways into his side. The cold had set in again and he knew he had to get shelter soon or he would die from exposure.

At last, he came to a cleft in the hillside where the ground was reasonably flat. Even better was an enormous oak tree which stood one hundred and fifty feet tall and almost as wide. Strands of yellow mistletoe decorated its crown and ran down the lengths of its sides. The trunk was as thick as the mountain itself. Corvus half-ran and half-hobbled to the reach of the ancient boughs where he collapsed in exhaustion. He almost began to laugh when he realized that the mighty oak had weathered the storm so well that the ground beneath it was bone dry. He closed his eyes and settled into his recuperation, while an unknown voice soothed his transition.

"Restings, my friend. Bury your hardships here at my roots. Believe me when I say that all shall be well. I have stood here for ages and seen many storms. The worst ones were mighty and twice on occasion I was nearly pulled from this earth. My roots have grown deeper and deeper with time, and what hasn't killed me has strengthened my poise. Whatever your worry, leave it behind. The strongest trees grow strongest in deep soil."

The words floated through his head as he drifted into a deep and emotionless sleep. Corvus slept in the comfortable blackness with surrender and relief. He slept for hours unattended by his mind and its troubles, and he heard nothing of the storm that swirled around him like a furious hurricane.

Late in the night a dream came to him. Gentle flickering lights penetrated the even darkness and they approached the dreamer with steady resolve. These lights became candles and soon the outline of a table could be seen. Upon the table was a banquet of food. Corvus reached out and pulled off a succulent piece of meat and placed the peppery skin into his mouth. Before long, he was eating everything in sight.

A familiar voice permeated his feasting mind. "I am sooo happy," said the voice.

Corvus looked up to see the smiling face of Obiticus. His appearance surprised Corvus. The old man was wearing a black and white three-piece suit and his hair was smartly combed. The chain of a watch hung out of his pocket, and between his fingers, Obiticus twirled a silver monocle. The light from the candles reflected in the glass of the monocle and flashed sporadically yet predictably against the black backdrop of the dream.

Obiticus's expression did not match his appearance. His eyes were like a child's, wide and incredulous, and his smile, though genuine, was unusually large - it hung open like a barn door. Obiticus looked so ridiculous that Corvus couldn't help but laugh. Obiticus didn't seem to mind at all.

"Such cause for celebration, indeed!" Obiticus said, mistaking Corvus's amusement for his own. "I knew you would do it. I knew you would leave them. Oh, but at last. For heaven's sake, I thought I would have to drag you out myself. You have taken your sweet time - but don't judge me too soon, this watch I wear isn't even real!" Obiticus said and began laughing uncontrollably. Regaining his composure, he said in-between giggles, "As if anything were."

"Obiticus," Corvus said. "Something terrible has happened. I have left the village forever. I can never return, nor do I want to," but as he said that he thought of Celina. He saw her now, standing in the moonlit meadow, her moonlit face expressing a love that mirrored his own. He had promised that he would return for her, but now that promise seemed more like the dream.

"Oh, return you shall, no question about that," Obiticus said. "You have everything to return for. It is *your* village after all."

"*My* village?" he asked.

"Yours for you and mine for me. We all have our own creations, just as we all have our own *perceptions* of our creations. The trick is discerning what is ours and what is not. In The White Village there is one dominant creation and it is most certainly not yours."

Corvus thought of Mallory and felt the anger rise up within him. "All of those people believe in his lies," he said clenching his fists.

"He has stolen your world from *you*, young man," Obiticus said, his expression changing. He was now alongside Corvus, and he spoke to him calmly and quietly as a teacher or parent. "Everything that you represent in the eyes of the villagers is because of him. But woe to you who has accepted their projections. Now not even *you* cannot identify who you truly are. You see yourself as a villain who is also a hero - a boy with the power to call crows, an outcast, a dreamer, a fighter, a rebel. Who *are* you?" he asked, almost mockingly. "Are you a meaning already defined? Your eyes reflect your value, yet they are the one thing you cannot see."

"Obiticus, my awareness has changed so much these last days that I feel further from the truth than ever before. I know more about the forest than I do about myself."

"And what could you possibly know about the forest?" Obiticus asked skeptically.

"I know that it is dangerous, and unpredictable, and full of illusion."

Obiticus chuckled. "That sounds more like a biography. Mine or yours I cannot say," he chuckled again. "The madness of the forest is only your own. Whatever you have brought with you from the village will follow you along. You must abandon your madness or it will consume you entirely."

"Then how have *you* survived?" Corvus asked, mirroring his skepticism.

"I was much fatter in my youth," Obiticus said with a wink. "But then again, I knew where to go. I learned a secret or two along my journey. The two I will share, the one I will not. The secret you need is etched on a paper which I will gladly give to you."

"Do you mean the map?" Corvus asked.

"You know of the map?" Obiticus said with covetous confusion.

Corvus sighed. "You have given it to me already, Obiticus."

Obiticus furled his brow. "*Did* I? Why would I give you what I haven't remembered? My keeping of secrets is coming undone with age. Be that as it may, assure an old man that you still have it in your possession, or I will be forced to dream another up for you."

"I do."

Obiticus grinned madly. "Thenyoumustfollowitscourse," he said, the words spilling out of his mouth in excitement.

"What is so important about this map?" Corvus asked.

"It will lead you to your past - it will lead you...to your father."

"My *father*?" Corvus exclaimed. "You know of my father?"

"I knew your father well," Obiticus said, revealing a hidden smile. "He was much like you when he came out of the forest - distraught, deceived, and afraid of his own power. He is out there, Corvus, waiting for you to find him."

The body of Obiticus began to dissolve and fade away.

"Wait!" Corvus shouted. "What if I cannot follow the map?"

"There is no cannot on this journey. You must arrive at the map's end with haste or the illusions of the forest will eat away your sides. You are much thinner than I once was, you know," he said with concern.

"Will I see you again?" Corvus asked.

"It is hard to say. I have arrived in this dream through the one remaining Dreamer's Lotus in my possession. I used to have many, but the other night I nearly ate them all. I cannot recall my errand nor my ending, but it is a common blunder for old men to make in the midst of their making. It is part of the territory though, you see? The forest is timeless and I often forget that I even exist. Best to remember that you do while you can. It is easy to exist in the collective, for everyone can witness your existence. But in here all alone it can take tremendous focus to assert one's own sanity."

As his hands melted into smoke, he smiled broadly again. "I will see you soon, I hope. Many dangers it seems, out and about, traipsing around in the darkness. Your journey can only be won from within, for out there, everything is but a reaction of the mind."

Corvus watched Obiticus disappear entirely, but for a moment afterwards he could hear Obiticus still calling to him from the other side. "Abandon the symbols for now, Corvus. They will do you no good in this place."

Chapter Nineteen

When Corvus woke up the sun was halfway over a blue sky. He stretched his arms and looked up to admire the impressive oak which he had slept under. "You saved my life," he said, examining its massive trunk. "Without you, I would have frozen to death."

A breeze moved across the mountain and through the leaves that fluttered above him. The wind blew stronger and a branch touched his head.

"Without me, you wouldn't even be here."

The leaves rustled loudly. Corvus turned around, but nobody was there.

"Hello?" he called out.

"Hello."

Corvus spun around, looking for Mallory. Mallory *had* to be nearby, hiding, watching him. Corvus pulled the smooth stone out of his pack and gripped it tightly, ready to throw it if attacked.

"That is not the sacrifice for your troubles."

Corvus turned around again. The voice sounded like it was coming from behind the tree.

"You have come here with troubles, yet believe your troubles have come to you. Your problems are yours because you have created them. If you wish to see a difference you must offer your value."

"My value?" Corvus asked, still looking for the source of the voice.

"I have thousands of leaves and I depend on them for my life. They are my most valuable possession, yet every year I give them away. They fall to the ground and decay, enriching the soil, and the next spring I grow taller and stronger. Whatever you want in your environment, you *must put it there first. You must give something of yourself. If you are a part of this world, which you are, one day you will be asked to make a sacrifice of your own."*

Corvus raised his eyebrow as he considered the words. They sure didn't sound like Mallory's. Corvus looked up at the massive mountain behind the tree. He was so small and insignificant out here. Maybe the forest was starting to get to him.

Corvus turned around and walked out from beneath the tree and into the open. He had a spectacular view of his surroundings. From what he could tell, Corvus had found the only shelter on the entire mountainside.

Down below he could see a maze of canyons covered by a canopy of trees. All around him were mountains. He saw no sign of the village and had no idea which way he had come from. He was lost. He looked up at the sky and thought of his crows. He needed them now more than ever before, but they were nowhere to be found. He would have to guide himself.

Obiticus and the dream trickled through his memory. Corvus reached into his bag and pulled out the brittle map and examined it closely. There was no legend or key or *any* indication of what was what. At the bottom of the map was a small square where the trail began. "This must be The White Village," Corvus thought. Upside down Vs crowded the center of the map. "And these have got to be the mountains," Corvus said, looking across the canyon. "That is all *I* see, anyway." His finger followed the path. "More mountains to climb," he said with a sigh.

He noticed that at the top of the map the dotted line ended at a large X. The X was smeared with dirt, oil, and grime as if Obiticus had spent countless hours pining over its location. Corvus saw no V's near the X. Instead, there were rectangles, many of them, which Corvus thought looked similar to the square that represented The White Village. This couldn't be a map to another village. Villages are small. Was it possible that Obiticus had given Corvus a map to The Great City? Knowing Obiticus, it was likely. That meant that Corvus's father was alive on the other side of the forest!

If he was going to get anywhere, Corvus first needed to figure out where he was. He looked up the steep mountainside. Maybe at the top he could get a better view. He picked up his bag, and began his climb.

*   *   *   *   *   *

The mountainside was rocky and steep. He climbed in the sun for about an hour until the trees overtook him and obscured his view. A thick forest of scraggly pines held the mountainside together and he used the narrow trunks to pull himself along. The higher he climbed the darker it became. He couldn't help but feel like he was climbing a ladder to nowhere.

He walked like this for hours. The mountainside was so steep that he was forced to rest often. By noon his water bottle was nearly empty. He sat down and ate a sandwich, thinking about the world he was leaving behind. He pulled out the smooth stone and rubbed it thoughtfully while worries crowded his head. Thinking of his dream, Corvus wondered if Obiticus was right, that the forest would eventually consume his mind entirely.

At that moment, Corvus heard a soft and gentle tune like a delicate staccato tapping at the air. He spun around in a circle, trying to discern where the music was coming from. From what he could tell it sounded like it was coming from just a short distance up the mountain. He gathered his stuff and started to climb.

The hillside transformed as he moved. The trees thinned and the ground changed from pine needles into stone. Soon, Corvus was moving over granite boulders that increased in size as he climbed. With no trees to obstruct his view, Corvus could see out across the canyon again and what he saw was remarkable. The mountains had expanded in scope, along with the sky. The sight of it all left him breathless and he stood still for a moment and listened to the beautiful music. The mountains and music and sky blended together like something intangible taking form and being touched for the first time. The lucidity of it all wrapped itself around his ego and his mind and his beliefs. There were no symbols for something like this. This was complete, this was eternal, and somehow, in this moment, so was he. It was a strange sensation - he was fully present yet had not a care in the world.

The music melted into his mind and Corvus took several hypnotized steps towards the mountains which were speaking to him like grandparents. They spoke of his path and the stand he must take, that he too was a mountain and must never give up. Corvus opened his arms in embrace as his foot stepped over the boulder and into the air. From out of nowhere, a powerful gust of wind whooshed into his chest and a voice bellowed, "*Wake-up!*"

Corvus stumbled back several meters. He looked around but saw no one, yet he knew that someone had warned him. Corvus peered out at the mountains and down the side of the one he was standing on. His feet poked over the boulder which rolled away and out of sight – Corvus was standing on a cliff! He delicately took a step back as he began to realize what had almost happened.

The music still tickled the air, unaware and unaffected that some stranger had almost fallen off the mountain. Corvus was now more determined than ever to discover the source of the music. He noticed a worn path in the stone that intersected with the one he had climbed up. Corvus walked along this new path that meandered across the rocky region. He followed the rising sound of the music until he came to an opening in the rock. A *cave!* Who could possibly live up here? Another outcast? An animal? Was it another of Mallory's clever tricks? Corvus put his hand to his mouth. "Hello? Is – is someone there?"

The music stopped. It stopped so suddenly that Corvus knew at once that he had made a mistake. He wanted to turn around, but his feet held him to the earth like iron rods. A slow and steady stream of mist poured out from the floor of the cave's opening. Corvus's eyes widened. He could not believe what he was seeing. Fear urged him to run, but a terrible curiosity possessed him.

"H – Hello?" he called out again, this time more quietly.

The darkness of the forest swallowed the last of the sunlight. A soft but undeniable sound could be heard from within the cave. Corvus's heart skipped a beat as he recognized the noise – it was the sound of breathing! Corvus lifted his heel and began a silent back-peddle, but the voice that emerged from the cave held him still as a statue.

"Do you know where you are?" the voice asked, its tone dark and unwelcoming.

No. He didn't. "I – I heard your music."

"Do you know where you are??" Its impatience was increasing.

"I do not," he stammered. "Perhaps you can tell me. I am looking for The Great City. I thought I could see it from above at the top of the mountain."

"The Great City!" the voice roared. *"It once was my home, I lived where it stands. Now it is metal, a living machine. It expands and devours, much like a disease. Your kind is all needing, for you live in your mind, always are seeking, but you never see what you find."*

"I have been advised to go there," Corvus continued. "A friend has told me that if I can make it to The Great City then the visions of the forest will not consume me."

Two large yellow eyes appeared out of the blackness of the cave and from behind them two thick curled horns came into the subtle light. Corvus's heart leapt into his throat. It was the satyr he had seen with Thomas. The satyr's voice was low and menacing. *"Your friend is probably right. Your sight and your sonar do not lead you true, and so the forest and I shall dispatch a journey for you."*

Corvus sensed something strange. It felt as if he was shaking, but he wasn't.

But he was.

"Your crows are not here to help you now," the creature said.

A deafening sound below him made him jump - the rock at his feet was cracking apart! Corvus ran at breakneck speed along the path while giant rocks tumbled off the mountain. The path he had taken was nothing but air now. His only escape was further up the mountain. Rocks the size of houses careened past him as he scrambled up the hillside. If he could just get another hundred meters he would at least be off the stone outcropping.

His path ended abruptly. A giant boulder had splintered away and fallen leaving a thousand foot drop where the path had been. Behind him, the hillside shook like an angry giant. The gap in the path was about ten feet wide, too far to jump, but if he didn't think of something fast his fate would be the same as the falling boulders.

Corvus looked desperately for a solution until his eyes settled upon a hollow log lying along the cliff's edge. He dashed over. The log was long and large but it was moveable, filled with the hollow hallways of termites. Corvus turned the log perpendicular to the gap and pushed with all his strength until it reached to the other side. The log wobbled as the mountainside shook. Corvus held his breath and stepped onto the log, hoping it wouldn't break when he got to the center. He had no choice. He had to go now.

A familiar voice behind him severed his concentration. "Be careful. It's a dangerous crossing."

Corvus nearly fell but caught his balance just in time. When he turned his head he couldn't believe his eyes.

"*Obiticus!?* What are *you* doing here?"

Obiticus widened his eyes with surprise. "What am *I* doing here? What are *you* doing here?"

The ground rumbled. Corvus looked at Obiticus in anger. "Are you *mad* or just trying to kill me?"

Obiticus laughed. "*Kill* you? You're as important to me as your crows are to you."

The log tilted and Corvus fell, but his right hand grabbed the wood tightly as his feet dangled beneath him.

"Corvus!" Obiticus yelled. "Stop playing around!"

Corvus gritted his teeth and pulled himself back onto the log and stood up. The log's wobble was worsening. Corvus stood in the center doing his best not to look down, knowing that the abyss lay beneath him like an ocean. He tried not to think about the rotten log, or the fall, or Obiticus. He just watched the other side and willed himself toward it. Booming noises could be heard behind him, sounds of the mountain falling apart. Panic gripped him when he saw that the log was sliding off the other edge. Corvus jumped and waited for his life to flash before his eyes, but instead his feet touched solid ground. He sprinted up the hillside. When he was sure he was safe he turned around, but Obiticus was gone.

Was it possible that his mind was playing tricks on him?

Corvus pulled the smooth stone out of his pocket and gripped it tightly. Waves of terror and exhilaration washed over him. He had never felt so alive in his life. He brushed his arms and patted his legs and laughed loudly. He had made it! Perhaps this stone was bringing him luck.

He turned around and walked quickly up the mountain under the forest trees. He wanted to make as much distance between himself and the satyr as possible. The sun was going down, but he knew he couldn't be much further from the top of the mountain. Corvus bounded up the hill hoping to make it there before dark.

Chapter Twenty

The remaining ascent proved much more difficult. He hiked uphill for hours ducking under brush, going around vegetation too thick to crawl through, and untangling himself from briars and snags. The terrain was both ambiguous and confusing, populated with identical rocks and logs and flowers and trees. He was grateful, however, that his current mission was straightforward – the only way he could possibly get lost was if he stopped climbing uphill. The trees became more ominous the higher he climbed and he could not help but wonder if these giants somehow knew that he came from the clan that prided itself in chopping them down.

His last few steps to the summit were heavy and labored and he dragged his feet behind him like old anchors. The sun had set several hours ago, but there was just enough light for him to see his surroundings. The top of the mountain was covered in trees - there was no view.

He sat down in exhaustion on a pile of pine needles. He was gripped by a powerful thirst and cursed the fact that he was out of water. A wave of hopelessness washed over him. He had climbed all this way for nothing. He would never find his father now. He fell over backwards and looked up at the prickly sky shrouded by the branches of the tall pine trees. He fell asleep almost immediately.

In the depth of a troubled dream, a red dragon appeared out of the darkness above him. Behind the dragon, Corvus could see a mountain of golden treasures. These treasures were not coins or jewels or anything physical, rather they emitted a sense of knowledge and knowing, a coveted wisdom revealed out of reach. The winged serpent was massive and hideous, and it sailed toward him like a nautical ship in the sky. Its eyes glared down at Corvus and it opened its reptilian mouth and spewed out a stream of molten fire. Helpless, Corvus watched the hot flames rise into a wall around him. Corvus spun, the dream spun, and the spinning tail of the dragon wrapped around the young dreamer like a red copper coil. Corvus could feel the pressure against his ribs and the serrated scales against his skin. He looked up pleadingly, begging the dragon to release him, but the dragon only smiled with an all-knowing smile, and its long thin teeth protruded out of a long thin grin. Corvus knew this smile well – it belonged to Mallory.

"Do you see, Corvus?" Mallory slithered. "Are you beginning to appreciate the power of the mind? Even though you dream, the pain is more real than you could ever imagine."

The pressure around his body was unbearable. He felt that any minute his spirit would collapse and perhaps be consumed by the wicked victor. As if reading his mind, the dragon opened its mouth to reveal row upon row of razor sharp teeth. A cauldron of fire could be seen in the depths of its throat. With the last of his strength Corvus willed himself to awaken, until finally, moments before the dragon's mouth enveloped him, he did.

Corvus awoke in a sweat. Darkness prevailed around him. The dream crawled through his mind like the poisonous serpent he had just escaped. He knew that if he allowed his thoughts to run rampant, he would manifest his own demise in moments. Sounds in the forest echoed between the trees and strange birds could be heard between the branches. The unknown of this place challenged him to his core.

He rebelled against sleep until morning. Corvus knew that he could not survive the nights like this much longer. He looked up at the twilight sky and saw a reflection of his own struggle against the darkness and the pursuit to break into some sense of meaning. He screamed a silent plea into the air, begging the universe for some sort of sign to continue on, to strengthen a cause that he did not yet recognize in this darkest hour of self-doubt.

A narrow column of light broke over the distant mountain and strands of luminescence parted through the upper branches of the tallest cedar on the summit. Corvus propped himself up on his elbows. He realized that if he could somehow climb that tree he might be able to see across the mountains, and *perhaps*, discern his location. He slung his bag over his shoulder and approached the massive cedar. The aroma was intoxicating. The tree's lowest branch was several feet over his outstretched arms. Climbing it would prove to be more difficult than he had first thought. Taking a moment he thought about how to proceed and after a few minutes he had an idea. He held onto one strap of his bag and tossed the rest of the bag over the lowest branch, leaving the other strap dangling over his head. With both straps in his hands he was able to pull himself up onto the branch.

It took Corvus several hours to get to the top. The higher he climbed, the brighter the light above him became. He knew that if he could get up just a bit higher he would be able to see out across the forest.

The last branch was out of reach but Corvus felt confident that he could use his bag as he had in the beginning. He tossed the bag up and watched it come down the other side. Grabbing both straps he started to swing his weight so he could climb up, but as he did so, the top of the bag came open. He tried to restart, but as he moved, his hand slipped and he nearly fell. His feet dangled in the air like vines and he watched helplessly as his last sandwich fell out of the bag and tumbled to the ground.

With the last of his strength, Corvus pulled himself up onto the thick branch. Sunlight washed over him. He was standing on one of the tallest trees on the top of a mountain. His view was nearly panoramic. He saw that this mountain was part of a long chain of mountains that spread out for as far as he could see. They were beautifully rugged and moved along the landscape like the spine of a snake, but to Corvus's dismay, there was no sign of civilization.

"It's quite a view," said a voice.

Corvus spun around and nearly fell off the branch.

"Be careful," Obiticus said quickly. "You don't want to fall."

Corvus couldn't believe his eyes. "*You* again! Obiticus, what are you *doing* here?"

"I came to see what you were looking at. More of the same, it seems to me."

Corvus almost grabbed Obiticus by the shoulders and shook him. "Stop sneaking up on me! That's twice you've almost killed me."

Obiticus baulked. "There isn't anyone out *there* that can do *anything* to you. It's all in here," he said, pointing at his bald head. He looked at Corvus strangely. "Are you OK? You seem a bit...stressed."

"Of course I'm a bit stressed!" Corvus screamed. "I'm hearing voices, seeing strange creatures, and apparently having a conversation with someone who isn't even here."

The old man laughed. "Of course I am here," he said. "Where else would I be?"

"Not in a tree two hundred feet off the ground," Corvus said with frustration.

Obiticus waved his hand in the air. "Oh posh. I'm crazy about trees."

Corvus crossed his arms. "Then why are you floating?"

Obiticus looked down. Sure enough, he was suspended beyond the reach of the branch. "Oh my!" he gasped. "I haven't floated in ages." He looked at Corvus with a bit of distress in his eyes. "I am *terrified* of heights," he said. Slowly, he began to disappear. After a few moments, he was gone entirely.

Corvus sat down on the branch. He was hungry, thirsty, and going crazy. He closed his eyes, but remembering the nightmares that plagued him the night before, he stiffened his posture and did his best to stay awake. He wedged himself into the crook of several branches that came together against the trunk of the tree. Corvus looked down. The vastness of the tree and the sky and the earth below him spun in wider and wider circles until he was dizzy. He did not have the energy to climb down, but he could not allow himself to fall asleep.

Hours passed and somewhere behind him the sun disappeared. Without cover from the other trees the cold wind bit into his skin like old nails. He pulled his legs into his chest and curled into a ball, fighting back fatigue by looking at the stars. They flickered and danced as they came through the night, taking their place among the constellations. He saw heroes, and hunters, and symbolic stories etched across the sky. Soon, he was floating among them, and it was then that he knew that he had fallen asleep.

Corvus drifted from one constellation to the next like a boat in the ocean of space. The symbols were conscious it seemed, and they acknowledged his presence as he passed by them. The Great Bear called from above to say his hello, while below the fishes sent wishes that The Boy would find his way home to his star. In the distance The Boy could see the constellation Corvus. It called to him through the silence.

The Boy hesitated.

"Go," the stars told him.

"But its meaning alludes me," said The Boy.

"Some symbols come to us to show us the way. Others remind us of what we already know. If you want to awaken then surrender your fears. Display a new dream in the heavens for the people below."

The Boy gazed out at the cosmos in wonder. The stories of the owls and virgins and serpents and kings each had their own myth emblazoned in the sky. The Crow, however, was black against the night and could barely be seen. The Boy wondered how anything so mysterious could ever be understood. When at last The Crow spoke to The Boy its words emerged like crystals of light. "I am the wisdom that is already yours. The only symbol you need is yourself. You are on the right path, young dreamer," The Crow said. "You shall find all that you are searching for, as long as you are ready to look with open eyes."

The Crow was perched on the tail of a snake and above The Crow was Draco The Dragon. The Dragon was long and immense and its body extended over the rim of the sky. Its tail twitched and flickered to life and the stars in its mouth became brighter and brighter. The Dragon detached itself from its fixed spot in the heavens and sailed over The Crow. It lowered its legs and opened its claws, preparing to ensnare its prey, but The Crow disintegrated into the darkness. The Dragon roared in anger not knowing where The Crow had gone, but The Boy could feel The Crow now flying within him. The Dragon looked down at The Boy and bellowed, "You do not belong here in The Sky. Your worth and your purpose are not made for this world. This world is designed by those who can see. Your dream is not your own - your mind is mine now, Little Crow." The Dragon opened its mouth and spewed out a torrent of fire.

The Boy closed his eyes as the heat rushed toward him. In the darkness of his inner space The Boy could see a star glowing and growing like the birth of a sign, and around the star a circle had begun to appear. The Boy passed through the circle which burst into flames as The Dragon's fire engulfed the last of the dream.

*   *   *   *   *   *

Corvus awoke with a yell, the dream still running through his mind like a raging river. He stood up and patted himself down frantically as if his clothes were on fire. Certain he had made it safely out of the dream, Corvus collapsed back into the tree. His stomach ached and his head hurt from dehydration. Corvus knew he could not descend the tree because in this condition he could easily fall. He looked out across the forest. The shadows of the steep mountains retreated with the coming dawn and the stillness of the morning quieted him. Corvus sighed and settled comfortably into the tree. "At least I am alive," he said.

"Life is the greatest sign of all."

Corvus bolted upright. He looked over his shoulder, expecting to see Obiticus, but there was nothing - no one.

"It is a sign you are in good company," the voice said again.

"Who *is* that?" Corvus cried out. "Where are you coming from?"

"From all around you," it said calmly. *"From the earth, from the sky. From within. From without."* A soft glow emanated off the tree.

"Is it *you*?" Corvus asked the tree.

The tree did not answer verbally. Instead, a resounding *yes* reverberated deep within Corvus's core. He swooned slightly - he was communicating with another tree! He felt dizzy and thought he might fall. The branches below him were spinning like wooden propellers.

"Be careful!" the tree warned. *"You are up very high with no wings to carry you to safety."*

Corvus felt like a cinched belt was wrapped around his head. "What is *happening*?" Corvus screamed. He stood up and shook his fist at the air. "Obiticus! Mallory!" he called out to the sky. "Where are you? What *is* this madness?"

"I sense that the you you are using, is not actually you. Be sure that your bark serves your service - no need for your ego to protect old beliefs. The world thrives alongside you while you doubt its existence. Doubt is your madness, young one. The meanings you seek are not in your head. If you want to see the world as it is then step out of your mind and into the forest."

Corvus sat down and stared at the spinning branches below him. "How?" he asked.

"Trust," said the tree. *"Trust your own guidance. Surrender your meanings and abandon your anger and doubt."*

"But what if I cannot trust?" he asked. "It is hard not to doubt that I am talking to a tree."

"And it is hard for this tree not to doubt that you can actually hear me. We have been talking to you for a while, you know? Everything in this world is conscious and aware. Does the thunder not speak to the rain? Do the birds not confer with the wind? These are things that anyone can see for themselves. Your problem with trust, I suspect, stems from your roots which are entwined with your kind. You have mistaken their beliefs for your own

and still use them to stand on."

"I am not the beliefs of my village!" Corvus said, slamming his fist onto the branch.

"Oh?" said the tree. *"Please tell me then, what it is that makes you you? Is it your hair? Your brain? How about the trillions of cells in your body - are they you?"*

Corvus stared at the tree, considering its words.

"At first glance you might think that I am just a tree. You can see my bark, and my branches, and my cones lying on the ground. But what about the things you cannot see - the insects beneath my bark, the mushrooms along my roots, the water in my veins? These things are a part of me just like my branches are, but they are not who I am. There is more to this world than what the eyes can see, just as there is more to you than what others perceive. An essence within you awaits your awakening."

"So how do I awaken?" Corvus asked, his voice bordering desperation.

"You will only discover your truth when you finally see who you are not."

The soft glow from the tree dissolved and the voice was gone. Below him the branches stopped spinning. Corvus stood up and looked out across the horizon. He squinted his eyes, following a beam of sunlight piercing the clouds. Was he seeing what he thought he saw? Far in the distance, hidden in a cul-de-sac of towering mountain, sunlight reflected upon blue water. Excited, Corvus reached into his bag and pulled out the map and examined it. He couldn't believe his eyes - there it was! A large and obscure lake, the only one on the map, rested to the east halfway along the trail to The Great City. Corvus studied the mountains carefully. He could follow the ridge he was on for a short distance and then travel down the other side. Eventually, he would be able to follow the large canyon to the north until he came to a river which would guide him to the turnoff for the lake. Tingling warmth spread over his body. He felt it, he trusted it - this was the right way.

Chapter Twenty One

Corvus ran briskly along the length of the mountain ridge, weaving his way through the tall trees until he came to a steep cliff. Lichens and colorful moss clung to the jagged sides of ancient boulders strewn about the mountainside like broken marbles. In the checkered distance above the opposing precipice he could see vultures circling in the air, riding the warm thermals up and down the mountain slopes.

Thirst gripped him like a bad dream. He felt dizzy. A light breeze blew against his face and he spread his arms out to his sides, feeling the air rush underneath them. He felt like a lost rodent in the maze of his mind. Should he continue down on foot? Should he jump off the cliff? Could he fly? Corvus squawked into the canyon and a loud lonely echo returned. He wondered who he was calling to and he wondered who was calling back.

He thought often of his crow as he traveled down the mountain, punishing himself again and again for Korbin's death, only to turn his turmoil onto Mallory in an endless cycle of self-destruction and vengeance. By the time Corvus got to the bottom of the mountain, the darkness had taken over. Walking became a slow and tedious process. Corvus traveled through endless brush and branches that longed to entangle him. On either side of him, steep granite walls of rock towered toward the sky. He felt claustrophobic. From every direction the dense darkness bellowed its deafening silence, pulling at his nerves, testing his patience.

At last, Corvus came to a small brook. He fell to his knees and splashed water over his face and body. He drank the water down in deep gulps of satisfaction. When he was finished he fell backwards into the water which trickled around his body as he looked up at the dark canopy.

Emptiness gnawed at his stomach. It had been over a day since he last ate. Corvus had never gathered food in the forest before, but he knew he would have to if he wanted to survive. In the thinnest shade, blades of grass clumped together and grew at various lengths. Where the grass was the shortest Corvus was pleased to see several dozen dandelions. He remembered someone in the village had once told him that the dandelion was a wonderful plant because most of it was edible.

Corvus approached the dandelions and took a knee beside them. He admired the yellow flower that mirrored the sun that could not be seen. His admiration did not last long, however, and his hunger soon got the best of him. He tore off a green leaf and popped it into his mouth with insatiable hunger.

An angry cry stopped him in mid-bite. Corvus looked around startled. Was someone watching him? Was there someone else in the forest, someone hurt? After a brief pause he resumed his position and pulled off the rest of the leaves and ate them. Again he heard the same scream and Corvus jumped with a start. "Who's there?" he shouted. "Is someone hurt?"

"Monster!" came the reply.

Was it possible the *dandelion* was talking to him?

"Of course I am talking to you!" it shouted angrily. *"You would too if someone were tearing your limbs away."*

"But you are a plant," he said.

"What difference does that *make?"* the dandelion yelled angrily. *"I am still alive! Did you think that just because I do not walk around and get lost in the forest that I do not feel pain?"*

He *had* thought that. Why wouldn't he have?

"Show a little respect next time. Try asking instead of just taking. A little communication goes a long way; it shows that you acknowledge us and that you actually care. You will find that we are much friendlier when treated kindly. You are a part of this world, you know? You should start acting like it."

Corvus was bewildered. First he was talking to a tree and now a flower. What next, the moon? This forest really was making him crazy, and this dandelion was downright mad.

"You know, a bit of humility might make your journey easier. Everything around you is aware that you are here. We all know who you are and where you come from."

Corvus looked around, disconcerted that he was being watched. "From the village, you mean?"

"From the peeeopllle," the flower said slowly. *"You come from the people and their meaningless beliefs. In fact, they aren't even beliefs. They're projections."*

"Projections?" Corvus asked.

"Unlike the rest of the creatures that live on this earth, people have decided to live inside their heads. They find comfort there, perhaps because there are so many voices inside to talk to. Sometimes the loudest voice confuses the person into believing that the voice is actually who they are. But it is not. It is only a voice in their mind and this know-it-all voice projects its assumptions onto the outside world, unwittingly perpetuating its own suffering."

"How?"

"The voice assumes that the outside world is simply not as smart as it *is. Obviously, this assumption can lead to disastrous results."*

"Like what?" he asked.

"Geez, like all sorts of things. Like separation, violence, denial - destruction of the natural world. Need more examples?"

Corvus didn't think so. "Well not everyone has this voice," he said. *"I* don't."

    "Oh really? Well how about that? What about beliefs? Got any of those?"
Corvus nodded.
    "If you still have a belief then you still have a voice."
    "So I am supposed to discard everything I believe in?" he asked
skeptically.
    *"That would be a good start. Your beliefs are coming from the external world
which means they are not your own. If you have a belief, then you are projecting it onto
reality, period. The problem is, reality is not what you think it to be. It is something* far
greater, far more complex. It cannot be boxed into a neat little belief. Not the real *reality."*
    "What is the *real* reality?" the boy asked.
    *"It is everything and it is nothing. It is the All that you can and cannot see. It is
the essence of the universe.* Your *essence is very real, young person."*
    "But isn't that just a belief?"
    "Ahh," said the dandelion. *"There is a very big difference between truth and
belief. Truth permeates this universe with every breath you take. It dwells in your heart and
animates your life. It embodies the symbols that guide you. Truth is what brought you to this
world and what will take you away from it. Eventually, all beliefs are dissolved by truth.
Do not let your perception of your own greatness limit you. Surrender your beliefs. You will
be surprised by what you find."*
    Corvus looked at the little flower between his feet. He sensed a great
wisdom from its words. Perhaps he could learn to start over somehow. Now
away from the collective beliefs of The White Village he was free to create a
new identity, one that couldn't be defined.
    *"It takes courage for a human to listen to a plant. For that I am grateful. I do not
blame you for your ignorance, nor should you blame yourself. Forgiveness is a truth you must
learn. Now please, before you go, take the rest of my leaves and the flower to strengthen your
passage."*
    "But won't you die?" Corvus asked.
    "That too, is just a belief."
    Corvus pulled off the yellow flower and placed it in his mouth. As he
chewed it he noticed another dandelion next to his foot that was white and
full of seeds. Carefully, and with great respect, Corvus pulled it out of the
ground and brought it up to his lips. He exhaled a long gentle blow into the
white fuzz and watched with child-like wonder as the seeds floated into the
air and out of sight.
    Corvus walked along the fertile soil and politely inquired with other
edible plants if it was acceptable to eat what they had to offer. After doing
this several times he found that many plants would beckon him forward
before he could even ask them for help. The further he walked the more
natural it became to communicate with the forest around him. Everything
glowed with a newness unlike anything he had ever seen.
    He followed the brook as he traveled and the brook swelled in size
the further he went. The sounds of the stream filled the canyon with a

peaceful water lullaby that cooed him to its fragile edge. Corvus cupped his hands and pulled out a small bowl of cold water and lifted it to his lips. He felt it grip the insides of his mouth and run down his throat like an old song.

"Thank you for your water," he said gently to the stream. A sunbeam hit the surface of the water, scattering light in all directions. Corvus thought he could hear the sounds of a harp and he realized it was coming from the brook. Filled with an incredible peace he lowered his hands again to drink. As he did, he noticed a fish the size of his forearm dart to the side and take shelter beside a rock on the riverbed. Would it be OK to eat this fish, he wondered?

"Dear fish," he said, hoping his words could be heard underwater. "I see you swimming below. I come to you with a great favor, that you may release yourself from this river season and feed a hungry human who desperately needs to eat."

The response came back to him clearly. *"I see you, looking down from up above. I myself have wondered what it would be like to live on that side of the veil. I acknowledge your acknowledgement and I am grateful for it, truly. I say to you that I am happy to serve you with your request."*

Corvus smiled. This was easier than he thought! All he had to do was ask. Corvus reached down into the brook and set his hands on either side of the fish, but the moment his fingers touched the fish's scales, the creature darted out of his hands and swam to the other side of the stream. Corvus carefully crossed the stream and tried again. Once more, the fish evaded his attempt.

Corvus scratched his head. "I thought you said it was OK to catch you."

"I did, but you will have to use your own brain to do that. If you think I am just going to hop out of the water and into your mouth then you should go back to eating plants."

Corvus looked around until he found a long stick he could use as a spear and then stood on a rock to survey the fish. After a moment he threw the spear. He wasn't even close. In fact, the fish hadn't even budged. Corvus found another stick and tried again, but when he released the spear, Corvus lost his balance and fell painfully into the cold stream. He sat up in pain, cursing his poor fishing skills. "And to think this was going to be easy!" he thought in frustration.

"Go with the flow."

He looked at the brook and grinned. "The advice never stops, does it?" he thought.

Corvus looked downstream and noticed that the brook narrowed into a bottleneck before emptying into a larger pool. Corvus tightened the bottleneck by stacking rocks along the river until the passage was only a foot wide. He took off his pants and lowered them into the stream after tying off the pant legs. His plan was to corral the fish into the bottleneck so that the fish would swim into the waist of his pants and get caught in the legs. Using rocks and sticks he secured his pants so they would stay firmly in place. He returned to where he had seen the fish.

"*Ready to try again?*" the fish asked, its tone almost playful.

Corvus lowered his hands into the water. At the last minute, he opened his fingers suddenly to frighten the fish. The fish turned around and swam in the direction of the bottleneck. Corvus repeated this process several times until, low and behold, the fish swam into the pant leg. Corvus quickly reached into the water and gripped the opening tightly with one hand and yanked the pants, along with the trapped fish, out of the stream. He walked several meters away from the shore to be sure that the fish could not escape back to its watery home.

Corvus pulled the fish out triumphantly and held it in the air with one hand, admiring the silver scales that glistened in the beam of sunlight. He watched as the gills of the fish moved uselessly, trying to filter the water that was no longer there.

"*It is incredible,*" he felt the fish say, "*to no longer be in the reality I have always known. It is...transcendental.*"

Corvus looked into the fish's eyes. Its eyes were large and lidless, so drastically different than his own. In them, he saw his own reflection and he heard himself softly gasp, his own breath mixing with the music of the brook in the background.

"I will make it quick," he promised. He held the fish up to the sky and thanked it for the teaching and nourishment it had given with its life. Corvus struck it against a blunt rock and did so once more for good measure. After a moment the movement of its gills stopped.

Corvus carried his cold clothes in one hand and gripped the fish tightly in the other. He was so hungry he could eat the fish raw, but the thought of a fire and a warm meal tugged at his senses. He had seen his aunt make fire plenty of times, but he couldn't remember her methods for starting a flame. Knowing he first needed dry wood to burn, Corvus set off to collect some tinder.

It didn't take long to find a pile of dry debris. Corvus set down the fish and his clothing and began pulling the larger logs off the pile to get to the drier sticks underneath. He was halfway through the heap when his hand ran over the scales of a long red snake.

Corvus yelled in surprise and backed away. Not only was he naked, but he also had nothing to protect himself with. Who knows what this snake could be capable of! The snake slithered over a long flat piece of wood, darting its tongue up and down, its eyes focused on the person who had disturbed its sleep.

"Get out of here!" Corvus shouted, with nothing more to brandish than his fearful voice.

"*Sssorry,*" said the snake. "*But this is my home and here I will ssstay. If I bother you then I sssuggest you ssshed your opinions.*"

Composing himself, Corvus tried again. "I came looking for firewood, though I have never made fire by myself. I need help," he admitted. "I don't know what I am doing."

The snake slithered closer. *"I can ssssee that. You might call to the air to bring you fire from the ssssky, but if the clouds do not agree that the time is right, you will wait for many moons. Better to create on your own. You have all that you need."*

"You mean wood?" Corvus asked.

"Hands," said the snake. *"When you rub them together, do they not produce heat?"*

Corvus opened his eyes with realization. He bowed his head to the snake in gratitude. "Thank you," he said. "It is surprising to receive such wisdom from a creature about parts of a body it doesn't even have."

"We sshare more than you know," the snake said, and then slithered away.

Corvus found a flat piece of driftwood along the riverbank and brought it over to a level spot in the forest. After a careful search he found some tinder, a long stick, and a thick piece of bark with a hollow crevice on one side. He put the tinder on the driftwood and then positioned the stick against the tinder. He placed the bark at the top end of the stick and then rested his chin on the bark to keep the stick from moving. Starting slowly and building speed, he rubbed his hands back and forth. It took him several attempts, but after a while the first trail of smoke appeared. Overjoyed, Corvus lifted the tinder to examine it, but after a moment the smoke disappeared. A gentle breeze blew through the forest and Corvus understood at once. He needed to breathe life into his creation.

After another try, Corvus had built a fire. He watched with enjoyment as the fire grew stronger while he added more fuel. Already it crackled loudly. He gazed into its inner glow and sat mesmerized by the rising flames. *"The more you focus on me, the stronger I become. It is like this with all things. Your intention creates your experience. If you center your focus on any one thing for long enough, you will find that it manifests in your physical reality. But take caution! One must control their focus just as one tends a fire. Do not allow your worries or desires to run rampant, for if they do, they may manifest in unexpected ways. If you fear the fire it will burn down your home, but if you are a careful steward, then the creatures of this world will beckon to your call."*

Corvus ate the fish slowly, savoring the delicate flavor as the fire softly crackled in the forest darkness. Individual flames twisted and danced together until none could be distinguished from the next. The fire's many meanings circled through his mind like currents of heat mixing with the winds of the cold forest air. This fire could destroy every living thing in the forest while simultaneously creating fertile conditions for all life. By understanding the nature of its essence it could be cultivated and used for many purposes. It had no more inherent evil than the crows – it all depended on the nature of the sacrifice.

His stomach now full, Corvus stretched out his legs and relaxed. He watched the smoke billow into the air and witnessed the individual sparks of fire rise and disappear. He did this for some time until he began to nod off, but moments before he fell asleep he heard the tune of a flute carry through his camp. At first, he thought he was dreaming, but after shaking his head and standing up he realized that he wasn't. The music seemed to come from all around him. The tune seemed louder in one direction and then again in another. Something was out there…and it could see him. His heartbeat quickened and his hands clammed up. Corvus knew. It was the satyr.

Corvus found the smooth stone and took a delicate step away from his camp. The glow of the fire receded, but the music did not. Around him the vertical columns of trees rose into the intangible sky. He used these shields to the best of his ability, hiding behind them as he moved further away from the fire. His heart was beating wildly now. He did not have a plan if he happened to encounter the terrible beast, but his fear was so entwined with his curiosity that he had no choice but to continue onward.

Suddenly, the bushes beside him rustled with movement and Corvus gasped like a frightened deer. He bolted forward, running blindly through the darkness and then ducked behind a tree. He looked behind him, desperately searching for the fire. Its subtle glow mimicked the illusion he was trying to escape from. Corvus knew the creature was watching him, knew that it could attack him at any moment. He needed to return to the fire, but the snapping of a twig sent him into a panic and he darted through the brush. Behind him he could hear the movement of the creature's pursuit.

It felt like he was running for his life. The deeper he went, the blacker the forest became, but he ran on, determined to lose the satyr. The canyon narrowed further as he proceeded, the rock walls rising at right angles. Large boulders created a maze that he ran through aimlessly, until at last, he came to the base of a hundred foot cliff. He was trapped.

The music ended abruptly and the sound of scuffling footsteps could be heard coming his way. Corvus stood with his back to the cliff in the small den of enclosed vegetation. The light from the far off fire just barely bled through the darkness creating dangerous impressions and stark silhouettes. Looming vines and tall trees taunted his vulnerability. The rustle ahead of him was growing steadily. Bushes were being pulled apart now. Whatever was coming through the brush was enormous.

Terror constricted his senses and fears of the unknown pervaded Corvus's mind. Nothing he had ever experienced before compared to the fear he now felt. Unable to face it, he turned away and looked up at the high stone wall and begged it for help. Behind him he could hear the immense figure break through the branches and he watched in horror as its shadow completely enveloped him and crept up the wall like an awakening smoke. In the dim light Corvus could see the monstrous outline of the miserable beast.

An unfamiliar voice percolated through the shadow and wrapped itself around his mind. *"Wherever you go, I will follow you. Your fear is so pungent I could smell you underwater."*

"W - why do you hunt me?" Corvus asked the shadow on the wall. His whole body was shaking like a leaf.

"It appears that we hunt one another. Was it not you who sought me?"

"No!" Corvus yelled. "I was seeking the source of the music. Believe me, I want nothing to do with *you*."

"Then why do you allow fear to guide you? When you use fear as your quiver, do not be surprised by what it lances. Your terror matches your creations." The creature's shadow pulled back its lips and its mouth opened like a cavern, revealing a dense row of thick and sharp teeth. It was so close that its strong musky stench surrounded the moment like a thick cloud. It stepped forward. *"Enough discussion,"* it said, saliva dripping off its jaw in globs. *"The time has come for me to eat."*

Corvus held his hands out to the shadow, as if *it* were the real threat. "Wait! Aren't you supposed to ask permission?" he shouted.

The creature laughed. *"Fear has many questions, yet none of its answers are logical. Do not kid yourself into thinking that your wishes will help you escape - only the truth of your own illusions can help you now. Stop hiding behind your blindness. See me for what I am!!!"*

The creature's words shook him to his core, not because they were terrifying, but because they were precise. In this moment, Corvus understood the fear of the villagers. They were afraid of something they couldn't define. How could Corvus possibly survive what he did not understand? He must face his fear, surrender to this shadow, and accept the truth for what it was. Turning around, he saw the tremendous beast paces from his face. He could smell its breath. He could feel the heat rising off of its body. He could see the large dark eyes, and in them, he could see the reflection of a boy pushed to the brink of his fear, though for an instant, he saw the boy recognize what he was seeing. It was a *massive* bear.

All at once, Corvus began to hallucinate. The boundaries of the grotto that he and the bear shared started to blur, and the vegetation behind the bear dissolved. The dark earth below his feet transformed into a milky white floor. Corvus watched in shock and fascination as the milky whiteness crawled over to where the bear was standing like a frost spreading across the ground. The white ether climbed into the background and over their heads, until the light overtook Corvus entirely. He fell away from the bear like a tree falling into the earth, but unlike a tree, Corvus made no contact with the world around him. Instead, he fell into his body and into an awareness that dwelled within his cells. He found himself gazing at strange spiraled stepladders - coalescing wonders which seemed to be the very building blocks of his being. He realized that his body was made up of these tiny snakes, and as he observed them, they started to sing. Their distinct vibration resonated in his mind like an ancient understanding, as if *he* was the one that was singing.

"You are with us and among us," they all said together. *"You are the energy that is our creation, and we are your creators. Trust your inner wisdom and know that you are whole and complete. Do not fear your illusions, but make them your allies. We beings of the snake are the generators of desire and the keepers of your wisdom. When you learn that you create from within, all will be well. Be not afraid for all of creation is one. Be not afraid, Corvus, be not afraid."*

The snake-like ladders fluttered and danced between the physical and the intangible. They sang in harmonic rhythm like the pulse of creation, their tone changing with the speed of his thoughts. He saw that his thinking affected their formula, and as his awareness expanded, he realized that these ladders were the keepers of his beliefs. Their frequency radiated all around him, a frequency which was also his own. He heard the timbre of his own fear and the song of his hope. He could see clearly that his programs of fear no longer served him and that he would have to recreate them. He traveled through his veins at the speed of thought, spinning the wisdom of the forest into the coding of his make-up. At last, he sailed out of his body like a spirit in transition. He floated over the bear and the boy's body in the whiteness of the eternal present. He saw the snakes swirling in the bear's being and he saw that he and the creature were intimately intertwined.

He dropped like a rock without warning back into his body. All around him the whiteness prevailed. The bear was expressionless as it approached him but Corvus stood settled and still. He noticed that as the bear walked it left large imprints of darkness.

The bear's snout was less than a foot away from Corvus when it spoke. *"You are beginning to understand,"* said the bear. *"You and I are one in the same - flesh and blood, spirit and spirals. Within and without we create our existence together. We are inherently connected, whether you know it or not, whether you want it or not. One cannot deny that we all share this planet and that we each carry our own meanings, yet our realities have been separate for so long that we have become strangers to one another. No longer do we understand the basis of the other's understandings. This ignorance is a dangerous thing for us both because we shall ultimately become what we fear."*

The bear's breath seemed to swallow the boy whole as it spoke. *"Our reunion does not have to be a collision. We do not have to find each other in the night of our fears, rebelling against the inevitable. It is inevitable, you know? Man and beast will come together again, one way or another. Humans have mistreated our kind so long, but you are already forgiven. We creatures of the forest are prepared to accept you, but your distrust in us only broadens our distance."*

"My fear is also their own," Corvus said insightfully, standing now fully in his power. "I have been conditioned into believing that the forest is a place to be feared and that the beliefs of the Elders are the foundations of survival and meaning. Though I now know this to be false, there still exists an entire community that believes otherwise. How can I separate myself from that which has created me?"

"But don't you see?" said the bear. *"You will never be separate. Nothing is*

separate. By shaping yourself you shape the world - your own evolution evolves the collective. Seek alignment with truth and the rest will follow. But beware," said the bear. *"Those not in alignment will seek control over your truth. It manifests as we speak. They sense your wisdom coming into being - it is a wisdom that will change their world forever. Wield your truth wisely, for the world you create is your responsibility, and your creations have consequences."*

The bushes behind the bear rustled and a small cub emerged into the clearing. Corvus stared at the cub until it dawned on him that this fearsome terrible bear was actually a mother. The cub wandered slowly over to its parent and stood alongside her hind leg. Its large innocent eyes looked up at Corvus.

The white light pulsed around them as the boy spoke. "My perception changes with my understandings. It is my desire to align with whatever meaning I am to become. There are still challenges to face and beliefs to break down." He looked at the cub. "I know that I am young and that my path is long and uncertain. My hope is that one day my dreams will better the world for us all. I suppose that when I find myself in paradise I will know that I have reached my goal."

"Your dream will benefit not only yourself. Know that your path will lead you through unknown country. Along the journey of life there is always challenge and death. Understand, however, that there are many varieties of death, and some are essential to our growth. I bless you on this journey. May you have courage and resolve, strength and bondage, that you may unite all things within, so that all things external may one day come together and flourish as one. Your eyes are deeper than you can imagine, older than you suspect. One day you will return to teach them, but there is something else you must do, something else you must see."

The light around the bear dissipated and the vegetation returned. Once again, Corvus and the bear existed in a grotto in a moment like any other. The bear took a step backward, put its nose into the air and sniffed. Smelling nothing of interest, it returned into the brush and disappeared, its cub following carefully behind.

Chapter Twenty Two

As the days dragged on, Corvus began to feel a rhythm that was so real and so tangible that he could almost predict what would happen from one moment to the next. He became accustomed to the waves of energy that appeared throughout the day. He saw that this energy not only affected all things, but was orchestrated and acted out by all things. A gentle wind would precede a flock of birds, which would summon an animal from hiding and guide it to water. The water would take the animal's intention downstream, caressing the rocks as it did so, reminding them of their importance in the riverbed. The reminded stones would remind the fish of the blessings of an animated body, compelling the fish to swim and dance out of the water after insects which fluttered over the surface of the river. The insects would scatter into the air and ask the wind for safety, which would take their prayer through the rest of the forest, until it reached a boy with grandfather eyes looking for a sign.

More and more, Corvus recognized that his own thoughts and actions were intrinsically intertwined to the Great External. If he were nervous or agitated, he would not see any signs of wildlife, but if he remained calm and serene he often saw creatures he had never before seen. He became astutely aware of the hints and secrets that nature displayed in her cunning game of ebb and flow. The more he observed the more he realized that he was a participant in this game and that his own energy was woven with the creatures of the forest. When he set his gaze firmly onto a tree branch, only a short amount of time would pass before a bird would sit where he was looking. He realized that indeed the universe spoke in symbols, but if he was able to suspend his fears and beliefs, open his heart and truly listen, the universe simply spoke.

The spirits of the forest accepted him graciously, perhaps because he was no longer afraid of them. He shared communion with the wind and listened to the echoes of wisdom from the thunder. He could hear the individual lives of the riverbank stones as the chattering water rolled over them in fancy and delight. He learned the names of the many trees that graced the land and understood that they each had their own teachings to give. It was as if every tree spoke for the whole of its species, yet all of them were unique in their own way.

The farther he traveled into the forest, the more birds he encountered. Sparrows flittered and twittered in the tall branches of the pine trees, sharing songs with him of the days before his time. Robins taught him about the virtues of simplicity and new beginnings, while the jays gave him insights into fastidiousness and opportunity.

On rare occasions, when the forest canopy opened up, he witnessed the paths of large raptors. He became enamored by the flight of the falcons that spoke to him only with their dazzling displays of agility and pursuit. Hawks shared with him the lessons of insight and caution, and every now and then, Corvus would spot an eagle soaring high over them all, watching all from above, unconcerned with such trivial things as symbols and time.

Not once did he see a crow. Most days, he hardly noticed their absence, so engulfed was he in the beauty of the forest and its many lessons. It was as if the old days were entirely severed from his present life. Occasionally, Corvus would reminisce about sitting below the old tree, training his birds with his whistles in the days when he was just beginning his simpler understandings. He thought little about The White Village or the villagers, but at times Elder Mallory would creep into his memory. In the beginning this troubled Corvus, but the more time he spent in the forest, the more he understood that if it *hadn't* been for Mallory's persecution, Corvus would never have learned the true meaning of the collective. Here in the forest everything was whole and complete. All existed for him, and through his efforts and pursuits of new understandings, he found that he existed for the All.

* * * * * *

On a night like any other, Corvus fell asleep and floated through the forest, carried by a wind that came from home. The wind brought him to a wooden boat and he stood on the boat which floated inches over a black lake. In the lake he could see the reflection of the stars and the moon in the perfect stillness of the indigo water. The stars, he felt, knew him by name, and they shone down from up above and danced in his eyes. He lived in this dream for a time undefined. The boat hovered softly over the cold old water, water that waited from somewhere beyond. He wondered if the water were actually the sky and if the moon below him could be held in his hand.

Ripples came and went and came again, until the water surface parted and fingers appeared. His breath caught in his chest as an old memory materialized before him. The boat kissed the brim of the water when Celina crested through the skin of the lake. Her body flickered with light and she rose out of the water, dry and complete. At last, her bare feet stood upon the surface. Around her head was the dreamer's scarf.

"I have found you," she said to him. Her smile was exactly the same -

it was truly her. No apparition could ever compare. No idea or belief, sign or projection could ever take the place of the only Celina he had ever loved.

"It has taken some practice," Celina said, her smile never leaving her face. "I have spent so many nights trying to reach you, but all I could ever find was a boy with glass eyes. I almost gave up until a crow came to my window. I put *it* in my mind and it led me to you."

Corvus could hardly speak he was so happy to see her. Celina had found him in his own dream, but now it was theirs and they shared it together. He held his arms out to her as he spoke. "Celina. It is such a gift to see you again. This is one of the few dreams I have had that I do not want to wake from. My time in this forest has affected me greatly. I have learned so much in just a few short days."

She looked at him strangely. "Short days? Corvus you have been gone for weeks, nearly a month."

Her words troubled him and tiny ripples nicked across the water. "But that cannot be. I left just the other night."

Celina shook her head. "The next full moon comes in two days. The old lunar cycle is nearly complete." She looked at him with concern. "So much has happened since I have seen you last, Corvus. Your absence has created quite a stir."

"What has happened?" he asked her with interest.

Celina sighed. "Elder Mallory has not given up his search for you. Quite the opposite. He has led multiple parties into the forest to find you. He is so desperate to retrieve you that he has allowed people to look for you without his guidance – even women and children have gone into the wilderness unattended! Mallory has warned us that if we do not bring you back ourselves then your twisted beliefs will destroy the village from the other side. At first, the people believed him because they were afraid. They feared that your crows would inhabit their dreams and make them crazy...like Jeremy," she said, unable to meet Corvus's eyes. "But then after a while, something happened. Some of the villagers who went into the forest heard voices. Mallory told them they were crazy, but so many people have heard the voices that it is undeniable. I heard them myself!" Celina said in a hush. "I was only meters away from one of the Elders when the very ground I was walking on began to speak to me. Its voice was distant but kind and it said, 'You must learn to walk on your own two feet.'" She sighed again, overwhelmed by what she was saying.

"The Elders merely tell us that we are sleepwalking dreamers with no concept of madness, simpletons who don't understand the signs. But the villagers are demanding answers and Mallory is growing nervous. People cannot stop talking about your crows, Corvus. They are wondering if the crows spoke to you as the creatures of the forest spoke to them." Celina lowered her voice. "The people are starting to wonder if the Elders are unable or *unwilling* to hear the voices themselves. Things are becoming suspicious. The other day Mallory called a meeting. He said the signs had told him that you were still alive and that you were using magic on the village, one that causes madness. He said the safest place for us to be was in the church, and that *no one* was allowed inside the forest except the Elders. At first we thought the Elders were searching for you to bring you back, but instead, the Elders returned with animals trapped in cages."

"Animals in cages?" he asked. "What for?"

"For your crows."

"My *crows?*" he asked.

"The crows left when you did, Corvus, all but one, though I think I am the only person who has seen it. It is a mysterious bird and remains hidden in the shadows. I have spotted it on several occasions, but I am still unsure of its meaning."

"It is the one that killed my aunt," Corvus said. "I am certain of it."

"I cannot say, but it is not this crow they are after. Mallory's meanings are many. He seeks to reclaim the trust of his village while at the same time replacing your power with his own. Mallory is after your flock, Corvus. He believes that if he can call the crows back to the village then he can destroy them, and thus, destroy you."

"But what is he going to do with the animals?" Corvus asked again.

"He is going to burn them alive over the ash eye."

Corvus swooned. Just the thought of such a thing made him nauseous. "But *why?*"

"I overheard him talking to Elder Moore," she said. "He says that you are not like the other outcasts and that you will not be forgotten. Mallory believes that your visions and the forest's illusions are merging. He suspects that the forest is somehow protecting you from your madness. He believes that if he destroys the animals, he is destroying the essence of what aids you."

Corvus's mind was racing. He could see the animals in his mind's eye now, hundreds of them stacked upon each other in wire cages, hungry and thirsty, calling for help. It was a twisted act, but not one without reason. Mallory's magic was twofold, Corvus knew. What he did in one world he must symbolically do in the next.

The ripples scattered across the water like frightened fish. Below them, the lake began to glow a deep ruby red. Corvus realized at once what was happening. "Celina!" he called. "You must go. It is *him*. He is coming. If he knows that you are here with me he will punish you in ways we cannot comprehend."

She looked at Corvus and knew that he was right. "Please be careful, my love. I have come with warnings yet they seem to only manifest in your disfavor."

"It is all right, Celina. Whatever madness he brings I will deal with myself. But you must go - please."

The red glowing water boiled and roiled below her feet as the red beast swam up from the depths of the lake. The light grew bigger and brighter and rumbled louder and louder and Corvus shouted to Celina that he loved her, and when she disappeared, the dragon crashed out of the water like a rocket of fire. The great dragon sailed up into the air, its wings bowed back with air-lined precision, climbing higher and higher as if it would pierce the sky. At last, it reached its zenith and it turned around with a coy curl and looked down at the little boat that floated on the indigo water. It opened its mouth into a wide gruesome grin, and as it began its descent, the dragon spoke through the dream.

"You cannot escape me, Corvus, nor can you escape the consequences of your actions. You have left a wake in your departure. You are so much like your father it is sickening. He also wanted to change my meanings of the signs and allow the people to blunder through their own misinterpretations. He wanted to destroy everything, just as you do, and now my poor village is on the precipice of ruin. Your dream *must* be unwoven."

"You cannot blame me for questioning the universe," Corvus shouted up at the dragon. "It is our birthright to know the truth of this world and our place within it."

The moonlight caught in the dragon's eye as it spoke. "I have stewarded The White Village for so long that the villagers are practically my children. I have kept them safe by protecting them from truths they would never understand. The mind cannot comprehend how a human so simple and flawed could possibly exist in a universe so perfect and vast. To think about such a thing is enough to make one insane - there is no answer to this mystery, *trust* me, I have searched for it. Many times I have attempted to coax out the heart of the Maiden and reveal her love to me, but this earth does not want to know me." Suddenly, a tear fell from the dragon's eye and crystallized into a star, though Corvus was the only one to notice.

"She does not want to know *any* of us," the dragon groaned. "She senses our poverty. She watches our struggle while everything around us survives in fecundity. If the animals and plants know their meaning, then how can it be that we humans, creatures of the *greatest* mind, cannot even understand the reason of our own existence? It is this very quest for purpose that has perpetuated all of our misery. I may be halfway blind to the wisdom of the signs, but I am still a guide. I have given my people understanding by giving their universe meaning, and somehow, it has given them meaning as well. I have worked too long to allow you to destroy my design. I cannot sit idly by while the ripples of your thoughts and your dreams seep into the psyche of the village. People cannot return to create for themselves, for if they did, our world would look like the land on the other side - a metropolis so great and so vast yet so utterly meaningless that it swallows everything of worth."

"If only you would tell people the truth," Corvus said. "Tell them what you have done and I swear they will forgive you. If *I* can forgive you then so can they, and together, collectively, we could create heaven on earth. I finally understand that I am part of the whole and I want nothing more than to share my gifts with this world."

"This world does not want your crows, Corvus. But I do," the dragon gleamed. "They will come to me with ease, in from the shadows that shelter your eyes. Your eyes *too* will be mine, for your vision is obscured by what you refuse to understand. I send you now a crow of my own to guide your journey to its ultimate end. May your own madness reveal the dream you refuse to awaken from."

The dragon was directly overhead and it swept down in a vertical plunge. It opened its mouth and from the bottom of its belly it expelled a red-hot crow forged out of glass like a disfigured phoenix. The crow opened its beak, but the crow could not caw because it wasn't alive. The cold night of the dream cooled the crow at once and the black glass crashed upon the wooden boat and shattered upon the boy with grandfather eyes.

Chapter Twenty Three

Corvus opened his eyes. He felt dizzy. The forest swirled and swayed around him as if he had just consumed a Dreamer's Lotus. The trees around him were dancing it seemed, moving in a slow and steady rhythm that equaled the pace of his breathing. He rubbed his eyes with his hands. He looked into the forest, waiting for this vision to taper and calm. As he sat there, he noticed a movement that was not in synch with the rest of the illusion. A hairy red creature weaved through the tree trunks and moved nimbly over and around the thick vegetation. Corvus reached into his pocket and grabbed the smooth stone, hoping to use it to defend himself if he needed to.

The creature was small and it approached Corvus without fear. It stuck its nose in the dirt and sniffed just meters away from Corvus's feet. It circled him once, and then again, until complete with its survey, it scrambled back towards the woods. Corvus called out to it.

"Hey. Where are you going? You have nothing to say? No news from the forest?"

The fox turned around. *"Oh there is always news. News to you but not to me. Many things change in this forest, but they are no concern of mine. Mine is a fox's way. My concerns are my own. Yours it seems, are much more complex."*

Corvus sat up. "What do you mean by that?"

The fox cocked its head. *"Your mind plays tricks on you. It has created concerns out of illusion. One must see things as they are. An animal track is not the animal; do you see what I mean? You follow more tracks than you can count. Perhaps it would be better if you focused on your own."*

Corvus scratched his head. The remnants of a forgotten dream ebbed through his mind. There was something he was supposed to do, some message he was supposed to receive.

"Did you see someone out there?" he asked the fox in a daze.

The fox shook its head. *"Any news of mine will only cause discomfort, I suspect. If I were more fox-like today I might send you off on a faraway chase, following behind in laughter, but truth be told I have pups to care for. Let me just say that there is something out there that seeks your pursuit. But take it from me, better to pursue a rabbit in a hole, than a bird in the sky."*

"Caw!"

Corvus jerked his head up. His eyes penetrated the branches of the trees and the leaves in the canopy to the one place in the sky where the faintest hint of blue remained. The black outline of a bird darted through the heavens and disappeared.

Corvus could hear the bird still cawing as it flew away. He scrambled to his feet, grabbed his bag and ran after the crow, bounding over fallen logs like a deer. Corvus screamed and tried to whistle but he was too excited and out of breath. The stream widened the further he ran. Without warning the crow veered off to the right. Corvus left the stream and scooted over a pile of rocks as he continued his pursuit. The crow was gaining distance. He ran faster. He *had* to stop it, he *had* to find out where it was going. Perhaps it would talk to him like the rest of the creatures.

But the crow's caw was barely audible now. Corvus looked upward as he ran, hoping to see the black outline in the sky when a soft and loose web hanging between two trees clutched his face. Corvus's foot caught under the root of a dead tree and he fell, sprawling head first into leaf duff. His ankle throbbed in pain and he touched it tenderly, still thinking about the crow which was now long gone.

He set his hand on the ground and looked up at the hidden sky while he pulled the strands of web off his face in frustration. He hung his head in self-pity and stared into the forest floor. Next to his hand the ground moved. As his eyes came into focus Corvus saw an enormous hairy brown spider only inches from his hand. The spider lifted its two front legs and arched its body upwards. On its stomach was a white circle.

"*Oooooo,*" it said with a strange whisper. "*Beee caaaareful.*" Corvus backed away but the spider inched closer. "*You must always take care in the forest,*" it whispered. "*Many dangers abound for those unaware. Be careful what you chase after. What you catch is not always your own.*"

Still a bit shaken from the surprise, he said, "I saw a crow."

"*Crow?*" the spider asked. "*No crows in this part of the forest.*"

"But I *saw* it. I *heard* it," Corvus insisted. "It was flying in that direction," he pointed. "Perhaps I can still find it."

"*Just as the fly perceives safe passage?*" the spider asked. "*Do not deceive yourself. The forest is woven with riddles. It can be hard to discern what is what. You are going* deeper *into the forest, remember. You may not find your way back.*" The spider advanced slowly.

"But the crow was my guide," Corvus said. "If I can find it then it will guide me to safety."

"*Do not be so sure,*" said the spider. "*I have caught many victims who were guided right into my web.*"

Corvus slammed his hand into the dirt in frustration. "Stop it! It is not the way that you say it is. The crow has been with me my entire life. It has been my only friend. It is my protector, my *vision*. If I can find it, then I will finally be able to see who I really am."

"*My sympathies for your growing madness,*" the spider said. "*You can no longer contain it, it seems. It flies out of your control."* The spider lifted its fangs and reared back.

Corvus gripped the flat stone in his hand tightly. He was prepared to throw it at the spider if it decided to attack him. "Be careful," he told it. "I will use this if I have to."

"Go ahead, then. Let us just see what all you can accomplish with that rock of yours. Your ignorance propels you further away from that which you seek."

Corvus held the rock behind his ear, his arm ready and coiled like a spring.

"Caw!"

He looked up. High above him he saw the stoic posture of a large black bird sitting high in the branches.

The spider sprung, leaping onto Corvus's arm and sinking its fangs deep into his skin. Corvus cried out in pain. He flailed his arms in every direction, casting off the spider which landed several feet away and scurried under a rock. Corvus looked down and saw two dark blue spots on his arm where the spider had bitten him. The bite was soft and tender to the touch. He stood up and placed his weight on his good leg.

"Caw!"

He looked up in time to watch the crow fly from its perch and sail off deeper into the forest.

"Wait!" he called after the crow. "Stop!" But the crow was gone. Corvus hurried in the direction of the bird's flight, limping at a rapid pace deeper into the forest, brushing back spider webs and low branches as he moved. He ignored the pain in his leg, and his arm, and the gnawing knowing that turned in his stomach like a caterpillar without a cocoon. Plants called out to him to stop. Trees coaxed him to reconsider, but Corvus was blind to reason. Still able to hear the dim sound of the crow, he bumbled through the brush like a lost fawn certain of its mother's call.

At last, the thicket of trees thinned. Up ahead he could still hear the crow. Its caw, soft and rhythmic, lulled his senses into a dreamlike state. The spider's venom moved through his veins in a similar fashion pushed along by the rapid pulse of his beating heart. Corvus stepped into the clearing.

The crow stood tall and erect upon a wide wooden stump. Its wings were stretched out as if it were about to take flight, yet it was a flight that would never be taken. This crow was a statue carved out of stone and it stood well over ten feet high. Corvus limped into the clearing, trying to understand the meaning of this circumstance. He stood below the statue now, looking up at its big stone eyes and wondering if they could somehow see him.

A powerful gust of wind raced through the clearing and on its heels was a hideous howl. Its meaning was fierce and unforgiving and Corvus knew the sound was not human but born of the forest. It was the sound of the satyr, and it was approaching. But Corvus only returned his gaze to the statue and put his hand upon the cold stone. In this moment he did not remember the dragon in the dream or the spider's poison which swam through his blood, nor did he care about the satyr which would surely find him if he didn't get going. He only thought about the crow, its meaning, and his own.

The sound of his name broke apart his concentration. Obiticus emerged from behind the statue. He was wearing the wolf-skin around his shoulders and he looked at Corvus with a strange but friendly smile. Somehow, Corvus was not surprised to see him, in fact, he was almost grateful. It seemed to Corvus that Obiticus was protecting him somehow. Corvus reached out his hand and touched Obiticus on the shoulder and felt the subtle warmth of his body. He sighed with relief. This was the real Obiticus and not another illusion.

"Obiticus, what luck to find you here! What is happening?" he asked. "I heard and followed a crow through the forest but have found only this statue. A part of me thinks that Mallory has sent this as a sign, though what significance it has I cannot say. The darkness of this place taxes my mind."

Obiticus took Corvus's hand. He held it tenderly and looked into Corvus's eyes with a mixture of worry and affection. "Mallory will do anything to maintain his power. He wants you to return so he can burn you like the forest he cuts down." Obiticus smiled, revealing half a mouthful of teeth. "Return you shall, but not yet," he said, a bony finger in the air. "First you must find your father and discover who you *really* are. In The Great City you will find all that you are to become. There is no darkness in The Great City. Quite the contrary, it is saturated by the sun. I will take you there, Corvus. I will take you away from the dangers of this place, away from the creations of madmen and alchemists. There are skills you must learn there," Obiticus said knowingly. "The Great City is a place of *potential!* It is a land of commerce where a person can trade one meaning for the next. With practice you will be able to create any meaning you wish."

"That sounds like what Elder Mallory has done," Corvus said skeptically.

"Elder Mallory has done his disservice through lies and deception. In The Great City, *everyone* shares their deceptions – and besides, in The Great City no one studies the signs, because in that place, there is only *one* symbol."

"Really?" Corvus asked, now intrigued. "What is it?"

"Aaahh," Obiticus said. "I have your interest now, I see. Well, you will just have to follow me and find out for yourself. Rest assured, Corvus, it is a powerful symbol, one that can get you everything you have ever desired."

A cloud of emotion and fog circled the boy like strands of the spider's web. He felt dizzy again.

"Come, Corvus," Obiticus said. "Quickly. The creature advances."

Corvus heard it too. The wind whipped through the clearing again, carrying the satyr's roar behind it. A loud crack in the statue made Corvus look up just in time to see the wings of the stone crow break at the shoulder blades. Obiticus shouted and pushed Corvus out of the way. The wings tumbled down and fell to the ground, one of them landing where they had both been standing. Corvus stared solemnly at the broken wings on the dirt as if *he* had been the statue, now mourning his inability to fly.

Obiticus, however, was not looking at the wings. Instead he was staring over Corvus's shoulder at the creature that was breaking through the branches and into the clearing. Its thick horns were curled like sharpened cones and smoke poured out of its nostrils as it stepped in front of the two humans. The satyr stood almost as high as the stone statue. Obiticus tugged at Corvus's arm, but Corvus was lulled into place by the sound of the satyr's voice, its words floating out of its mouth like the tune of its flute.

Its large eyes looked at Corvus's. *"I have tracked you for days. Amazed have I been by your course of displays. Intense your epiphanies, but woe to your mind - your kind has rewinded your madness."*

"Let's move!" Obiticus said, still pulling Corvus by the arm, but so entranced by the creature's words, Corvus would not budge.

Now the creature was looking at Obiticus. *"Old man, I have seen you before, in the woods. Planning for something, - up to no good. Then before, at the edge where The City now stands. I watched you reign down over your fellow man. But that place has destroyed you old man, yet that's where you go? You know I cannot allow your arrival or The City's madness you will bring in return. My song sings the end of your survival, unless all of your meanings you burn."*

Obiticus turned around. "Run!" he yelled. He pulled Corvus by the arm and nearly tripped over the wings of the crow. Corvus followed clumsily behind, the spider's venom sapping his need for haste. Behind them, they could hear the satyr's roar and the ground at their feet began to rumble.

"This way!" Obiticus said, casting the wolf's head over his shoulder.

Trees uprooted before them and fell in their path. They ducked and receded against the falling firs and darted beneath the crashing cedars. Corvus looked over his shoulder as Obiticus pulled him onwards. The satyr nimbly dodged the falling debris and lifted a wooden flute to his lips and began to play. Corvus knew the hypnotic tune would persuade them to stop running, but Obiticus was unaffected by the music and led the way with surprising agility. Corvus could only hope that Obiticus knew where he was going.

They ran for a long time until at last they reached the same stream Corvus had left. The stream, however, was no longer a stream. What had once been a slow flow of water around stepping-stones was now a fast moving current that pushed against large boulders the size of houses.

"We have to cross!" Obiticus yelled above the din of the current.

"Are you *crazy?*" Corvus screamed. "I can barely swim. Can you?"

"No," Obiticus admitted, but he pointed a hundred yards downstream to a narrow point in the river. A thousand pounds of water pressure squeezed between a small passageway of two enormous rocks. "We can cross there to the other side."

Corvus didn't believe it. The cross that Obiticus was suggesting would be no easy feat. Both of them would have to jump nearly six feet from one slick rock to another. Corvus rebelled but Obiticus was already pulling him along the noisy shoreline, closer to their transition point. Behind them, the trees were toppling over like dominoes. The satyr would soon see them.

They were both standing on the large rock and looked down at the river below them. Two enormous pillows of whitewater crested just inches below the top of the rock. The rest of the water flooded violently through the narrow passageway and downstream the river coalesced into a barrage of unnavigable chaos.

Obiticus was the first to go. He stood on the slick rock and tested his footing. He looked back at Corvus with a smile, but even Corvus could tell that Obiticus was hiding his worry. "Just remember," he said, "don't look down."

Obiticus swung his arms a few times and then bounded nimbly over the river and onto the other side. "No problem!" he shouted, obviously relieved. He held out his hand. "Now it's your turn." Corvus looked at Obiticus's thin wrinkled hand and wondered if it would snap off if he took it. "Come on!" Obiticus yelled.

Below the old man's hand, Corvus watched the water cascade in violent spasms. He didn't know if he could do this. Was it the spider's venom that dulled his senses? Was it the depth of the forest? How had he become so afraid? All around him the boundaries of the wilderness ebbed and flowed like the pulse of the river. Even the river itself seemed to take on strange properties. Was it flowing backwards? Corvus felt dizzy and had to take a knee on the rock to avoid falling into the whitewater.

"It's here!" he heard Obiticus shouting. "Corvus, you *have* to jump!"

The creature was only a hundred yards away from them, standing at the riverbank, watching them with curious amusement. Corvus became lost in the creature's eyes. He wondered why they were enemies and what had caused such a deep rift between them, man and this steward of the forest. The only thing Corvus knew was that this creature would do anything to prevent him from arriving at The Great City.

Obiticus still called to him from the other side. "Hurry, Corvus. The time is now!"

Still looking at the satyr, Corvus hesitated. The creature held the young man's gaze and lifted the wooden flute to his lips.

Corvus jumped.

He plummeted into the middle of the fast current and tumbled downwards, crashing into rocks and obstacles as he careened along the unknown waterway like a branch in the arms of a hurricane. At last, his head popped out of the water and he sucked in a mouthful of air only to be pulled under again. The river spun him in every direction, and it was only when he felt the last of his life remaining that the water would push him up to the surface, as if prolonging the inevitable. Corvus somehow felt that the river was consciously trying to kill him. It was in the midst of this desperate thought that he heard a voice.

"Cease your struggle and go with the flow. You too must learn the current of life. Your perception of struggle binds you to the illusions of man. Not everything is as it seems. You believe that this water will kill you, but what is death if not a rebirth? It is only in our most desperate moments of existence that we truly learn what we are capable of. You are supported in more ways than you know, but the demons of ignorance must be dissolved in the waters of awareness if you are to pass through to the other side."

He felt his feet being pushed downstream as his head came out of the water again. Around him the water rolled with steep rapids. Corvus did as he was advised and surrendered his movement to the current of the river. Had he known that imminent death was just downstream he would have been kicking furiously for either side, but it was the river that ultimately pushed him to safety. His body was rushed forcefully into a powerful eddy and he could feel the charging water release him from its grip. He wrapped his arms around a nearby rock and managed to plant his feet into the rocky riverbed. He stood up straight now and took several long determined steps to the river's edge where he collapsed onto his hands and knees and began vomiting up whatever water he had swallowed.

He sat down and watched the powerful river run past him. Corvus could not believe that he was alive, not to mention that he had made it to the other side of the river. He had no idea how far he had traveled, but he sensed he had been washed downstream a great distance because neither Obiticus nor the satyr were anywhere in sight.

Chapter Twenty Four

The water raged by, pummeling its way downstream on its way to the deeper unknown. Corvus watched its movement in a trance. His body was exhausted, though his mind was unaware of its fatigue. He babbled incoherently to himself and the darkness, frustrated by its lack of conversation and appeasement. Corvus leaned back in a dramatic stretch and tilted his head up toward the sky, but the sky refused his gaze and concealed itself behind the thick layer of trees. It was time to continue on, he figured, though he had no idea where he was.

Corvus walked along the river for miles in a strange and rhythmic daze, whistling absently to himself as he continued downstream. The bite on his arm had swelled considerably, but Corvus hardly noticed. The world around him was much more fascinating. He grinned a drugged grin when one of the trees uprooted and walked beside him. He tried to talk to the walking tree, but could not understand its language. He smiled down at the rocks and their awkward rocky faces, hoping they would speak and share wisdom, but they said nothing. He felt that the forest had changed, somehow.

The farther he walked, the more dark and narrow the canyon became. The trees bent with the climbing sides of the mountain, hiding all but the faintest of light. At times large boulders blocked his path forcing him to change his route to get around them. Tired, Corvus stopped to rest. He sensed that he was not well and he closed his eyes, hoping to find some semblance of stability within.

When Corvus opened them again he saw a red outline weaving through the trees headed in his direction. He held out his hand, wanting to pet the red fur of the fox, hoping that it remembered his language and would speak to him kindly. As this creature approached, Corvus saw that it was larger than what he had first perceived. Corvus could see that instead of paws it had hands, and instead of fur it wore clothing. This strange redheaded person walked on all fours and scampered nearby to sniff the surroundings. When at last it came into focus, Corvus recognized a familiar individual he had almost forgotten about.

"Hello, Corvus."

"Is that you, Jeremy?" Corvus asked in surprise.

Jeremy sat down and scratched his ear with his back leg. "I have been searching everywhere for you. You are not an easy one to find. The Elders told me to look in the forest, but they didn't say what part."

"The *Elders* sent you?"

Jeremy nodded his head enthusiastically. "Elder Mallory has taught me how to dream. He has been my teacher," he said proudly.

"This is a dream?" Corvus asked.

"It *better* be," Jeremy said. "I sure wouldn't want to be out here otherwise." He looked at Corvus oddly. "You didn't know this was a dream?"

Corvus's silence answered Jeremy's question.

"Tsk Tsk," he said shaking his head. "You are worse off than Mallory thought you were." Jeremy scratched his ear with his back leg again.

"Why did he send you?" Corvus asked.

"Because he wants me to give you something, something that you lost." Jeremy reached behind his back and pulled out a long black feather. It shimmered in his hand as he gave it to Corvus. It was the same exact feather Korbin had given to him when they had first met. Corvus held it at the tips of his fingers and gazed at it like a painting. It suddenly reminded him of Celina's drawing which he had lost crossing the river.

"Snap out of it," Jeremy said impatiently. "I'm supposed to give you a message, too."

"A message?"

"I am supposed to tell you that you can have it back. Your crow, that is."

Corvus widened his eyes. "You mean Korbin?" he asked.

"If that's the dead one, then yes." Jeremy grinned suddenly, remembering the death of Korbin. "Mallory says you can get it back. But you must do something first."

The very idea of seeing Korbin brought back a flood of memories. Emotions crowded his mind - hope, anxiety, guilt, remorse. He could get Korbin back? How was that it even possible? Korbin was *dead*.

"Do what? What must I do?" he asked.

Jeremy locked his eyes into Corvus's. "You must...fly." The madness in Jeremy's eyes swirled into Corvus's.

"Fly?" Corvus asked with confusion.

"And your bird will come find you," Jeremy stated matter-of-factly.

Corvus fingered the feather, looking at it, talking to it. It would be beautiful to see Korbin again, he thought. "How? I mean, how am I supposed to fly?" he asked.

Jeremy shrugged. "How should I know? Flap your wings, I guess - climb a tree and jump, I suppose." Jeremy stepped back. "So that's that," he said. "You got my message and now you can try and fly. See ya later, Corvus." Jeremy began to leave, but then stopped and turned around. He looked at his enemy with a strange expression. "By the way, I never got to thank you, Corvus," he said with a weird smile.

"Thank me?"

"For the dream you sent me, a while back. I know it was you who sent it. It's OK. I'm grateful. It has changed me in a powerful way, Corvus. I am not the same person I used to be. I'm not like *them* anymore, believing everything I'm told, living in someone else's fantasy. Now *I* am a dreamer," he said with delight looking into the air above him. His look transformed into an eerie sneer. "And I am learning that my dreams have plummeting consequences."

*   *   *   *   *   *

Corvus woke up with a start. The darkness around him was absolute. He couldn't tell why, but he felt strange. He stood up and marched off in a random direction, perhaps hoping to reunite with the vision or to find the crow that was promised to him. He *must* learn to fly. Corvus flapped his arms up and down faster and faster. He flapped as he walked and he tripped and fell three times on this quest. After the third time he stopped walking and flapping and listened to the silence. He whistled out into the dark stillness, his dissonant staccato echoing between the trees like stones on wood.

Above him, the sound of feathers broke through the stillness. Corvus twirled around in the darkness, trying to see his crow.

The sound stopped.

"*Who?*" he heard through the nothing.

Corvus crouched down and listened.

"*Who?*" it said again. "*I see you. Can you see me? Can you see at all?*"

Corvus could see nothing in this terrible darkness. "Is that you, Korbin? Where *are* you?" he called.

"*Who me? Why right in front of you,*" came the reply.

"Then why not show yourself?" Corvus demanded.

"*Just because you cannot see me does not mean that I am hiding. Your struggle with the darkness blinds you. You have become so accustomed to your own ignorance that you cannot see the truth, even when it is right before your eyes. When will you trust your own vision?*"

Corvus took a deep breath and relaxed his grip on the stone in his hand. From out of the blackness he watched as two large circles materialized, each with the dimmest speck of light within them. They hovered high in the branches of a nearby tree. He had never seen eyes so big before. They were enormous!

"*So you see me now,*" it said. "*Tell me, what does your vision reveal?*"

Corvus put the stone back in his pocket. "You are not the bird I was searching for."

"*Though I am the bird you have found. We owls share the secrets of this forest, and even in the darkest of woods we see many things. For example, I see a boy with eyes like my own. They are eyes so deep and so old that many wonder how a child like you could possibly possess them. Wear them you do, but use them, at times, you do not. You see what others want you to see, but you have yet to see the truth you carry within you."*

"And what truth is that?"

"You possess a powerful gift, one that your people do not fully understand. Their reality is locked in the fear of the natural world, yet here is a boy who can beckon that world to his calling. This gift is tremendous indeed. You have the potential to unite the kingdoms of man and earth. You have learned that the symbols are filled with the spirit of life, and that the spirit of life cannot be defined. This is the secret that has been revealed to you, yet there is one more to confront. Open your heart and your eyes and trust that even in the darkest places, the truth can be found."

Chapter Twenty Five

Corvus could not remember when he had fallen asleep, but when he woke up, he saw two dark eyes looking intently at him.

"Corvus!" It was Obiticus. His large eyes were full of worry and his strong boney hands gripped the boy's arms tightly.

Corvus batted them away and sat up. "Obiticus? What are you doing?"

"Oh my!" he said. "I was in fear. I saw you lying down. And then I saw your arm. You have been bitten! I know that mark. The spider that delivers it is deadly. I was bitten once myself, but I cannot remember what I had done to deserve it," he said, gazing into the distance.

Corvus looked down at his arm. The swelling had reduced, but only mildly. After a moment, he noticed that the dizziness that had enveloped him yesterday was nearly gone. All that was left was a slight headache, most likely from hunger.

"I am fine," he said, still not fully present. He was thinking of the owl.

"'*Fine,*'" Obiticus said, mimicking him. "You fell into the river's cauldron and you are 'fine'? You are lucky to have survived, you know?" Yesterday's events began to come back to him…the statue, the satyr, the river. Corvus felt as if he had already spent years away from The White Village. "You were able to escape from the creature?" he asked Obiticus.

"I have tricks of my own," Obiticus winked. "I too carry a whistle."

Corvus raised an eyebrow, but before he could say anything, Obiticus reached out his hand and pulled him up. "Come come," he said. "We must continue our march. The creature will find us if we don't get going."

Corvus obeyed and stood up, but not before he saw the black feather resting at his feet. Perplexed, he leaned down and picked it up. He touched the silky material with his fingers, thinking about the dream, wondering if he could fly.

"Where did you get *that?* Obiticus asked with covetous intrigue.

"This was a gift," Corvus said, putting it away. "Let's get going."

They walked downstream together at a slow but steady pace. As they progressed, the canyon narrowed and steepened and the river coursed past them with charging ferocity. Enormous boulders that had once been part of the mountain now littered the canyon floor, further narrowing the passageway. The morning darkness lengthened like a tunnel.

Corvus wondered if the satyr was still following them and he replayed the encounter in the clearing as they walked. "Obiticus," he said. "Why did the satyr say that you once 'reigned down over your fellow man?' What did that mean? Have you seen this creature before?"

Obiticus talked over his shoulder as they walked. "I have seen this creature once before, but long ago. He is the guardian of the forest and he meets most pilgrims that pass through his land. He takes unkindly to our kind, as of course you know by now. He thinks we are evil, that we deem its destruction or some other such nonsense. Personally, I want to partake in none of his mischief. And to answer your former question of the latter, I am *certain* that he has seen me before, because I have felt his prying eyes in the wilderness from time to time. He cannot be trusted."

"But you reigned over men?" Corvus asked for a second time.

"The creature has keener eyes than I once gave it credit for. Perhaps he saw me from the edge of the forest, perhaps in a dream, I do not know." Obiticus stopped walking and turned to face Corvus. "There was a time, Corvus, when I was a much different man. It was a time long ago when I lived where I take you now. The Great City does something to your awareness," he said, looking over Corvus's shoulder and into the darkness of the forest. "It changes your mind in a curious way, for you see, when you are in that wonderful place you realize that *anything* is possible. *Anything*." He looked at Corvus for a long time and in his eyes, Corvus could see part of the old man's story. Obiticus was standing in a large room at the top of a tall building, and he looked out over The Great City like a king or a powerful merchant.

Obiticus looked younger as he spoke and the sound of his voice rang to life as he continued his tale. "I was once a man who could create anything my mind could imagine. My knowledge of the symbols was like the arrows in my quiver - I could transform the world before my eyes, never in my life have I been so happy..."

The age returned to his voice and he looked at the ground. "But then, something happened. I was forced to leave the city due to the unfolding of certain events. I was no longer the same person. After so many years of constant creation, my mind was at capacity – I could no longer contain it. I knew that I must take my new knowledge back to the forest, but when I returned I found it was impossible to relearn what I had once taken for granted. These days my creations are dull and lifelike, as you have seen. They lack the luster that only spirit provides. Rock and stone are not the same as flesh and blood."

Obiticus was looking expectantly at Corvus, but Corvus only looked blankly back at him, unaware of what he was referring to.

"Are you still with me boy?" Obiticus asked with wide eyes. "Do you follow my speech? I'm not out here talking to myself am I?" Obiticus said, poking his fingers into the air. "I talk of the stone crow, of course. What you saw was not my design. I wanted *flesh*, not stone. I wanted what I once had... The crow still comes to me on rare occasion, but not in the way that it used to. It once would land at my feet and follow the will of my dream. It used to soar - it used to dive with *determination!*" he said, with a fist in the air. "Now it is just a statue because I cannot make it my own again. The crow is yours now, Corvus, it is yours.

"If it is mine then what does it *mean*?" Corvus asked, his voice almost desperate.

Obiticus shook his head in frustration. "Can't some things just *be*? You seek to create and define the world around you, yet what have you created? You are alone, afraid, and nearly insane - all because you seek something that you will never find. Your meaning eludes you, and unless you surrender it to another, then it will haunt you to your end."

"Who would I surrender it to?" Corvus asked.

Obiticus looked at him carefully, innocently even. "To me," he said quietly.

"To *you?*" Corvus asked.

"I was the original dreamer, you know? Your crow was once mine and I could call it like the mountains call the clouds. I once told you that the crow is the meaning of life – it is *my meaning*, not yours. Its presence in your life has only perpetuated your suffering, but if you surrender your meaning now, then even Elder Mallory cannot control you. He *also* seeks your meaning. Where Mallory sees and interprets the world before him, *you* can actually *call* the world's creations to your whim. It is the one thing Mallory cannot do. His creations are mere illusions. Mine are made of stone. But you, Corvus, you are the wielder of the world around you. Embrace that fact, and see the world as it is. The crow belongs to *me*, Corvus. Surrender it to me and I will guide you where you need to go."

Corvus looked at the old man strangely. "The crow is not mine to surrender," he said.

"But of course it is," Obiticus refuted.

"It is not," Corvus said and walked on. "The crow is a rogue that has followed me since birth. Believe me, Obiticus, if I could surrender it I would have done so years ago. It is now in these moments that I need its presence most, yet as you can see, it is nowhere to be found. There was a time when I could call it, but I sacrificed this power through the fault of my ego. There is little I can do to set things right." He suddenly thought of Jeremy and Corvus brushed the feather in his pocket with his finger.

"There is plenty you can do to set things right," Obiticus said, his eyes shining with secrets. "You are a dreamer, like your father, and dreams are the fuel of the soul. They remind us that we are infinite beings with infinite potential, that we can create anything and that it is our birthright, our *birthright*, to do so. We do not have to remain bound by the boundaries that society has created for us," he said, getting riled up. "Like you, your father saw through the Elders' lies, but he did not know what to do about them."

Obiticus looked down at Corvus, holding his gaze tight. "Your father was distraught when I met him. In a state of great sadness he told me everything - about his banishment, the deceit of the Elders...the birth of his only son..." his voice trailed off. "He revealed the manner in which you were brought into this world and the impact it had on those who witnessed it. Elder Mallory called it a prophecy. Your father simply called it a sign. He believed that you would destroy the meaning of the village, after you had destroyed your own."

The old man's words hung in the air with looming conclusion. The river had calmed as they walked beside it and now flowed smoothly like a deep pool through the thick forest. "It soon became evident that your father knew more than what he let on. He knew that the crows would become powerful allies for you and that they had the potential to guide you to great things."

"He knows why they follow me..." Corvus said softly to himself.

"But he was afraid for you. He feared that because of his absence the Elders would use your crows against you." Obiticus smiled spontaneously. "I, on the other hand, was elated. It was as if my crows had returned to me through *you*. You see it had been years, *decades*, since I had last seen them - even though they were constantly perched on my memory. Oh, it was an incredible experience...to destroy a village with a dream. I was not wise enough in my youth, however, to make the village my own. I assumed through my own inexperience that the dream had done all the work for me," he said, shaking his head. "I was wrong. The crows had only created a clean slate to begin again. While I still slept in my dream, others more rooted in reality took advantage of my creation. Mallory saw the village ripe for the picking and he created a world of his own design. By that time my dream was gone, along with any hopes for a village of my own. It was then that I left.

"Years later, when I met your father, I knew that a new cycle had begun - my old dream of creation was being born again. Your father knew that he could never return to The White Village. Elder Mallory had threatened to kill you if your father ever did so. Your father *begged* me to help you somehow, and so, in the subtle darkness of the forest, I promised him that I would protect you and guide you. He was grateful for my protection, but reminded me that the *crow* was your guide, and that ultimately, it would determine your own understanding.

"I guided your father to The Great City myself, and when we got to the city's edge, I left him with a wooden box with a sacred symbol inside. I did this as a token of trust, a way of promising your father that one day I would bring you back to him. That symbol will become very important to you, Corvus, for its meaning is linked with your own." Obiticus smiled at Corvus and extended his hand dramatically over the river. The sound of the water had grown into a crashing crescendo. "And let me tell you, my dear boy, there is no better place to destroy your own meaning than in The Great City."

The wide river pushed through the last of the forest to meet an expansive horizon. Gentle ripples weaved over the edge of the water and breaking white waves pushed against the smoothed boulders that formed the edge of the transforming river. A soft and alluring mist hovered above. The sound and the water and the waves and the air merged together into an incredible creation of falling orchestrated chaos. Obiticus stared intently at the mighty waterfall, an unnerving expression on his face as if he sensed a danger he had been expecting.

Corvus hardly noticed. Instead, his gaze was transfixed on the horizon. Hundreds of miles from where he stood, Corvus could see a long and dark cloud that stretched across the sky like a brown snake. In the middle, the mountains opened up into a broad valley, and through the valley, Corvus could see tall and shiny structures that rose out of the earth like reflective trees - The Great City.

"You will come to learn that some things are worth waiting for," Obiticus said, now looking at Corvus. "I have waited a long time for you. I have nestled you in the arms of my dream and have followed your crows who no longer know me. Your meaning is also my own, Corvus. That is the beauty of this creation. We share it, you see? My creations are yours. I sent you the dream with the statue in the forest. I planted the language of the destiny you were born to fulfill - *Hokfeerus Edicus Sten*. It is who you are, young prophet. It is what you were born for."

The statue of the crow still stood in Corvus's mind. It was the stone crow in his dream which had first led him into the forest. "*Hokfeerus Edicus sten*," Corvus said slowly, stepping closer to the edge of the waterfall.

Obiticus eyed Corvus carefully, but attempting a smile he said, "Those words still carry the same power. The crows follow you because you are also a crow, Corvus. You possess everything they do. They witness the world objectively. They see what others cannot. Like you, they exist in a liminal state, unbound by the worlds of reality and dreams. They are the *true* creators, and with them, you too can create a world of boundless potential."

"Dash their fears upon themselves. Dissolve their dreams and fly," Corvus said quietly, his words carried away by the falling water. Jeremy's dream bled through his awareness. He looked up at Obiticus and studied him closely. The old man was hunched forward and his eyes stared into Corvus's with an impatient anxiety. Obiticus had replaced Corvus's meaning with his own. Could that mean that somewhere out there Korbin still existed, waiting for Corvus to redefine it? He fingered the feather in his pocket. In his other hand he gripped the smooth stone tightly.

"But you have forgotten your *purpose*," Obiticus said sadly and dramatically. He raised his arms into the air and looked up at the sky in torment. "I have done all in my power to remind you of your path, to train you into your truth. With the lotus I showed you how to dream. I coaxed out the anger that is such an *intrinsic* part of what you must become if you are to redefine the world, but *still* you resisted. I knew that if I could just get you to leave The White Village for good I could mentor your meaning and then the two of us together could return with the truth of our justice and outcast the out-casters once and for all."

"You wanted me to get banished?" Corvus asked, not understanding the old man's words.

Obiticus looked at him with sympathy. "Believe me when I say that your banishment was my last option - but some say that madness is an impatient Master. I had little desire to sacrifice your aunt, but it was my only choice."

"Sarah?" Corvus asked, confusion spreading over his face like a lost but persistent memory.

"It was the only crow that I have been able to create since the dawn of my dream. It flies between the worlds, but I cannot control it. Only you possess this gift. I beg of you, Corvus. Come with me and learn what you and your crows are truly capable of."

Corvus felt a tornado of emotions rising from the depths of his being. Obiticus had *murdered* his aunt? The muscles in his stomach tightened painfully and his hands became balled into iron fists until the sadness and anger and hopelessness exploded out of his body in a deafening scream. He spun around and glared at Obiticus as the familiar rage boiled within him - he wanted to grab the old man's neck and choke out the last of his life, but suddenly he thought of Korbin, and Jeremy, and everything which had led him to this moment. Corvus held his head in his hands as he stared over the waterfall. "What on earth can I *do*," he thought to himself in despair. "What on earth can I believe anymore?" All along he had thought it was Mallory, yet Mallory was innocent.

"Take care," Obiticus said, observing Corvus's proximity to the edge of oblivion. "This is where our journey shifts. This falling water is a landmark. From here we must go west, down into the Canyon of No Return, across the desert of tree-stumps, and into the valley where The Great City stands."

Corvus looked out at The Great City which called to them like a mechanical song without soul. Corvus took a step away from Obiticus and onto the ledge of the waterfall. A gentle flow of water ran over his feet. He could see the crow in his mind's eye, flying in circles around his head. It *wanted* him to jump, it wanted him to fly.

"Corvus..." Obiticus said. "Please, come down from there. We have much distance still to cover. The Great City...your *father*...awaits your arrival.

Do not do something foolish."

But Corvus hardly heard him now. He was looking down at the mist that shrouded the bottom of the canyon. The falling water spilled into the clouds and disappeared. There was no telling how far the drop was. Corvus lifted his arms and closed his eyes, feeling the air rush over his skin. He thought of the village and how it had shaped his beliefs. He thought of Celina and the blue color of her eyes. He thought of the Elders and everyone and everything in his life that had come to define him. He was not who they thought he was. He was not who *he* thought he was. Corvus looked up and stared at Obiticus. For the first and only time he wondered if he was actually looking at himself.

The old man struggled for words and shifted his weight, hoping to find balance in such a precarious situation. He reached out his arms, as if the boy were his child, and silently coaxed him to return to his version of sanity.

Corvus inhaled the misty air into his lungs. Still looking at Obiticus he said, "We can only fully begin to dream when we have truly awakened from our sleep." He pulled the smooth stone out of his pocket and threw it over the edge of the waterfall. He watched it sail into the air and disappear into the white mist. He pulled out the long black feather and clutched it between both hands.

Then he jumped.

Corvus could hear Obiticus shouting at him from above, denying the reality that Corvus had created. He fell faster and faster and that world left him almost immediately. The wind whipped at his hair and his clothes and his face, and he tumbled and somersaulted again and again unable to control his fall. The falling water fell upwards as he sped past it, and the rocks which jutted out of the cliff like broken elbows had become a blur, yet he still gripped the black feather in his hand, somehow convinced that he could fly.

Corvus stretched out his arms and held them steady against the wind until his fall had become a glide. Below him, the clouds covered the destiny of his descent, and he watched in fascination as his history played upon them like a movie screen. He saw the old aged tree at the top of the hill and the crows which sat upon the branches. He watched himself watch The White Village and saw the villagers watching him. Their world was also his own, their creations entwined with his. He gripped the feather tighter as he fell through the air. Was he the feather or the crow, the beliefs of a village or a boy without meaning? How could he separate himself from anything in this world if all was connected? He was the crow and the snake and trees and the sky. He was all of these things yet he was none of these things. He was the physical and the metaphysical – the dreamer and the dream, and now, somewhere in-between, he flew through this transition with full awareness that the last of creation was at play.

"*Corvus,*" a voice called. It came from somewhere above and he felt its echo move through his heart. He heard no other sound. Even the screaming wind that blew against his face had become silent.

"*Corvus,*" it said again. "*Can you fly yet?*"

"Korbin?" Corvus cried. "Is it really you?"

"*Perhaps,*" said the voice. "*I am somewhere in the All. I am somewhat yours, somewhat others', somewhat mine. I am many and I am none, yet I am most certainly somewhere and something. Which of the All do you wish to see?*"

He wanted to see his crow. He wanted the helper, the guide. He wanted the bird which flew through his dreams, but even his dreams were not wholly his own. How could his crow ever be? He had done to Korbin what the villagers had done to him. He had projected his questions and desires onto a riddle he did not fully understand, and until he could see the crow for what it truly was, his vision would be eternally clouded by his own beliefs. His only hope was to see without judgment and witness the world in all its perfection.

He arched his neck and yelled boldly into the sky, knowing that these words could be his last. "I search the sky for the crow which came out of the mystery for the first time. I seek the seer that flies through all my worlds. I recognize the Creator's Creation and the intelligence which animates it – that which allows me to see what's within and without, that which creates dreams and dreams creations. Korbin, I seek what makes you *you*. Your air, your wind – your *essence!*"

The wind was ripping away his layers of madness that clung to his identity like old clothes. He was no longer an omen, or caller, or dreamer, or hero, or villain. He was simply a boy falling through the sky. Korbin's feather flapped wildly in his hand. He knew that he must let it go, but if he did, then what would he be? Corvus's eyes remained fixed on the plume in his fist, knowing he had to make a choice, fully aware that below the clouds was the end of his fall. Corvus screamed as he sailed through the air and into the clouds where all edges and meanings were gone and dissolved. Closing his eyes, he released his grip on the feather, and let it go.

The feather floated in front of his face and time seemed to stop. He had not made impact, but somehow that now seemed irrelevant - he could hear cawing in the distance. They were coming for him, he knew, perhaps to guide him over to the other side.

A glossy black talon lowered from the heavens and appeared in front of his face. In the talon was the smooth stone that Corvus had thrown over the waterfall. The large black crow descended until its eyes were level with Corvus's. Korbin looked ancient and impeccable, as if just been born out of eternity. Regarding the stone, Korbin said, "*I caught this in the clouds thinking it was you, but I see that you are safe without it.*" With that, Korbin dropped the smooth stone into the air and out of sight.

"*You fly between both worlds now and you cannot continue as you have in the past. The forest has become a part of you; its wisdom swims through your creations. It has dreamt you into its existence, even though you were born to another collective. They too are still dreaming...*"

Corvus could see the rest of the crows emerge out of the clouds. Soon they were surrounding him, gliding above and below, escorting him through the cold air like guardian angels. He could feel their minds within his own and he felt his soul merge with the many, though the many were also somehow one.

"The Elders are expressing their vision now," Korbin said. *"They prepare to burn living creatures that once inhabited the forest. Elder Mallory believes that the essence of the forest can be incinerated and transformed into smoke. He plans to replace the illusions of the wilderness with his own. No creature will exist to defy him, no knowing child will remain to expose his lies. If he succeeds, you and everything you have come to symbolize will perish. But all is not without hope. Even in the darkest night, the sun waits to rise. The sky is for you, Corvus, it is yours to shine through just as we crows are yours to call. We will follow you wherever you must go, but this quest can only be taken on wings."*

Corvus stared deep into the dark eyes of the crow, and in them he could see his own reflection gliding in the air. Was it *possible*? Could such a transformation take place in this cusp of awareness, here between the dancing border of dreams and reality? He reached out his hand to Korbin and the crow fluttered onto his palm.

"It is time for you to guide yourself."

Feathers spread across the crown of his vision as the blackness of his eyes blended into that of the crow's. The wind moved over his skin like a silk cloth and tiny combs of air tickled the feathers that had begun to appear on his body. He wanted to cry out, wanted to speak but was terrified of what he would say. His throat felt like it was clamped shut and any moment he knew he would pass out and fall to his death, but he struggled and rebelled with the last of his life until a powerful realization swept over him: he must embrace this moment, for this moment, was *defining* him.

Corvus screamed at the top of his lungs, dislodging the block in his throat with a terrific and magnificent caw. He hovered in the air like a great spirit revealed, looking at himself in the reflection of the falling water. He let out a caw and then another caw and then another and another until it was joined by the sound of his kin. He flapped his wings and climbed higher and higher, up past the waterfall, past the tallest trees, and into the open sky. His murder followed closely behind him like the tail of a snake and they sailed away together to awaken the rest of the dream.

Chapter Twenty Six

The day was clear and eternal and the blue sky stretched to the edges of perceived perception. Corvus guided his crows over the mountains, following the path of the river back home. His black eyes scanned the earth below him. From such a height he felt as if he could see everything - every leaf on every tree, every animal in every hole, and every lie in every soul. His vision was more real and visceral than anything the Dreamer's Lotus could ever provoke and he felt that he existed in two places simultaneously: falling down the waterfall, and flying through the sky. Which one was the dream he did not know and if he had died and been reborn in the air then that was enough to exist for. For now, his existence meant merging one realm with another for the sake of them both. He could save them all, he knew - the animals, the villagers, even Mallory. Mallory didn't deserve to die. He was human, as were his mistakes, but his meaning was much more than that. Corvus did not know, however, if Mallory or the villagers would be able to surrender their beliefs, but perhaps they could if they were given a sign...

The murder of crows crested over the last of the high peaks that shadowed the tiny village like the knowing of a future fate. Up ahead in the distance, Corvus could see a single pillar of black smoke. The crows behind him cawed softly to the group and Corvus led their descent, keeping his eyes fixed on the black column near the center of the village.

As they approached the village Corvus could see that the smoke was not coming from the plaza but from the smoldering remains of a house. The building had burnt down days ago and consisted of little more than a pile of smoking black logs toppled together. Corvus's home had been burnt to the ground. He knew that Elder Mallory had burned down his home in a symbolic act of defiance, a general's message against an unknown guerrilla campaign of retribution. Corvus's physical history had been erased, and if Mallory had his way, whatever else that defined Corvus would be as well.

He led the crows between the clouds and the village, shrouding their presence and intent until all could be observed. Below them he could see the villagers gathered together in the center of the plaza standing in a ring around the ash eye, but the eye could not be seen - it was smothered by straw, and upon the straw, was a covered corral. Corvus did not need to look to know what was inside. His ears told him everything. Foxes and cats and deer and bear, rodents and skunks, owls and eagles, and a multitude of other voices howled out into the ethers, calling for help. How could any man do this, he wondered? Would Mallory burn down the forest as well? Could the Elders be so foolish to believe that they could burn everything they did not understand out of existence?

A fierce wind whipped across the plaza. The church door opened and Elder Mallory emerged with a staff of fire in his hand. The circle of arms parted and Mallory penetrated the human chain and approached the ash eye. He walked with a stoic resolve toward the plaza center, keeping his eyes trained on the animals in the corral.

As Corvus scoured the scene from above, he noticed that many of the boys were missing from the circle. Celina, however, could be seen with her back to the black stump of The Tree of Truth. She looked uneasy. Her hands were gripped tightly by her mother and father who stood on either side of her, their eyes, like everyone else's, were trained on Mallory. Celina looked desperately up at the empty sky for a sign, unaware that a murder of crows hovered behind the clouds.

Mallory stood paces away from the wooden corral. He clutched the flaming torch tightly in his hand and raised it high into the air, pointing it at the sky. "Our world is threatened," he said, his voice booming out of his chest and into the plaza. "It is as if our village stands below the walls of a cracking dam." He paced around the enclosed corral as he spoke, his words rising into the air like sparks from a bonfire. "The dam I speak of is the forest of illusion, and the widening crack is a boy in the forest. For weeks I have done everything in my power to retrieve this child so that the mind of the village may be purified. But in my haste to do so, I have betrayed the trust of my people and have led them into an illusion they were unprepared for. I did not realize it then, but the madness of the boy and the forest have become one. Together, they have planted visions and voices to contaminate your knowledge of the signs.

"Since he has left us, many of you have come to me with dreams to confess, and in these dreams there is always a crow. Many inquire if the meaning of the crow has changed now that the boy has left the village. I am here to tell you once again that it has *not*! The crow is a trickster and a thief – a demon from another world. It seeks to guide the ignorant deeper into their own forest of darkness, but in that forest you will only find the indefinable – a strange and dangerous child that seeks ownership of your dreams. *He* is the crow in your mind and he flies through the symbols before us now," Mallory said, pointing at the animals. "The forest has harbored his hiding, but no longer! The village's mind is united, and together, we shall purify the last of his nightmare."

As Mallory spoke, Corvus could see the villagers sway in unison as if an electrical current ran through their arms. It was a collective dream, Corvus realized. Mallory was orchestrating his beliefs like a conductor. His sermon opened the villagers' ears but blinded their vision. They could not see the world around them for what it was - their eyes were open for him alone.

Mallory's face was a contortion of hidden meanings, but he spoke with an absolute certainty that was impossible to ignore. "Our existence depends on our interpretation of the world we inhabit. In this dualistic universe, each creation has its place. The darkness stays in the night, just as the light of the sun guides our vision throughout the day. We too, have our place in this world, just as the creatures of the forest have theirs. Our place is the community of man. It is a reality separate from the illusion, a world woven by the rules and laws created by our ancestors years ago. But now the dream of one is affecting the many, and the rules which we have lived by are coming undone. The crow will continue to return as long as it believes that we are willing to redefine it. As its persistence penetrates our collective mind, only fire can return it back to the illusion from whence it came. These animals serve us as a symbolic reminder, that they too, have no place in our world."

Elder Mallory stepped boldly onto the straw that surrounded the corral. All he had to do was lower the torch. Mallory stared at the animals as he slowly waved the fire back and forth in front of his face like a torn veil in the wind. He wanted to see the fear in their eyes, perhaps hoping that somewhere within them he could recognize the boy that he hunted. Mallory wanted these creatures to beg him for mercy. He knew they were conscious and that they spoke to those willing to listen. If they would only sacrifice a bit of their wisdom, then perhaps he would reconsider their fate. Mallory was desperate to understand their meaning because he knew that their meaning was linked with his own. If only he knew who he was, if only She would tell him, if only She would love him as She loved the boy.

But as Mallory looked deeper and deeper into their eyes, he saw something that no fire could ever destroy. The longer he waited for them to speak, the clearer it became that they would not. He would gain no new wisdom today by burning them. These creatures came from a different understanding, and it was an understanding he could never control.

The old Elder stifled the anguish in his chest and pulled back his lips into an angry sneer and spit into the corral. Speaking both to the animals and to the boy on the other side of the veil, Mallory said quietly, "Whatever essence you maintain shall always be yours, but the meanings of my creations are believed by all! My fire will burn away your wisdom for good."

Mallory held out the torch and extended it over the straw.

From out of the bright day, two wide and steady wings sailed down over the plaza like a newborn sign. The strong black talons gripped the wooden staff and ripped it out of Mallory's hand and carried the fire off into the sky. It was Korbin.

Mallory shouted after his staff of fire and called out to Corvus, knowing that the dreamer observed him from somewhere above. Corvus led his crows through the clouds in a wide circle high above the plaza. He could see all possibilities now – victory, defeat, sacrifice, murder, martyrdom. None were separate, all were intertwined and the crows loomed behind him like dragons. They would do anything for him. Anything.

Celina's eyes looked up to the heavens. She could still see the dimmest light from the fire as the crow carried it higher into the sky. When the crow vanished into the clouds she looked at the villagers, hoping for some indication of their acknowledgement. Had they seen what had just happened? Did they understand what it meant? None of them seemed to. Their eyes were locked on Mallory's and a widening smile was spreading across the Elder's face like straw catching fire. Celina tried to wrench herself free, but her mother and father held her arms tightly. She looked nervously up at the sky as she thought of the boys who were hiding in the church. This was all a part of Mallory's plan, she knew. He *wanted* the crows to come.

The clouds parted and Corvus dropped down with his crows behind him like a string of dark omens. Mallory stepped behind the corral and knelt. His fingers gripped the wood tightly and he looked over the corral's edge like a child looking into the funnel of a tornado. They were coming straight for him. "Come," he said softly. "Fulfill my vision."

The villagers began to scream hysterically as the crows spread over the plaza like a black cape. Inches over the corral, the crows careened upward back into the sky. Corvus hovered hundreds of feet over the center of the plaza while crows circled around him like a current of wind. The villagers' hands remained linked and Corvus knew that the chain had to be broken if the animals were to be set free. He called his crows, and staying behind, watched his kin drop one by one out of the clouds.

They were halfway down when Mallory put his hands to his mouth and yelled, "Now!"

The wooden door of the church opened and thirteen boys brazenly stepped out and looked up to the sky. Each of them held a loaded bow in their hands and the boys followed the flying crows like professional marksmen. When their sights were set, arrows sailed into the air. Bows were reloaded and fired again.

The first arrow pierced the crow in the lead and it fell to the ground like a broken stone. Behind it, crows darted and swerved, but the relentless barrage of missiles sent them into a panic and scattered their flight. Now easy targets, the birds fell out of the sky like it was raining until the white stones in the plaza were littered with black bodies. The crows had fallen within the ring of arms and the villagers watched the scene before them in horror and disbelief. Many of the children were crying and even the boys near the church looked at the plaza in dismay. Black and bloody birds were everywhere. The boys' eyes revealed the dawning awareness of their role in the murder. Even Jeremy, who had shot the first crow, appeared distraught. He looked at his companions for acceptance, but they were looking for acceptance of their own. All eyes were on Mallory.

Mallory's eyes were on the sky. It was empty. He lowered his gaze and scanned the plaza like a vulture, searching for Corvus. There were dead crows everywhere. Mallory stood up and approached a fallen bird lying on a white stone. The crow had been shot in its neck and little bubbles of blood were coming out of its mouth - it was still alive and Mallory frowned. He put his foot on the crow's head and stepped down until he heard the soft crunch of the bird's skull and then moved on to the next one.

Celina could not bear to watch. After she had seen the first crow hit the plaza she refused to witness the rest of them fall. She had only looked up. As crows fell out of the sky, Celina could not take her eyes off the one crow that had not yet descended. A second sign was coming...

Mallory walked faster and faster from one bird to the next. "Where *is* he?" he grumbled, kicking the birds as he walked. Surely, Corvus was here. Elder Mallory stood up now, straight and defiant, and he scoured the plaza for the body of his enemy. But then, something hit him – hard! The Elder wobbled and swooned as he tried to stay standing. He touched the top of his head with his hand, wondering what could have hit him when an object near his foot caught his attention. "What on *earth?*" he said to himself.

On the ground was a flat stone, smooth enough to have been born in a river. Mallory leaned over and picked up the stone and rubbed it thoughtfully with his fingers.

"Look!" someone yelled.

Mallory raised his gaze to the villagers, whose arms still surrounded him. The villagers, however, were no longer looking at Mallory. They were staring at a blond girl with her back to the Tree of Truth.

"Look!" she screamed again.

Mallory's eyes widened with intensity as the full meaning of the experience hit him like the falling rock. From behind the clouds, a crow emerged. Korbin was fully aflame and he was descending upon the village like the sun itself. A long snake of black smoke trailed behind the burning crow which spiraled downwards like a falling comet. The flames crackled and snapped as the fire burned the black feathers away, and a loud and tremendous cawing filled the air like a siren. Down below, a little girl broke free from the circle and thrusting her arm into the air Celina screamed, "Look! Look! Look!"

The chain of arms split into pieces. The villagers raised their hands to shield their eyes from the blaze of the sun, but it was not the sun that blinded them - it was a sign they had never seen before.

"Archers!" Mallory yelled. "Archers! Fire! Fire! Take aim and fire!" But the archers did not move. They were just as entranced as the rest of the villagers. Mallory walked stiffly and quickly toward the church, looking over his shoulder at the burning crow in the sky. "That crow will fly into the church and set it ablaze!" he shouted.

The villagers were now gathered in small groups as they watched the burning spectacle approach. The fiery crow fell faster and faster and the closer it came the less it resembled a crow. Mallory yanked Jeremy's bow out of his hands and pushed him away. The old Elder pulled out an arrow and placed it into the bow, knowing he only had one shot. Mumbling a mixture of hope, magic, and prayer, Mallory released the arrow.

The arrow sailed through the air and caught the tip of Korbin's wing and the crow spiraled out of control. No one could take their eyes off the burning bird as it fell. It was both terrifying and beautiful, like a flaming meteor descending to earth. At last the crow crashed into the plaza and onto the straw with a tremendous thud. There was nothing left of Korbin that resembled a crow, only a smoldering black lump next to the corral. Within moments, the straw had ignited.

Corvus could only save the animals now - everything else had been lost. He sailed down to the plaza like a falcon and in an instant he was on top of the covered corral looking down at the animals between the wooden beams. The animals were out of control, crashing into each other and the corral in a panic. Corvus jumped onto the ground and into the fire. He could feel the heat crawl up his legs, singeing his feet and his feathers, but he would only stop if it killed him. He clawed at the straw and his sharp talons scratched at the fire and pulled it apart. He was fast and efficient and soon the fire was nearly out. His body was badly burned, but for now the animals were safe. Corvus knew, however, that there were coals beneath the straw that could reignite the fire at any moment. Corvus realized that the only way to save the animals for certain was to open the gate. If he could move the wooden latch that held the gate closed, then the animals could push the gate open and escape.

Corvus hopped onto a piece of wood next to the latch - but there was a problem. Sticking out of the gate at an awkward angle was a pinecone impaled on a stick. In order to get to the latch, the pinecone had to be moved out of the way.

Mallory could see the bird upon the gate, studying the pinecone, but he did nothing to stop it. Instead, a smile crept over his face.

Inside the corral, the animals were going berserk. *"Stop!"* they said. *"Stop! It is a trap!"*

It was too late. Corvus grabbed the pinecone with his beak and removed it. The stick that the pinecone was attached to fell away and a hidden lariat wrapped around Corvus's legs, flinging him into the air. He flapped his wings wildly trying to break free, but the cord held tightly to his legs.

In the blurry distance, a man in white approached him. Elder Mallory lifted Corvus close to his face and Corvus could smell the musty aroma of old tea on Mallory's breath. The old man peered into the crow's eyes, studying them closely, searching to see if they belonged to the boy.

Corvus could see himself in the eyes of the old man. It was the first time he had ever seen himself as an actual crow. Mallory's grip around Corvus's neck tightened as he unwound the cord around his legs. Corvus closed his eyes, ready to pass out.

"Waaaake uuup." The words came out slowly and seeped through Corvus's mind like the cold river water. "This is all just a dream, a *terrible* dream," he could hear Elder Mallory saying. "You do not exist alongside a murder of crows. Look at yourself. You are not a crow, but a *boy*. Wake up, boy, *wake up*!" The tightness around Corvus's neck slackened and Corvus took a deep breath and opened his eyes. "Don't you remember?" Mallory asked. "You have flown in from the shadows of your forested mind, into a vision you are no longer a part of. Return to your illusions, however you have left them."

Mallory squinted his eyes as he studied the crow. He could see the waterfall in the black eyes of the bird, as well as the falling boy who believed he could soar. "Oh," he said, a smile crawling onto his face. "You *cannot* return, can you? For if you did, you would fall for the last time. Well," he said, winking at the crow in his hand, "then I shall send you back to your illusions myself."

Corvus craned his neck up and looked into the man's eyes. "*Elder Mallory,*" Corvus said. "*I have come to save them. Elder, can you hear me? We can change all of this. We can be free.*"

But Mallory only continued to smile at the crow. He lifted Corvus high into the air and the villagers stared at the crow in the hand of their Elder. Mallory felt amazing. He had done it! He had saved his village. "This is The Crow!" Mallory shouted for all to hear, overwhelmed by a self-imposed sense of belonging. "Take a good look while you can, before I destroy this symbol once and for all. Someone bring me the fire!"

But the villagers were as still as the air. All eyes were looking at Corvus.

"*Elder Mallory!*" Corvus called. "*Tell them the truth. Give the people a chance to know what is real and what is illusion. Don't do this, you must not set fire to that which is meaningful,*" he pleaded, but Mallory could hear none of it and instead walked slowly toward the ash eye. Inside the corral, the animals stared without movement. Corvus looked at them sadly hoping they could forgive him for his failure to save them.

The Elder brought Corvus down to his chest and lowered his voice to say something. "I think it would be good if you watched the animals burn with your own eyes. They are here for you, you know, just as you are here for them. It is all so intrinsically intertwined!" Mallory said, a wave of fascination and delight suddenly passing over his face. "There is so much to *know*, so much to *learn*. Why, it is the very reason we study the signs in the first place. If we can understand our creations in this world, then we can see the world as we see ourselves."

He lifted the crow over his head. From Corvus's perspective, Mallory looked small and out of place - simpler, gentler. His thin hair was only a light cover for his balding head, and with his arms outstretched in front of him he almost looked like a father holding his child. Mallory was even smiling.

It was in this moment of certain finality that Corvus saw himself in the arms of his dying mother. Her departure left a lasting impression on a boy who would one day grow up to see the world in symbols. Without a parent to explain that the earth was *also* his mother, the meaning of the external world was just as ambiguous as his own.

Corvus danced between the worlds and he shifted and swayed from his birth to his death. He saw himself falling in the waterfall now, and deep in the pool below him he could see something glowing and calling his name. Its beautiful light reached him from within the pool, singing a wisdom he had somehow known all along.

You are well. You are well. You are worthy and well. All creations are one, as all Ones create.

He was in the plaza again. Mallory's hands gripped Corvus's bones tighter. His body ached and his spirit ebbed with exhaustion, but Corvus was no longer afraid.

"Your flight is over, fowl," Mallory said. "I am going to tear off your wings and set fire to the symbols."

Corvus looked into Mallory's eyes one last time. *"You too are a symbol, and within that symbol I see myself, but that reflection is not me. I am the light I carry within - it is the light that helps me see."*

Mallory stared curiously at the bird in his hands. The crow's eyes were so deep and so black, eternal - profound. Involuntarily, Mallory gasped. He could see himself in the reflection of the crow's eyes. He unconsciously raised his hand and touched his temple. He felt lost yet unconcerned with where he was going. He squinted suddenly and a shadow passed over his face - another bird could be seen in the crow's eyes.

Elder Mallory did not know it was there it until it was upon him, but by then it was too late. The crow hit him with the force of a hammer and buried its thick black talons into Mallory's porous face. Blood squirted out immediately and the Elder screamed and batted his arms wildly, trying to free himself from his assailant. The crow was blacker than the darkest dream and Mallory was spinning and screaming in anguish and he fell to his knees, tearing at the crow that wouldn't release him, throwing Corvus out of his hands amidst the chaos.

At last, the terrible bird pulled itself loose and flew a few meters away, safely out of range from Mallory's flailing arms. Corvus could see the crow clearly from where he was and he recognized it at once. It was the very same crow which had killed his aunt. It belonged to Obiticus, Corvus knew, because in the crow's glossy talon was Mallory's right eye. It lowered its beak and pecked at the eye and scraped it against the red-stained stones. After a moment it looked up and watched the Elder roll around in agony and then turned down to peck at the eye again. After a moment, the crow looked up and saw Corvus. Bits of eye hung from its beak. Corvus stared back at the mysterious black bird, a bird that looked so strikingly similar to himself.

The crow ruffled its feathers and squawked menacingly. It pecked at the eye as it looked nervously back and forth between Mallory and Corvus. Its eyes bored into Corvus's and it squawked again loudly, threateningly. The crow gripped the eye tightly with its talon and hopped away toward Mallory. No one had come to his aid, but Mallory was still shouting in pain. For a moment Corvus thought the crow was going to attack him again, but the crow simply watched the Elder with patient interest. At last, it took flight. It rose quickly into the air and flew off toward the far-reaching forest, carrying Elder Mallory's eye in its talon.

Corvus looked up at the sky. He was exhausted and his vision ebbed and flowed between darkness and sight. His legs were burnt beyond recognition and he knew he was dying. Corvus closed his eyes, ready to surrender to the Great Unknown, when a pair of warm hands curled around his body and lifted him off the ground. When he opened his eyes again he saw Celina.

"Everything is alright," she cooed to him. Celina placed her other hand upon his back and softly pet his feathers. "Everything is fine," she said softly. Corvus felt himself falling away and he closed his eyes. Celina tilted her head and rested her cheek against his body. Her long blond hair draped over his face, and when he opened his eyes again he could only see streaks of the world beyond her. He saw the villagers still standing in the plaza. They were staring at Celina in wonder, whispering and murmuring to themselves about the girl holding the crow.

From the back of the crowd, a little boy pushed his way to the front. He wanted to see the sign for himself. When he got past the mass of villagers the boy saw Celina holding the crow in her arms, rocking it like a child. The boy walked softly and slowly across the plaza, never taking his eyes off the crow. When he came within arm's reach, he stopped. Finally, Thomas said, "I saw this crow try to save the animals. This is not the symbol we once knew. Perhaps," Thomas said to Celina, "it is not as they say it is. Maybe the meanings are meant to be free."

Thomas stepped toward the corral. He sensed that he entire community was watching him. The animals too eyed the boy carefully as he placed his hand against the gate. Standing on the other side of the corral was a massive brown bear and Thomas knew the bear could very well kill him as soon as he set it free. But Thomas had seen the burning crow that had fallen from the sky, and no Elder or Book of Signs could change that. Today, he was no longer afraid.

With a labored push, Thomas opened the large wooden gate and backed away. The villagers held their breath. Inside the corral, the animals were still. They looked at their doorway to freedom with patient caution. The heavy brown bear raised its snout and sniffed the air and then stepped out of the gate toward Thomas. The young boy did not move even though the bear was only an arm length away. At last, the silence was broken, but it was not the bear that spoke. It was Thomas.

"You are free now," Thomas said, "and because of that so am I, free to see the signs as they truly are." The bear took a step toward Thomas and pushed its head into the boy's chest. Slowly, delicately, Thomas set his hands into the thick fur of the bear and embraced it. One by one, the animals emerged out of their captivity. They walked across the red and white stones toward the villagers who studied them closely. Within moments the soft sounds of starting conversations could be heard. The villagers were speaking to the animals - the signs were being redefined.

Celina still held the crow in her arms. She rocked it softly back and forth as she whistled a strange staccato that a boy with grandfather eyes had once taught her. She leaned her head down and whispered quietly to the crow.

"I know you can hear me, Corvus, and I know why you came." She looked at the villagers and the animals. "This village will never be the same," she said, a tear rolling down her cheek. "They are beginning to see the world as it really is, without all the reasons and meaning. I love you," she said to him. She squeezed the crow tightly next to her chest, knowing that soon she would have to let him go, and knowing equally as well that he may never return. "You belong in the forest," she told him. "Maybe one day I will find you there, or maybe one day you will come back for me. For now, this dream is complete, and a new one begins."

Celina looked up at the sky. The sun was hidden by the clouds, but a powerful light blasted out from the corners of the shadows. "You were meant to fly, Corvus. Your flight guides those down below, those of us who share your dream of the unknown. You who observe are *also* watched," she said with a smile. "We see your discoveries in our own world. Go now," she said. "There is much more in this life to embrace and embody."

Celina bent her knees bringing Corvus down to her waist. He watched her with careful consideration, knowing that when he saw her again, neither of them would be the same. For now, she was setting him free. Celina sprung up and lifted her arms to the sky as she threw Corvus into the air with a spirited laugh, releasing him back into the vision. He felt himself rise and he opened his wings one last time as he watched The White Village below him disappear from sight.

*   *   *   *   *   *

The clouds roared past him and the icy air blew against his face like a hurricane. Corvus was falling again without wings. Strange pulses of a recent past permeated his mind, though his memory as a crow was both distant and vague. As he fell through a funnel of clouds he could the dark silhouette of a bird flying slowly in his direction. Corvus reached out with his mind and asked the bird to breach the misty boundary that separated them. When at last the bird did so, Corvus saw that it was not the bird he had expected to see. It was not a crow, but a dove, and it hovered above the abyss and Corvus could see that the dove's eyes were as white as its wings. No words were said, no song was sung – its presence was communication enough. It circled him now, faster and faster as Corvus fell through the clouds. The mist parted and below him he could see the shining reflection of the sun on white waters. His body lifted up and his feet came down and he dropped like a rock into the water below the cascade.

The force of the fall ripped his clothes from his body. Corvus felt none of the impact. He did not feel the cold icy water, nor did he sense the cocoon of bubbles which surrounded him as he sank deeper and deeper. He was only aware of an all-pervasive darkness that surrounded him like the shroud of death.

An eternity passed and he was awakened only by a sense of falling. It was not the kind of chaotic or fearful falling that a living body experiences. It was something else. He sensed he was sinking into the final ending of a long and infinite journey. It was a homecoming of some kind and at the end there was a light. The light glowed below him as he sank effortlessly toward it. It seemed to call to him like a faraway sun at the edge of a dark universe. It grew as he approached it and his eyes opened up and an indigo blue bled through the blackness of his surroundings and a shaft of light cut through the water.

Now an ancient and subtle pain spun through his awareness. He wondered how pain could possibly exist in this world away from the living, but he felt it, it was real - it was *life* moving inside of him. It buzzed and it hummed and it burned through his body like wildfire, igniting his cells and his senses with both pleasure and immeasurable pain. Everything inside of him shook. A powerful pressure compressed his chest. He knew somehow that he was sinking away from safety, but the beautiful light was just below him now.

The edge of the universe was a flat and barren land. There was no light, no life – nothing, nothing other than the glowing orb beneath him. He felt his feet sink into a thick and viscous muck and he came down upon his knees and settled into what looked like a position of prayer. The light was all around him, illuminating his body making it look ghostly and white. For a hidden instant, the pain was gone and he felt he could stay here forever, though he knew he was here for a reason…

Corvus plunged his arm into the muck until he felt his hand clench something solid. He yanked the object out of the earth like a tree root and his nerves flickered to life - his heart pounded relentlessly, his chest constricted his lungs like a vice. Corvus pushed his feet against the ground and kicked his legs furiously, holding the orb tightly in his hand. Twilight blue surrounded him on all sides and he swam for his life up the light ladder which led to the sun. At last, Corvus exploded out of the water and crashed down with a tremendous splash, sending waves in all directions.

Corvus floated on his back and gazed up at the blue sky and the clouds dissolving in front of the sun. Behind him, the waterfall fell into a distant white noise. All around him mountains scaled the world at right angles, climbing into the upper reaches of the sky, their sides shrouded in a carpet of green trees. From what he could tell from his limited perspective, Corvus had jumped into a large lake. He looked at the waterfall behind him and followed it up to the sky and into the clouds. The memories came back to him all at once. He saw himself walking alone through the forest, saw the animals and the plants and the things they had taught him – and there, at his memory's edge, was Obiticus. Could the old outcast still be up there, Corvus wondered?

For the first time, Corvus looked at the object in his hand. It was a beautiful quartz crystal, clear, eternal, and flawless. When he turned it, the crystal scattered the sunlight in a million different directions. Inside of it, he could see his own transparent reflection.

The lake seemed to shiver and a cool breeze brushed across the surface of the water. Corvus rolled onto his back and placed the crystal on his chest. Micro ripples bounced around his body. He looked up at the sky. Now calm, Corvus could feel the spirit of the lake whispering out to him.

"You are the first of your kind to visit these waters in a great many years." It was a feminine voice, gentle and calm, though an awesome power lay beneath the words. *"These waters will soothe you and renew your strength. You are here now, and so you shall be. All things return from where they have come from."*

"Am I dead?" Corvus asked. "Is this heaven?"

"Dead? No. But heaven, well..." The lake paused, overcome by the beauty of the word. *"Heaven is the origin, the garden of our beginnings, a place where all is awareness. All creatures conspire to harmonize for each creature knows they are part of the same organism, an ever-evolving experience of existence in perfection."*

A gentle song blew across the water and through his hair and Corvus looked into the infinite sky as he listened to the words. *"This crystal is a gift,"* the voice said. *"You have found it in the murky blackness which lies at the bottom of every vessel. Those who are brave enough to seek and are willing to confront their own ignorance shall all be rewarded with the charms of new beginnings. This crystal will tell you many beautiful things, all of which you already know. Understand that it is merely a representation, a symbol, of what you harbor within."*

The wind slowly began to die down and the ripples around his body trickled away. The voice was almost gone, but before it left She said, *"Born through the waters of awareness and pain, you have gained a new alley, a child who has lived in the eyes of a sage, a creator and dreamer who can see all things in all ways. And when the time comes to guide once more, you will know the path to take, for truth be with you forever."*

When Corvus got to the opposite shore, the sky had become a magnificent collage of colors that mixed across the cloudy canvas like the painting of a dream. The pink sun sank into the edge of the sky, guiding the clouds to carry these colors back to their origins.

That night he slept next to the water, using the shore as his blanket. As he passed into sleep he could feel the soft sand soothing his transition. *"Every life is an allegory for those who have not lived it. Surrender your story, which is a myth for this world. You have left them a gift - one that will guide them for ages. Let the dreams of your beginnings dissolve in your sleep, and allow those who awaken to make meaning of their own."*

Epilogue

On a still clear morning, Corvus rose from the soft sand and approached the water to wash himself. The sun was high in the cloudless air and small birds flittered over the surface of the lake. Corvus stretched his arms and sighed. He leaned over and took several handfuls of cold water and splashed it onto his face. He looked down at his reflection. Corvus's hair had grown past his shoulders and a thin beard covered his once youthful appearance. He was handsome, he saw, and it pleased him to see that he was growing into his ideal.

"*Handsome indeed, my child,*" said the lake, "*though no more handsome than I,*" She chided. A rush of warm air sailed over the lake and through his hair. Corvus dove into the water with a laugh and swam out as far as he could. When he became tired he rested and floated on his back and looked up at the mountains and the incredible beauty of the world around him, a world he belonged to. At times the lake would sooth him with Her loving voice and recite in a steady rhythm, "*You are here, you are here, and now you are here.*" Other times Corvus simply settled into silence.

Today the wind was strong.

"*My child, you are changing. You are becoming a man. The world changes alongside of you - it always has and always will. The water which comes into my body will eventually follow the flow out. With time, everything transforms.*

"*Long ago, these shores were lined with human settlements. They were few at first but quickly grew. Shelters became camps, camps became a village, and the village became a town. They were a pleasant people, though ignorant in their ways. They did not understand that their own health and happiness was tied to the well-being of the place they inhabited. They could not comprehend that co-existence is a mutual agreement, and that the land has needs of its own. Instead of stewarding the surplus of their territory, they exploited it. Creatures were killed without consideration. Trees were shaved off the hillsides like tall grass. Eventually, the rains no longer came to greet the trees, and no water remained in the lake. The animals migrated away. With nothing left to consume, the people departed. The mountains shifted and fell, sealing off this place from the rest of the world, locking us in a reality far from the unconsciousness of man.*"

Corvus floated on his back and watched the sky as the spirit of the lake spoke to him. "Where did the people go?" he asked.

"The people traveled far far far from here to the most beautiful part of the forest. They gathered others with them as they moved along, determined to find the perfect home. At last, they reached the edge of the forest where it met the ocean's shore. Never before had they seen anything so beautiful. Convinced they had arrived in heaven they began to build again."

"What happened?"

"It is as this place once was. The trees are gone. The waters are poisoned. It has become a vast wasteland that the people call paradise, but the peoples' resources have run thin, and one day, they will return here for more."

Corvus swam back to the shore and spent the rest of his day gazing at the lake, thinking of what She had said to him. He closed his eyes and went within, going to his own inner lake and wondering what it would be like if it were also gone.

When he opened his eyes again the sun was behind the mountain and a full moon was cresting over the eastern hills. Behind him his crystal reflected the moon's light. He kept his crystal on an altar of stones, and upon the stones was an assortment of flowers and feathers and herbs. Corvus sat down in front of his altar and remained there for hours, staring at the perfect prism before him.

When the light in the crystal shifted, Corvus turned around.

The satyr standing in front of him looked exactly the same. In fact, it didn't look like it had aged a day. Its horns were shiny and polished, its face clean and impeccable. Its hands were empty, but a small satchel on its hip carried a wooden flute. It stood silent and still and it watched Corvus intently.

Corvus stood up slowly, never taking his eyes off the satyr's. The moon was directly over both of them now and its full body showered them with light. Even in the pale darkness, Corvus could see the satyr was agitated, though about what, he could not tell.

Corvus lifted his hands to his waist so his palms faced the sky and he bowed his head with humility. Choosing his words wisely, he said, "I have learned many things and seen many signs since I saw you last. My understandings are more complete now. You have been on my path in the past, but fear has propelled me away. Whatever news you have, whatever message you bring, I am willing to receive it, and help if I can."

The satyr shifted its weight and the moonlight caught in its eye. *"You are taller these days,"* it said. *"The ways of your essence has shifted your shape and your spirit now carries your flesh. No less are you now than when before you began, but the test that is coming will make you a man."*

Corvus looked at the satyr carefully, but before he could ask what the creature meant, the satyr continued. *"I too have my lessons, in that world and this. So long I believed I could dismiss what I hated. Yet despite my jaded views of the men in this world, my ignorance imbued the sickness they carried. Inactions will prove our creations undone."* The satyr's expression darkened. *"Those with the symbol of sickness carry an illness our way. It cannot be fought, it cannot be burned – only now do I know it can only be learned."*

The satyr pulled the wooden whistle from his satchel and raised it to his lips. He played a song with a tuneful tempo and Corvus noticed that the stars began to flicker. After nearly ten minutes of playing, the satyr lowered the flute and looked at Corvus.

"I can only survive in the safety of my forest. The lives of this land are mine to attend. I amend what I can, but I cannot for long. The others are coming until all they have taken, and so I have played you a song to awaken the next leg of your path. Only a human can stop them, one of their own. Your father has tried, but he can no longer see what has been shone."

With that, the satyr dashed away. Corvus yelled after it to stop, but the creature continued until it was over a mound and out of sight. Corvus took off in the satyr's direction. When he reached the mound, Corvus could see the creature standing in the distance overlooking a meadow. Its flute was to its lips and Corvus could hear the tuneful tempo playing in the night air.

By the time Corvus arrived at the meadow, the music had stopped. He and the satyr stood side-by-side looking out over the field. The field was aglow by the light of the moon, and upon it, were hundreds, if not thousands, of the Dreamer's Lotus.

A long low gasp escaped from his mouth like wind from a cave as Corvus understood what he was seeing. He had come to this field many times, but never before had he seen such an incredible sight. He was so entranced by what he saw, that by the time he turned to see the satyr, it was gone.

Corvus walked slowly toward the large patch, stepping so lightly on the soft grass that he made not a sound. He knelt on one knee and examined the flower below him. Corvus held out his hand and stroked the soft petals of the large lotus. The edges of the flower glowed in the moonlight.

"What wonder to see you," he said. "You still grow in the night of my mind, though at times I realize I have forgotten about you altogether," he said. "I am honored to find you here."

"And we are honored that you have found us. You have been awake for so long that you have forgotten the importance of The Dream. The cycle you are in comes to an end. The time to transition into new understandings begins." The lotus's words hung on his mind like jewelry. *"You may take as many of us as you like, but you must do so quickly, for our life force is at its strongest at night, and by sunrise, we will disappear back into the daydream."*

Tenderly, he cupped the flower in his hands and pulled the short roots out of the ground. He was humble and pulled only three flowers out of the earth and carried them with utmost care back to his sanctuary. He laid the three flowers at the base of his altar and gazed at them in silence. It had been years since he had dreamt, longer than he could remember, and he knew that once that path was reignited there was no turning back. The potential of the lotus frightened him greatly although the rest of his soul ached with curiosity. This wasn't just an everyday occurrence. This was a sign, one that had come to him for a reason.

He picked up a lotus and held it in his lap. The flower glowed like the moon.

"I am everything that you have yet to reveal to yourself. I am the secret you will not confront. You who find me have sought me since the beginning." The lotus spoke in certainties, as if it knew the depth of all souls in all worlds. *"Before you began this journey of spirit in a world of matter, you understood the challenge of expansion. You have come from a faraway place, young traveler, and in the beginning you made a promise to yourself – but that promise is for you to determine and it is up to you to decide if you shall fulfill it or not."*

Corvus cupped the lotus in both hands and lifted it above his head. The petals reflected the color of the moon, both of them mysterious and proud, their meanings bound by darkness. The moon was at its zenith and the fullness of the celestial body conveyed clearly the lesson of the moment. The skylight of the heavens would surrender later this evening and retreat into its cycle of death and rebirth. Corvus, on the other hand, would not touch the deadly center of the Dreamer's Lotus.

Corvus pulled off a corner of the lotus petal and placed it carefully onto his tongue. The familiar taste of berry pulsed through his mouth. *"More,"* the lotus told him. *"You have been awake for a long time and it will take more than just a bite to shake your subconscious free."*

He pulled off two petals, thinking this would be enough.

"More."

He pulled off a third, but the lotus interrupted his action.

"You must consume them all."

Sweat formed on the palms of his hands. "But it might kill me," he said, his voice saturated with concern.

"Death comes from carelessness. It is nature's warning system, a way of managing the elements of ignorance. A snake's venom warns others who are not familiar with it just as the center of the lotus is poisonous for a reason. But since you act with consciousness in this most sacred act, our wills are united."

"But such a quantity, is it not dangerous? I have never before taken so much. I do not know if I am ready."

"Only you can decide if you are ready. One evolves when in harmony with challenge and timing. If you are willing to travel into uncharted territory, then the gifts of insight will emerge like flowers on a moonlit meadow."

He crossed his legs and took three deep breaths to calm his mind. With all ten petals in his hand, he wrapped them into a tightly packed ball and placed them in his mouth after setting the deadly center to the side. Gentle electricity surged through his mouth. He felt small pinpricks of sensation tickle the palms of his hands and the balls of his feet. The sensation crawled up his arms and legs and into his heart. This was it, he knew, there was no turning back.

Corvus's vision blurred. His eyelids flickered. The lake began to fold and sway until it melted into the mountains. He felt himself spinning in circles though was still conscious enough to know that he was not moving. Strange and distant sounds could be heard all around him. Muffled voices called through the ethers, their origins unknown. A deep fatigue ran through his body yet his mind raced like the wings of a hummingbird. Lights appeared from the edges of darkness, sweeping in from the corners and enveloping him entirely. They moved up his arms and poured through his face and out the back of his head. He began to twitch and shake uncontrollably, and in a moment of great release he sighed and fell over backwards onto the soft sand of the lakeshore.

He flew out of his body as if ejected, sailing into the air and over the lake. Out of the body, his mind felt calmer and clearer, and he took this moment to regain his composure. This wasn't a dream, he realized. This was real. That was really his body that he was looking at and this lake was really his home.

On the horizon came the crow. Its black wings set against the night made it almost invisible, but the light in its eyes, an indigo blackness which shined like the moon in still waters, affirmed its presence. He and the crow floated side-by-side and Corvus reached out his arm to feel the crow's feathers. It was not Korbin, nor any other crow he had ever seen before. It was the archetype of all crows. It was the guide of the dreamer and before Corvus could speak, the crow looked down at the lake, motioning for Corvus to do the same.

One by one, the trees around the lake began to disappear, and left in their places were ghastly stumps marked by a red X. Corvus watched his body below decay and dissolve into the fine dust which surrounded a black and shallow lake. The mountaintops were severed clean, like mesa-top platforms to better view this terrible scene. Tears fell from the eyes of the crow to the barren earth like raindrops of acid. No longer was this a world of hope and potential. It was a vacant wasteland.

His heart felt like it was about to shatter. "Who could *do* this?" Corvus asked with overwhelm.

Now the crow flew around him in circles and as it did so it flickered like a white flame. Corvus watched the feathers fan out, and between the crow's wings the head of a dove emerged. Back and forth they existed, potent in their imagery, drawing out the many meanings of his own identity. The two forces of matter and spirit spun around him like a black and white painting of infinite potential.

"This is the work of your ancestors," the matter-spirit told him. It is a dream they created long ago, one that is being born into fruition by those left alive.

"What is the potential they wish to create?" he asked. "Can I see it?"

He felt the talons wrap around his mind and he climbed higher and higher in the sky until he came to a cloudy boundary of an unfamiliar existence. A pristine silence permeated this world. Glowing orbs surrounded him in space, their distance both mesmerizing and unimportant. Shining spheres passed him intentionally, yet he knew that they were universes unto themselves and that he was merely an observer.

The matter-spirit released him and hovered overhead.

"You have come to the land of awareness, a place of absolute potential. Be careful what you wish for, as it shall manifest instantly in this place."

Corvus emptied his mind until the purpose of his presence here became clear. "I have come to link the past and the future," he said carefully. "I have come for my ancestors. I am here for my father."

He watched in awe as an endless canvas of colors was painted before him. Great towers of light grew like living redwoods and rivers of energy could be seen running below them. Within moments an incredible city of light had manifested before his eyes. This place was older than time itself.

"This is the desire of the collective and the wish of your father. It is a symbol of humanity's divine potential and everything they strive for. It is the perfect union of matter and spirit, a place where will and creation thrive together as one. It is this place that your kind strives for, yet it is a place they have never known."

"Why?"

"Because man has forgotten that he is eternal, and so his creations reflect his own limitations. In the eyes of spirit, this can only be seen as the perpetuations of a strange and compelling madness."

All at once the city began to transform. The lights grew dim and coagulated together into dense dots of matter. The mist turned to smog and the sky which had once been white was now yellow and black. Strange machines strummed along on what was once a highway of light but was now a river of dark stagnation. Enormous buildings appeared out of the ground like metal trees shrouded in a thick layer of gray mist and smoke. A distant drone of mechanical drumming drifted through the black ethers. This was the source of true madness, Corvus knew. This was The Great City.

"My father is in there," he said to himself.

"There are many there who have lost their way. The Great City is like a machine and the people its cogs. It has become a land of sleep-walkers, a place so removed from the purpose of this world that it has become a collective nightmare. It cannot be contained," the spirit-matter said. *"It creeps to the edges of perceived perception. It is they who have dreamt the destruction of your home, and if left to their own devices, they shall destroy the very world they rely on to survive."*

"Can they be stopped?"

"The future is but a shadow in the night. Only when the sun rises can anything be said for certain. But there is always hope, for every spark can ignite a fire."

"I would like to go there and see it. For myself."

"Very well," said the spirit-matter. *"But even I will not follow you there."*

Corvus fell from the sky and was transported over the city like a feather in a high wind, swirling in erratic circles, plummeting into the blackness of the nether smoke, seeing the madness that the city maintained. Below him he saw thousands of people who traveled like termites in a strange and mechanized walk going nowhere all at once. Suddenly, he was alone and he found himself standing in the center of a room lined with mirrors. His reflections transformed as he paced in a circle around the room. In one mirror he saw a young boy with black eyes dressed in white clothes. In another mirror he watched his reflection transform into a wolf. The wolf's hide was thick and gray and its eyes were narrow with secrets. Long white teeth protruded out of its mouth and a low growl echoed against the glass. It paced in the mirror, mimicking the staggered thought that Corvus was now relying on to get him through these sets of illusions.

Suddenly, all of the lights went out except one. Corvus turned around. At the far end of the room a man behind the mirror looked out at the strange young person with the dark familiar eyes. Very slowly the man put his hand against the glass and Corvus could see a terrible scar across the palm. Corvus walked toward the man until he could feel the coolness coming off of the mirror. The man was tall and gaunt, his hair uncombed, and in his eyes was a bewildered look as if he had forgotten what he was about to say.

"Your eyes..." the man finally said in a daze. "They - they resemble my father's. Are, are you my father?" he asked.

Corvus looked deep into the man's eyes. He pitied him greatly in this moment. This was not the great figure he had been seeking. Instead a hollow man in tattered clothing looked through a two-way mirror at the son he could not recognize. For an instant Corvus wanted to abandon this pursuit, to fly away from this wretched place and forget the madness that stared back at him with such frightening clarity. He did not know what wisdom, if any, his father had for him, but he knew that this man's reflection had to be seen.

"I came to find you, Father," Corvus said. "I have seen you before in my dreams, as this too is a dream, only somehow much more real. I now know that you do in fact still exist."

"Do I?" came the reply.

"Yes. As do we all, in one form or another."

They stared at each other for a long powerful moment while the dream spun around them like a singular mirror. Without warning, the man slammed his body against the glass, showing Corvus both of his disfigured palms. "Get me out of here!" he screamed. "You've got to get me out of here. I forget I'm even in this place, forget that I even exist." He was panting heavily and he looked into Corvus's eyes in desperation. "Within the madness there are moments of clarity, though they are fleeting and will soon be gone entirely. Few here exist who can maintain sanity for long – a sickness plagues the people. There is only one symbol in The Great City, *only one*, a deity worshipped over all things. This symbol is a creator and a destroyer, but eventually, all will be ruined. I am just one more victim of its destruction, though the curse of another keeps me imprisoned in this hollow illusion. I have become the symbol of a corrupted past that I no longer recognize." The man fell to the ground and pulling his knees into his chest, he began to weep.

Corvus bent to one knee and put his hand on the glass, hoping to coax the man to his senses. "Perhaps I can save you," Corvus said. "Perchance there is still time for meaning to be made."

"It is useless," he whispered. "For if you penetrated the illusion you would not return, for all things lay within the lie."

"But I have made it this far," Corvus said. "Perhaps one day I can..."

"No!" the man shouted. "No no no no! False hopes beget the false prophet and you, young magician, have only shared in the misery of an old man's waking nightmare." He stood up in a rage and began to pound his fists into the glass until a long thin crack began to appear. Corvus noticed a line of blood run down his hand, smudging the glass with a red stain.

He stopped and for a moment Corvus thought that the man had become frozen in time, until very slowly his lips began to move, and almost inaudibly, he said, "The depth of my illusion binds my mind, but the glass of madness reflects my sign. *Save me.*"

In one motion the man crashed both fists into the mirror, shattering the glass into a thousand pieces. Instantly, Corvus was transported away from this place and into the void. He felt himself falling faster and faster into the black abyss until he existed only in observation.

When he opened his eyes everything was perfectly still. The normal sounds of the birds in the trees or the wind on the air were absent. The mountains in the distance were visible yet strangely dark. Even Corvus's hands were shadowed somehow, though the day it most certainly was.

Carefully, cautiously, Corvus raised his head to look at the sky. Above him a perfect ring of fire circled a shadowed moon and a strange and powerful knowing permeated every corner of his being. He knew he was crossing a threshold to another transition that would lead him into a forest darker than any he had ever known.

He would travel to The Great City and rescue his father.

About the Author:

Mike Dickenson is a traveler, white-water raft guide, and permaculturalist. He also creates documentary films and leads courses in writing and storytelling through Commonlink Productions.

For more information please visit:
www.commonlinkproductions.com

Made in the USA
San Bernardino, CA
24 November 2014